A Novel of Barsoom®

DARK TIDES OF MARS

THE WORKS OF EDGAR RICE BURROUGHS

Tarzan® Series

Tarzan of the Apes
The Return of Tarzan
The Beasts of Tarzan
The Son of Tarzan
Tarzan and the Jewels of Opar
Jungle Tales of Tarzan
Tarzan the Untamed
Tarzan the Terrible
Tarzan and the Golden Lion
Tarzan and the Ant Men
Tarzan, Lord of the Jungle
Tarzan and the Lost Empire
Tarzan at the Earth's Core
Tarzan the Invincible
Tarzan Triumphant
Tarzan and the City of Gold
Tarzan and the Lion Man
Tarzan and the Leopard Men
Tarzan's Quest
Tarzan and the Forbidden City
Tarzan the Magnificent
Tarzan and "The Foreign Legion"
Tarzan and the Madman
Tarzan and the Castaways
Tarzan and the Tarzan Twins
Tarzan: The Lost Adventure (with Joe R. Lansdale)

Barsoom® Series

A Princess of Mars
The Gods of Mars
The Warlord of Mars
Thuvia, Maid of Mars
The Chessmen of Mars
The Master Mind of Mars
A Fighting Man of Mars
Swords of Mars
Synthetic Men of Mars
Llana of Gathol
John Carter of Mars

Pellucidar® Series

At the Earth's Core
Pellucidar
Tanar of Pellucidar
Tarzan at the Earth's Core
Back to the Stone Age
Land of Terror
Savage Pellucidar

Amtor™ Series

Pirates of Venus
Lost on Venus
Carson of Venus
Escape on Venus
The Wizard of Venus

Caspak™ Series
The Land That Time Forgot
The People That Time Forgot
Out of Time's Abyss

Va-nah™ Series
The Moon Maid
The Moon Men
The Red Hawk

The Mucker™ Series
The Mucker
The Return of the Mucker
The Oakdale Affair

The Custers™ Series
The Eternal Savage
The Mad King

The Apache Series
The War Chief
Apache Devil

Western Tales
The Bandit of Hell's Bend
The Deputy Sheriff of Comanche County

Historical Tales
The Outlaw of Torn
I Am a Barbarian

Parallel Worlds
Beyond Thirty
Minidoka: 937th Earl of One Mile Series M

Other Tales
The Cave Girl
The Monster Men
The Man-Eater
The Girl from Farris's
The Lad and the Lion
The Rider
The Efficiency Expert
The Girl from Hollywood
Jungle Girl
Beware!/The Scientists Revolt
Pirate Blood
Marcia of the Doorstep
You Lucky Girl!
Forgotten Tales of Love and Murder

The Wild Adventures *of* Edgar Rice Burroughs™

Tarzan: Return to Pal-ul-don
by Will Murray

Tarzan on the Precipice
by Michael A. Sanford

Tarzan Trilogy
by Thomas Zachek

Tarzan: The Greystoke Legacy Under Siege
by Ralph N. Laughlin and Ann E. Johnson

A Soldier of Poloda:
Further Adventures Beyond the Farthest Star
by Lee Strong

Swords Against the Moon Men
by Christopher Paul Carey

Untamed Pellucidar
by Lee Strong

Tarzan and the Revolution
by Thomas Zachek

Tarzan, Conqueror of Mars
by Will Murray

Tarzan and the Lion of Judah
by Gary A. Buckingham

Skies of Venus
by Neal Romanek

Tarzan: Back to Mars
by Will Murray

He closed with the hideous travesty of humanity.

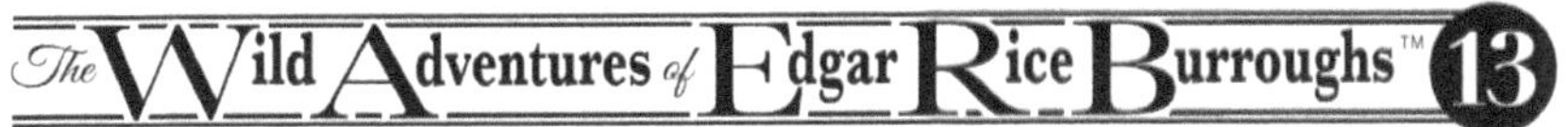

A Novel of Barsoom®

DARK TIDES OF MARS

CHRIS L ADAMS

Cover art and interior illustrations by
DOUGLAS KLAUBA

EDGAR RICE BURROUGHS, INC.
Publishers
TARZANA CALIFORNIA

DARK TIDES OF MARS: A NOVEL OF BARSOOM

Cover art by and interior illustrations by Douglas Klauba

Wild Adventures of Edgar Rice Burroughs Series Editor: James Sullos

Special thanks to Joan Bledig, Robert T. Garcia, Douglas Klauba, Janet Mann, James Sullos, Cathy Wilbanks, Charlotte Wilbanks, Mike Wolfer, and Bill Wormstedt for their valuable assistance in producing this book.

First standard hardcover edition

Published by Edgar Rice Burroughs, Inc.,
Tarzana, California

EdgarRiceBurroughs.com

ISBN-13: 978-1-945462-60-3

- 9 8 7 6 5 4 3 2 1 -

To these four, special folks who read the rough manuscript of this novel in its early days, supporting me with their feedback while enduring months of listening to me go on about plot dilemmas and character names. Each of them encouraged me to contact the estate of Edgar Rice Burroughs to learn if there was any interest in publishing the story . . . Thankfully, there was.

For the record, Seth is the first person to have read what eventually became *Dark Tides of Mars*, reading a chapter at a time as I would finish writing them. Thank you all.

Melisa Adams
Scott Belton
Shawn Bragg
Seth Valentine

A Note on Measurements

Measurements in this novel are given in Barsoomian units. While these terms should be understandable via context, their specific Earth equivalents may be found below for the curious Jasoomian reader.

haad A Barsoomian "mile" (equivalent to about 1,949 feet).

sofad A Barsoomian "foot" (equivalent to about 11.694 inches).

tal A Barsoomian "second" (equivalent to about .885 seconds)

xat A Barsoomian "minute" (equivalent to about 2 minutes, 57 seconds).

zode A Barsoomian "hour" (equivalent to about 2 hours, 27 minutes, 42 seconds).

TABLE OF CONTENTS

Prologue

WITH THE LIGHT OF THURIA shining down softly as she carved a swift path through the skies of Barsoom, a trio of mounted men trotted rapidly along an ancient road that descended the desiccated coastline of an extinct sea, making their way out to what were once its great deeps. The ancient path they followed was not the oldest fixture within view since, besides circling about the occasional rock formation dotting the landscape, it also wended its way beneath the even more ancient remains of a primordial wharf whose great piers and decks reared their massive components far over the heads of the riders and their swift thoats.

"How is it, John Carter," asked Tardos Mors, Jeddak of Helium, "that you are so confident he will pass this way tonight? The idea seemed credible when we set out earlier that your powers of deduction might indeed derive when and where he might pass this eve; but the light has waned, and night is upon us, and now it seems less so, and that more likely as not we shall never see him, nor he, us, but instead that we shall in all likelihood pass like thoats in the night."

Bathed in Thuria's swift-moving and dancing moonbeams, whose rapid movement lent such nimbleness to their fleetly moving shadows as to veritably make them seem alive, John Carter smiled at the Barsoomian colloquialism, given its similarity to an Earthly saying with which he was familiar.

"I know him," he replied. "Also, as I have made the trip in his company, both to and from his city, I know he prefers it. And after traveling it myself, I have found this the most interesting route of those I've taken by thoat. Not, mind you, because it is the quickest, because it isn't, but rather because it offers vistas of great beauty that are not lost upon me, nor are they lost on those of his race."

"I, too, have taken this road," added the third rider, "but not alone for its natural beauties which are, in truth, profound. I find it interesting to bypass dead cities, and there is one in this direction that I enjoy seeing."

"And what city might that be, Carthoris of Helium?" asked Tardos Mors, who happened to be the young man's great grandfather.

"Hold," cautioned John Carter with a raised hand who, alone of any man alive, might speak thus to the Jeddak of Helium with impunity. Carter halted his beast upon the crest of a hillock they were crossing. Before him, for as far as the eye could see under the influence of the quirky movement of Thuria's dashing moonbeams, hill and dale rolled upward and downward into darkened valleys, disappearing in the distance toward a horizon that appeared black but for the moonlit hilltops. The men stared in the direction indicated by Carter.

"I don't see anything," offered Carthoris after a moment.

"Neither do I, now," replied his father, who on this world went by many names, not the least of which was Warlord of Barsoom.

"Why not wait here a tal or two and see if he appears?" suggested Tardos Mors. "By the way, John Carter, do not forget to send me that recommendation for our special envoy. You seemed to feel you had a perfect candidate when we last spoke on the topic. The day of the summit approaches, as you know."

"I have not forgotten," replied John Carter, scanning the crests of the hills before them, each illuminated by moonlight with a diminishing brightness in direct ratio to the distance from those rounded points to where they sat upon their mounts. "There! I saw it again. A fleet flash of motion gliding over yon hill. It disappeared into the valley at its feet."

"There he is, I see him!" cried Carthoris, pointing, his smile greatly resembling that of his mighty sire's. "You were right, father."

All three looked in the direction indicated, where across the dead sea bottom raced a green man, mounted on a thoat. His tusks, sparkling in the moonlight, were a vivid white against the deep olive of his skin which, in the moonlit night, appeared a solid black but for glints of color as cast back to their questing eyes by beneficent Thuria. Even at this distance they saw he had slung across his back a rifle with its unbelievably long barrel such as is popular with the green men, typically made of skeel and gleaming forandus.

His apparel, they knew, would be scant, for like themselves he wore it not out of a sense of propriety or a belief that it covered any indecency, for indeed his kind cared nothing for such refined sentiments. Rather, he wore his scant war harness because it supported the sword that banged upon his hip and against the side of his thoat; also, it held his pouch and a dagger. From his middle right arm—for the man was equipped by nature with a set of intermediary limbs—he held couched a forty-sofad-long lance.

Shortly he topped the last rise, having closed the distance to the trio considerably, so much so that they could see his face plainly. So grim was his expression, so stern and so martial was his appearance that, as he catapulted over the little rise and then down the declivity, they expected to see a hundred thousand more of his kind at his heels, following him into battle. But behind him were no others.

"Father," queried Carthoris, "did you not send Pakk Bantos, Dwar of the *Cquikuss*, with the invitation to fetch him to Helium?"

"I did," his father replied, "but rather than travel in one of the grand and newly built ships of our navy, he sent word that he preferred instead to make the journey upon his war thoat in the manner in which he and his tribe are accustomed of old to travel, and that he would leave a couple of weeks before he was expected, for who can say what might lie along a man's path?"

"You mean to say," asked Tardos Mors, "that you used that tiny bit of information to calculate his arrival here, tonight, and that you cut it to such a nicety as to time his arrival nearly to the precise tal? Astonishing!"

Carter only smiled as they continued to await the new arrival.

"Well, where is he?" asked Carthoris after a reasonable amount of time had passed and still the newcomer did not appear.

"You don't think a banth lay in wait for him at the bottom of that dark valley?" suggested Tardos Mors.

"The banth that might take me unawares treads not the wastes of Barsoom," someone said behind them.

The surprised men turned quickly their mounts.

John Carter shook his head and grinned. "I should have expected that old trick."

"I spotted you three from the top of a rise three hills distant," observed the voice. "But come! We have haads to travel ere we are done riding this night!" With that the green man spun his thoat and shot down the path leading toward distant Helium.

All that night the men rode as might ones hounded by something grim and disastrous—and who is to say that they were not? When at last they topped the final rise in the well-worn trail outside the city, they brought up their thoats, their padded feet—soundless on the ochre moss of a dead sea bottom—stirring up a cloud of dust as they slid to a stop in the middle of the oft-traveled trail.

For just a moment the four riders paused, naked but for their war harness, bristling with swords, spears, and radium guns—a scene so barbaric as to appear almost out of a bygone age when seen against the backdrop of the amazing, fanciful city in the distance, whose towers reared into a cloudless sky, and whose air was already a-thrum with fliers, even at this early hour.

Without sound—for the commands were issued telepathically—the beasts leaped forward at terrific speed, voicing all manner of bays and grunts as they did so, their tails extended straight out behind them. John Carter let out a war whoop as was his custom in the days when he lived in Virginia, while the red men, Carthoris and Tardos Mors, held their peace. But the green man with whom they had ridden all night and whom they had sallied forth at a late hour yestereve to greet on the road, in the sheer exuberance of health and vigor, raised his own face to the heavens and voiced a shout.

Tars Tarkas had come to Helium.

Chapter One

En Garde!

THE CLASH AND CLANG of steel on steel reverberated down halls of polished marble in resounding echoes, emanating from the training room of John Carter, Warlord of Barsoom. A man walked briskly down those halls, glancing to neither left nor right at the spectacular murals painted upon these hallowed walls over the centuries by savants in the field of artistic endeavor, his quickening stride evidence that he was late to some appointment.

As he entered the room it looked as though pure bedlam had been unleashed, while the noise was a thunderous din made up of the shouts and grunts of men and the metallic slithering of blades running across blades.

Over it all presided the Warlord, upon his features the half-smile that was always present whenever he drew steel. He enjoyed imparting some measure of his nigh-godlike prowess with the blade to his friends and to fellow members of the Navy of Helium, especially those belonging to the personal retinue of Dejah Thoris, his mate, the resplendent daughter of Mors Kajak. To this end, he held such sessions as his busy schedule allowed.

Noticing instantly the arrival of the latecomer, John Carter barked, "Grab your gear, Dat Voga, and jump in there!"

Dat Voga wasted no time. Within moments he was caparisoned like his fellows and, practice foil in hand, leaping among their numbers as directed and battling as if his life depended on it.

One who observed the action for very long would see that chaos did not reign as it might first appear. Instead, one would discern that the motions were skillfully devised. The men whirled, riposted, sprang, rolled, and thrust—always moving, never standing still so as not to present static targets as they actively sought openings in their opponents' guards. John Carter acted as choreographer, moving among the men, yet staying out of their way, offering any instruction he deemed necessary.

"Keep your feet evenly placed, Kal Vak! Lean into him a bit but maintain your balance. Moss Fet! Keep the point of your sword where you can see it; hold it too wide or too low, you leave yourself wide open for a thrust. Excellent, Dat Voga!" observed the Warlord.

Attached to the harness of each warrior, directly over his heart, was a pouch. Occasionally, one would see a swordsman find an opening, and then the blunt tip of a training sword would squash his opponent's pouch, causing what appeared to be a small amount of "gore" to gush over the stricken man's chest, marking him as defeated. At this point the stricken man would leave the melee and watch the remainder of the mock battle from one of the benches along the walls.

During a pause, where John Carter offered instructions to one of the trainees, a man, scroll in hand, approached the entrance to the training room. Dat Voga recognized him as an official of the palace and guessed the scroll contained orders sealed by Tardos Mors, Jeddak of Helium. As the man entered the training room, the two guards saluted him, their right hands coming up and across to their left shoulders.

Passing between the guards, the man went to one side where he stood, an interested spectator. That he enjoyed the swordsmanship on display was evident from the smile on his face as he followed first one pair of fighting men and then another. But the fact that he remained on his feet rather than taking advantage of the many settees placed about the room told Dat Voga that his attendance here was predicated on business, not idle pleasure.

One of Dat Voga's conferees, the one whose guard had been defeated, now received some one-on-one instruction from John Carter as the others watched and listened. Carter did not berate the man, for it is through mistakes that one learns. But the Warlord reminded the student that mistakes in this grim business often end in death. Carter had seen the man's mistake and now he reenacted how he *should* have responded to his opponent's actions. In Dat Voga's mind, Carter seemed endowed with superhuman powers of sight and deduction when it came to swordplay, for he seemed to miss nothing.

Without appearing to have noticed the man on the sideline whom Dat Voga had watched curiously from the corner of his eye while Carter turned Moss Fet's mistake into a teachable moment, the Warlord called a halt to the exercises. "That will be it for today. All of you performed very well," he commended. Then he turned and strode straight over to the man standing near the entrance, where Dat Voga heard him greet the man with, "Kaor, Koh Vast!"

The actions of the training exercise had carried Dat Voga to the side of the room where Koh Vast was standing so he heard both John Carter's greeting and the man's response.

"Kaor, John Carter," said Koh Vast. "It is always such a pleasure to see your great skill in action. I have no doubt that these sessions will save many lives in the future—without doubt, many lives in this very room."

John Carter glanced at the men, as good-natured bantering carried on between the victors and those who had had their targets burst. "It's a service I'm all too glad to render for my adopted country. So, Koh Vast, what brings you here from the jeddak? That scroll you're carrying looks official."

Koh Vast nodded and handed the parchment to Carter.

Having satisfied his curiosity as to the man's identity, Dat Voga, together with his comrades, removed and cleaned their training leathers, oiled their practice foils, and returned them to their storage racks upon the walls. There, the men whispered excitedly among themselves, discussing what might have brought this high official to a mere training room.

Taking furtive glances in the direction of Carter and Koh Vast, they saw the Warlord break the seal on the scroll and read. Once, Carter looked up at the men at the back of the training room, whereupon they all immediately engaged themselves in checking their sandals and searching for imaginary spots on the floor.

Finally, seeing the one he sought, Carter called out, "Dat Voga, would you come here, please."

At the sound of his name called aloud Dat Voga's heart leaped like a schoolchild collared by his instructor. Breaking away from the group of trainees, he approached the two who now stood awaiting him. But Dat Voga was no schoolchild. The young man was, in many ways, exemplary of his race. His thick hair was black, as were his eyes, and his skin bore the reddish copper pigmentation of the dominant race of Barsoom.

A fine example, wonderfully muscled, his eyes were quick, and it became obvious after looking into them that his mind possessed a keen intellect. His facial structure bespoke centuries of fine breeding, with strong features, perfect teeth and the clear complexion of health and vigor. He looked every bit a handsome noble, which he was, being the scion of the old aristocracy of Greater Helium.

Gazing at the parchment in John Carter's hand, he knit his brow, wondering how it could possibly pertain to him; Carter did not leave him long to guess. As soon as he paused before them, he handed Dat Voga the missive from the jeddak.

To John Carter, Warlord of Barsoom,

I have consulted with the Council of Jeds and decided to act upon your suggestion for the appointment for the position of ambassador to Ptarsas and Zoquan. That appointee is, per your endorsement, Padwar Dat Voga.

This I do in recognition of Dat Voga's aptitude in his aid to the Ministry of Sciences, and his noteworthy service in the Navy of Helium; but most importantly, in recognition of the endorsement of one whose word carries no little weight.

Please allow Dat Voga to read this commission if, as I am informed, he is in your presence. If such is not the case, Koh Vast is to deliver a duplicate copy to the padwar's quarters. The date for the summit to discuss the situation has been set that we might plan this great venture. Details will follow shortly.

Tardos Mors, Jeddak.

The bottom of the official notification carried the embossed seal of the Jeddak of Helium, and that of the Council of Jeds. After the young man finished reading, John Carter smiled at the stunned look on the padwar's face.

"I hope you don't mind that I recommended you, but I'm convinced you're the perfect man for this position. I didn't mention it to you prior to this as I didn't wish to see you disappointed should they have chosen to elect another."

Dat Voga smiled eagerly. "No, sir! It's an honor—and thank you. I hope your confidence has not been misplaced. Ptarsas and Zoquan? I don't recall those names. At any rate, I can't wait to learn more about this intriguing position."

"I am pleased," replied John Carter. "And you shall not have long to wait, by the sound of it. And if I didn't have every confidence in your ability, padwar, I'd have never made the recommendation."

Chapter Two

A Summit in Helium

THAT EVENING, A MESSENGER ARRIVED at the quarters of Padwar Dat Voga with an official invitation to the summit, detailing the time and location, John Carter having sent the padwar's acceptance via Koh Vast. For the scene of the meeting, it had been decided to utilize a room in the palace Dat Voga had only heard of—the official State Room of the Jeddak.

Soon he would not only see this fabled room in person, where decisions concerning every topic from wars to widows were settled; he would also meet individuals of royalty and science from all corners of Barsoom. It was a giddying prospect.

For the padwar, the summit could not come soon enough, but he admitted to himself that he was nervous. He heard the names of a few guests—celebrated jeddaks and odwars whose reputations preceded them. A gathering of scientists and representatives from the Council of Science in Greater Helium, which boasted members from all the allied countries, would also be present. Nor were these all; the complete list of dignitaries would have blanched the face of the most stalwart statesman, let alone a simple padwar.

The night of the meeting finally arrived. Wearing his best leathers, as well as a raven cape he occasionally wore to those few royal functions to which he was invited, he strapped on a matching dagger and sword and departed for the summit. Although he left early in hopes of being among the first to arrive, the dismayed young man discovered he was the last to make his appearance.

As he stepped through the doorway, a voice boomed, "Ah, here's Dat Voga. Let us begin!" The voice was that of Tardos Mors. With that announcement everyone found a seat at an immense table. The room was filled to capacity, with everyone staring at the young padwar—or at least, he felt so. The embarrassed young man felt the heat rise in his face at the thought that these important personages had been awaiting his arrival—a mere padwar.

The jeddak stood at the head of the table upon a raised dais before a rostrum; all were seated, and he began without delay. "All of you have some vague idea as to why you were invited here this evening, although very few of you are aware of all the details. The purpose of this summit is to lay the known facts before this elite panel and iron out a course of action. I call upon John Carter."

Carter strode to the podium as Tardos Mors took his seat. "Many of you," the Earthman began, "have heard related parts of the story of how, disguised as a red man and an assassin, I sought to bring down a house of slaughter in Zodanga known as the Assassin's Guild.

"In a freakish twist of fate, I became the hired killer of a brilliant, yet villainous, scientist by the name of Fal Sivas. Initially, I stuck to my role as I sought to utilize this man to locate the guild. But of almost as much interest, I learned of a ship he'd built, a vessel he claimed could travel to Thuria. It was a claim I soon proved to be no idle statement.

"While there I also learned that another great and equally evil mind was at work completing a similar ship—Gar Nal, an archrival of Fal Sivas. The guild, it seemed, had formed an alliance with Gar Nal, and having learned of my mission, they used their ship to kidnap my mate,

Dejah Thoris, as many will recall. They took her to our nearer moon to hold her for ransom. It was my discovery of this which led me to follow in the ship of Fal Sivas.

"Now, the purpose of relating this to you is not to re-acquaint you with my tales of derring-do; far from it. The point today is the science and physics behind those ships—specifically, the power source their engines utilized. I now yield the floor to the speaker for the Council of Science and one of our local historians. These men will elaborate on the specifics of these engines and their power source. That said, I call Siv Datron of Duhor, speaker for the Council of Science, and Val Statt of Ptarth, of the Society of History."

With a nod to each of these two gentlemen, Carter took his seat while they together rose and approached the rostrum. It was Siv Datron who explained that, while the ultimate disposal of these two unique ships had never been publicly divulged, they had been removed and taken to a remote location where they were studied by a team of specialists. Murmurs rose from the assembly at this admission, with someone exclaiming, "I wondered what happened to those ships!"

"What we learned as to their power sources," Siv Datron continued, "is that both had a remarkably similar design, no doubt due to the spies of Fal Sivas and Gar Nal stealing secrets from one another. Both engines utilized an extremely pure form of radium, and in greater quantities than standard fliers. After one trip to Thuria each during the occasion narrated by John Carter, followed by subsequent trips into orbit about the planet during testing, the method of releasing the energy resulted in significant depletion of the radium.

"So rapid was the loss that we deemed a dozen trips out of the atmosphere would see the complete depletion of the fuel source. We further determined that utilizing the ship within the atmosphere appeared to cause no appreciable decay of matter, thus deducing it to be the enormous amount of energy required to escape the planet's gravitational field and the atmosphere, thin though it be, which caused the rapid exhaustion."

At this point Siv Datron glanced to his historian counterpart. Val Statt, a wizened old scientist who had been a fixture in the Society of History for hundreds of years, stepped forward, fiddling comically with a set of large spectacles upon his nose that magnified his eyes, from his listeners' viewpoint, to nearly double their actual size.

"As many of you already know," he creaked, "radium has for ages been quite a mystery to the scientists of the modern day. We know how to use it for motors and exploding ammunition, for instance, and yet the simple task of generating light from it was lost during the cataclysms, following the shrinking and lamentable dissipation of our seas.

"We can step into the pits of a city such as Horz, built over a million years ago, and these amazing lights are still functioning today. I don't doubt they will continue to do so for another million years. It's likely these remarkable inventions will be the last artificial light on a dying world after we are long turned to dust, their dim radiance illuminating dark passages that meanwhile will not have been trod by Barsoomians for eons. We assume the ancients created their compound utilizing materials that simply no longer exist, hence their mystery."

At this point the old man paused to steady himself by placing his hands upon the podium and leaned in toward an audience now grown quiet and wholly absorbed after his compelling preamble.

"You may not recall from your history lessons the names of two cities I am about to mention. Their names have fallen off the map for thousands of years. I know of no communication with these two once great nations within our time. I refer to the ancient trade cities of Ptarsas and

Zoquan, one-time chief exporters of the highest quality radium on Barsoom, their ships plying the seas to bring their ore to the shores of cities hungry for the material.

"For, in the burgeoning days of motorized travel and during raw times of war, and for other uses such as the lighting I mentioned, the ancients could not get enough of it. The mountain ranges lying close to Ptarsas and Zoquan were aforetimes the richest sources in the world for this highly coveted ore. Once the ancient peoples realized its value, the economies of those nations became double that of any other metropolis in existence."

Val Statt paused for effect. "This condition continued up to the cataclysms." At this point the historian motioned to a young retainer who came forward with an urn, and a vessel for drinking. Val slowly poured water from the urn into the transparent vessel during which activity one could have heard a Barsoomian maiden's coif pin hit the floor.

"With the drying up of Barsoom's oceans and the ensuing decline of civilization, and in conjunction with the great longevity of radium, stores of which cities had hoarded for millennia, the importation dwindled and eventually radium trade ceased. Ptarsas and Zoquan fell out of communication with other nations due to the decreasing need for their ore and the great distances at which they resided. Their seemingly inexhaustible stores of radium were no longer required in the quantities they had been in the past."

Val Statt held up the vessel of water. "For lack of this, they were forgotten." He allowed his gaze to travel the table of members, eyeing each individually, his gaze lingering longer upon Dat Voga, or so thought the youth. Then, with a single motion, he tipped the vessel up and quaffed it dry. The plunk of the empty vessel as Val Statt brusquely sat it down shattered the tomb-like stillness of the room.

"A shame. You've heard the laudable exposition of Siv Datron relative to the requirements of these new spacecraft.

If our estimations are correct, we shall not only rival, but also surpass, the requirements of the past for radium. Those stores of ore I referred to have reached a state of near exhaustion! Thousands of years of usage have left their indelible mark."

Gasps and exclamations of surprise from the astounded listeners broke the stillness, with Tardos Mors having to call for order from the assembly. Val continued.

"What I am about to relay to you is of the utmost secrecy and not to be discussed with anyone outside of this dignified body. The stores of radium we have at our disposal will be utilized and gone within a few decades of powering these new types of craft. The engines of these spacecraft consume radium in greater quantities than the simple motors that have powered our vessels through the thin air of Barsoom for centuries. There is a noticeable depletion of quality radium from local sources after heavy mining over the course of thousands of years; new influxes are required.

"Although they are a half a world away, the time has come to rekindle relations with those cities if they still exist and bring them back into the fold of international trade. Our intent is to create the next evolution of craft, vessels not bound to the dead atmosphere of a dying world. If our races are to survive, we must come together to stem the tide of our own extinction. Our reproductive rates have fallen; our atmosphere plant has already experienced one near catastrophic failure. In short, the outlook is grim.

"John Carter has told us of life on Jasoom and Sasoom. We have reason to believe that Cosoom, even, is habitable. One day we foresee a time when we must sadly abandon our beloved Barsoom and flee to other worlds. It shall be a mass exodus the likes of which our solar system has never witnessed, made possible with the inventions of Fal Sivas and Gar Nal. Scoundrels though they were, they may have given us the means to save our races.

"Our success will come down to the efforts of two men. These two, whom I wish to bring before you, are Dat Voga, official Ambassador to Ptarsas and Zoquan for the Council for the Acquisition of Radium, and Prince Carthoris, Plenipotentiary to Ptarsas and Zoquan."

Excited murmurings erupted throughout the room as Carthoris and Dat Voga rose and advanced toward the front of the stateroom. The padwar, not realizing he would be required to stand before the assembly, rapidly assimilated the information he had learned. He hoped if he must speak that he would be able to do so astutely, but also realized that until he journeyed to these far cities, he would not have anything of real value to add to what had already been stated.

As Dat Voga followed Carthoris to the raised dais his eyes chanced to meet those of John Carter, where he sat next to Tars Tarkas. The Warlord smiled and nodded encouragement, a nod that the padwar nervously returned. He then let his gaze wander across the gathered assemblage, once more impressed with how quickly they had assembled this summit. He hated the idea of abandoning Barsoom, holding as it did everything dear to him. But, if it came down to that, he was prepared to do whatever was necessary to save every life on the planet.

Much of what they had been told this evening was common knowledge, but much he had found new and astounding. To run out of radium! It seemed incredible. As soon as Val Statt made that astonishing pronouncement, the young man understood for the first time the gravity of the responsibility that he and Carthoris had assumed.

As they met at the rostrum, Carthoris extended his arm to his compatriot. In Barsoomian fashion, each gripped the other upon the shoulder. Dat Voga had the utmost respect for the Warlord's son. His inventive genius he knew to be little short of uncanny; his swordsmanship, legendary, and exceeded only by that of his sire, while his honor, integrity, and service to Helium were renowned.

Still feeling unworthy of the title conferred upon him, the padwar felt overshadowed in some measure. At the same time, he was reassured knowing Carthoris would be there to lend his considerable support. An ovation of applause ensued as they took the stage, but quieted when Carthoris began speaking.

"As you've just heard, we are charged to reopen communication between Helium and her allies and the distant cities of Ptarsas and Zoquan. Having consulted ancient documents, we've narrowed down the location of Ptarsas, with Zoquan laying another seventy-five to a hundred haads further southwest. Our plan is to first locate and consult with Ptarsas, as that city is closest. After completing negotiations there, we intend to venture to Zoquan, hoping to enlist the aid of the former if trade talks have gone well.

"As many of you know, I inherited a bit of wanderlust from my father, being ever anxious to travel to the unknown corners of our planet, much of which remains unexplored. I look forward to visiting a region that, historically, stands out so prominently in the beginnings of the modernization of our world, although it is regretful that two cities largely responsible for that advancement were later forgotten."

Here Carthoris glanced at his fellow diplomat. "I'm delighted by the selection of Dat Voga as ambassador to these forgotten nations. I'm aware that most of you are unfamiliar with him, so let me say this by way of introduction: he is the son of Heliumetic nobility whose endeavors in the arts of science and physics come highly commended. His is the sort of keen intellect any nation would be proud to have sponsor her, and to represent her to her peers; you could not be better served.

"We all know our world is fraught with danger; it lurks in every corner of the globe. Dat Voga's military record is impregnable, the man being as versatile with the sword as he is with astrolabes and test tubes. Since we're sending him into the unknown, we wished to designate an ambassador who could think, or fight, his way out of any predicament. You see before you such a man.

"As to my own selection for this initial contact, the council believed that being the grandson of the Jeddak of Helium, and the son of the Warlord of Barsoom, my presence would lend strength and substance to our negotiations. I will be there to lend support to Ambassador Voga during this initial contact, after which I shall return to continue development on other projects also vital to our forthcoming ventures.

"Only the two of us shall undertake this journey. We didn't wish to show up at their city gate with an armada of warships and a fleet of cargo vessels, which might be construed as an act of war on one hand and downright presumptuous on the other. We haven't had contact with these people for Issus knows how long.

"We don't know what to expect. The theory has been propounded that we'll find deserted ruins, and that all this preamble will be for naught; that we'll merely have to begin mining this unclaimed ore for ourselves. While that's certainly possible, I hope it's not the case."

Carthoris described the route along which they were to proceed and how long the council should wait before, not having heard from them, scout vessels were sent in search. The Prince of Helium then indicated to the padwar that he had completed his delivery and smiled reassuringly at the young man. Dat Voga took the rostrum as Carthoris stepped to one side.

While feeling inadequate in a room full of people who were very much his senior in every respect, the padwar had no need to feel abashed. He did not realize it, but he had as much right to be here as every man and woman in attendance. His keen intellect, quiet reserve, military shrewdness, and trustworthy demeanor had all been taken into consideration in his selection; he had not been chosen lightly.

He began speaking. "Men and women of Helium, Ptarth and Zodanga! Men and women of Hastor, Gathol, and Tjanath! Of Duhor, Okar, and Thark! We have here tonight representatives, not only of the few I have named, but also of many other great nations of Barsoom. I give you greetings. To tell it to you straight from the thoat's mouth, I'm humbled at being chosen for this position.

"By my first ancestor, I swear to strive to my uttermost to succeed in this endeavor; indeed, it seems it will mean calamity to do any less. We've been enlightened this evening on matters of science and history related to this venture. But I say we're making history tonight, in this very room. This project is farther reaching then I ever dreamed, and I now believe the fate of all peoples of Barsoom hangs in the balance.

"Too, I am hopeful to renew commerce with two important cities. Even were the issues we've discussed not so grave, yet would I wish to reach forth the hand of beneficence and make new friends of these formerly great nations.

"I shall not address you at great length—I'm anxious to begin the necessary planning to commence this historic undertaking. And too, until I come to the former shores of Ptarsas, I haven't anything to report except that I won't rest until Carthoris and I are splitting the thin air of Barsoom to Ptarsas and Zoquan!"

Cries of "Hear, hear!" and "Dat Voga!" filled the room. Men and women exploded, leaping from their seats. The newly appointed ambassador drew his sword, held it over his head and shouted, "For Barsoom!" The refrain was picked up and repeated.

Dat Voga hoped that his short speech had inspired the heart of each at the table below him. From their reaction, it certainly seemed so. His own confidence was augmented with the knowledge that his inexperience with matters of state would be balanced by his scientific acuity, and the presence of Carthoris, who would be right by his side to advise him. Together, they were about to embark upon a momentous period in the history of their world, the beginnings of a new epoch in the annals of Barsoom.

Chapter Three

White Apes of Xanator

FOR TWO WEEKS after that initial meeting, the assembly continued to refine their plans. Carthoris plotted a course and readied a flier while Dat Voga honed his statecraft. It is quite probable there existed no better statesman to groom the young padwar than he whom the council called upon, that being Tars Tarkas, Jeddak of Thark.

While Tars Tarkas might have felt more at ease galloping across the ochre sea bottoms astride a war thoat than addressing officials and dignitaries, he could not disagree that he possessed a natural ability concerning these matters. His speeches had often been hailed as the most elegant of the assembly, a natural side effect of the archaic manner in which green men spoke in their day-to-day exchanges.

But, while a master himself, in a short time Tars Tarkas, alone with the youthful ambassador in the same chamber of state where they met the night of the summit, leaned back in his chair, a tone of obvious satisfaction in his voice.

"Dat Voga, your sword arm is articulate in the speech of war—this I have seen with my own eyes. Your mind is keener than the sword at your side, and now I have with my hearing verified another truth. To wit, I believe if you gain the ear of the Jeddak of Ptarsas for even a few moments, you will have, in that short duration, won your argument.

"I consider my work here complete. I wish I were to accompany you and Carthoris, as this expedition has all the earmarks of spice and adventure. Be that as it may, I bid thee safe journey. When next I see you," he intoned solemnly, "I shall clasp your shoulder, and thou mine, and I shall congratulate you, no doubt, on the successful conclusion of this mighty endeavor."

With that, Tars Tarkas flashed the youth a rare smile and, standing, strode from the room with the measured, lengthy strides of the Jeddak of the Hordes of Thark.

The last night before they were to depart, Dat Voga's closest friends took him out to shower him with food and gaiety that they might celebrate his fantastic promotion, and to bid him farewell in high fashion, for they knew not for how long he would be absent. He had always enjoyed the night life of Helium, but tonight it seemed different.

Thoughtful, he stood atop the roof of a high-rise in Greater Helium, leaning upon a balustrade with a glass of sompus wine sitting untouched at his elbow, staring out over the beautiful scenery of the brilliantly illuminated city. The vistas from this lofty prominence were stunning.

Although he had seen the sight every night of his life, tonight it seemed special, almost spectrally vibrant. It could not be due to the dangers of the expedition; those held no concern for him at all as he had the utmost confidence in the swords of Carthoris and himself. He considered that, because he was to venture forth as an official representative of Helium, perhaps the weight of responsibility . . . but, no, neither did that explain his strange mood.

He could not quite put a finger on it, but it felt to him as if, after tonight, he would never see Helium in quite the same manner. Sighing, he turned from the night sky and, still contemplating, returned to his friends.

The next morning dawned quick and bright, as did the

rising of the sun each day on Barsoom where the dwellers of that dusty world know neither twilight nor any long-delayed dawning, the sky's transition from inky blackness to full daylight, and vice versa, occurring almost instantly.

Old Val Statt and Siv Datron were both present to speed them on their journey, likewise Tardos Mors, John Carter, Tars Tarkas, and many other members of the assembly. They stood upon the towering hangar deck atop the palace.

Besides members of the assembly, the parents of Dat Voga were present. Dejah Thoris, too, arrived to see her only son off. Thuvia, once of Ptarth but now long since mate of Carthoris, stood opposite the princess at the side of her mighty mate, not wishing to miss a single opportunity of contact with him. They each understood the future to be at all times uncertain, and none could predict for how long these loved ones would be gone, or upon what day they might once again set foot in Helium.

Dat Voga noticed that the beautiful Dejah Thoris had joined his parents and was standing beside his mother. Both women watched proudly as their sons took their places aboard the open-cockpit, six-man flier.

This vessel, chosen from the fleet of Carthoris for its handy size, was perfect for the wants of the two men, having plenty of space aboard to accommodate any necessary gear. Supplies for a lengthy journey were stowed in their places. The markings upon the hull had been modified, with the insignia of the House of Carthoris having been removed, while in their place the ship now bore the insignia of each city represented by the assembly.

The vessel came equipped with the latest version of the destination control compass. This wonderful invention by Carthoris could be set to any point on the planet after which the pilot could lay down and go to sleep if he wished. He could do so confident the ship would guide itself perfectly to its destination.

During flight, the device's invisible waves quested for obstacles which, if detected, would cause the ship to either rise above or drop below the object, or even to increase or decrease velocity. The compass would intelligently deduce which would be the most efficient maneuver to prevent a collision.

If the compass could not compute a permutation that would result in avoiding the obstacle, it would revert to its final solution—that of sounding an alarm to alert the pilot. When it arrived at its destination, it would stop the ship and sound a different alarm to inform the pilot of his or her safe arrival.

The vessel held comfortable seating for six, with two seats abreast at the controls that allowed piloting from either position. The remaining four were in the passenger area, with two seats on either side of a narrow walkway running the length of the ship.

At the stern a gun mount had been affixed to the ship's frame. Here a simple bench was fitted to the decking; this was not intended for occupancy except under such contingencies as would require the manning of a gun. At present no cannon sat in the cradle, although the intended use of the position was obvious.

Their personal items stowed, the two men said their good-byes as the time loomed for their departure. Val Statt bombarded them with information with which they were thoroughly conversant. Others from the council alternately bid them farewell or gave them last moment advice. This they did right up until the small, stately skiff lifted from the hangar deck.

Dat Voga seated himself beside Carthoris, who for the time being manned the controls. The young padwar's heart pounded with excitement. Upon takeoff, they rose rapidly to five thousand sofads in elevation, at which point Carthoris turned the nose toward the southwest and opened up the throttle. With the velocity of a speeding projectile, their craft soon disappeared from the sight of those atop the hangar deck.

The two warriors recognized much of the terrain over which they flew. They had logged many zodes in this area on the backs of war thoats, in small fliers, and aboard the gargantuan vessels of war capable of carrying five thousand men—the mighty battleships of the navy.

Not wishing to waste any more time than necessary, they paused only as needed, spending most of their time in flight. One man took turns at the controls while the other ate or slept on a pile of silks and furs that served as a cushion against the hard forandus flooring, their harness safely buckled to the decking. It could be easily understood why this precaution was necessary. In the event the pilot must take any sort of drastic measure, or in the event of a midair collision, an untethered occupant could be pitched overboard to his death.

As their route would take them near the ancient city of Xanator, they decided to use the ruins as a waypoint, planning a short stop there to attend to their bodily needs, and to stretch their limbs. Always curious and wishing to break up the monotony of flying over haad after haad of trackless desert, the two felt it might be interesting to see the ruins.

Late afternoon loomed upon them on the day they finally reached the outskirts of the dead city. The sun was falling rapidly toward the horizon when they spotted a group of the great white apes squatting in the shade of a ruined building that must have been an imposing pile in its day.

The apes were notorious for haunting these glorious icons of Barsoom's past, making any exploration of the structures virtually impossible. From its foundations, the edifice rose for two hundred sofads, but much of the roof had collapsed into the interior. The remains of towers lay at each corner, all but one of which had completely collapsed.

The lone remaining tower reared five hundred sofads above the roofline of the main structure. With most of its approach destroyed, it was doubtful the tower had entertained visitors for thousands of years, unless some adventurous flier pilot had anchored to the tower and entered through one of the windows encircling the upper reaches.

The risk involved in doing so was considerable. If the tower were to collapse when one was inside, and the only means of escape was moored to the exterior . . . Dat Voga shuddered at the thought of riding that tower to the ground.

The two decided to land elsewhere due to the proximity of the white apes who rose at sight of them. The beasts began growling and grunting and moving about in a large avenue fronting the colossal edifice, possibly an ancient government building of some fashion, though it was impossible to say.

In passing by the alluring tower, they peeked through the openings ringing its top, glimpsing the familiar splashes of ancient murals upon the interior walls, along with the detritus and the dust of ages strewn about the dark, tantalizing interior. Carthoris gunned the controls and sent the skiff shooting out over the decrepit roof to search for another landing spot.

Realizing their altitude made them much more visible to eyes below, Carthoris sent the ship into a low dive, bringing them well below many of the rooftops as he looked for a place they could in safety leave the vessel. They flew onward over a maze of buildings, wishing to put distance between themselves and the apes before they set down.

Paramount and uppermost in each of their minds were the need for haste and the success of their undertaking. Any thoughts of exploring these interesting ruins out of mere curiosity must take a back seat to their mission. They flew on until they approached the edge of the original city, near what had once been a mighty sea wall. The terrain outside the wall dropped steeply where the sea floor sloped downward toward former deeps.

Here Carthoris discovered what might once have been the home of a noble. It appeared to be very much intact, having a low wall running around the squared-off property abutting the sea wall from which the setting sun must have once been visible across the waves of the Throxeus. Today, however, the sun would set over an ochre sea bottom. The dying rays cast long shadows behind them.

Dat Voga imagined how it must have been to live here a million years before with a beautiful, undulating sea gently lapping the wall below where he stood. He thought how the family must have spent a good deal of recreational time on this backside of their property overlooking the sea. Here of late he had given a lot of thought to ancient Barsoom, what with all the talk during the summit of his planet's past.

Above him, Thuria, the nearer moon, raced madly across the darkening firmament that shortly would blacken into a nighttime sky; her mate, Cluros, slow and stately, had barely crested above the distant horizon. The shadows cast by speeding Thuria were moving eerily over the ground. The two Heliumites disembarked, keeping their voices low to avoid any unwanted attention. Green hordes were known to frequent dead cities such as this, and one must always be wary of a sudden confrontation with the great white apes.

Those hideous creatures stood nearly sixteen sofads in height, were equipped by nature with an intermediary set of limbs such as those possessed by green men, and had an alarming shock of bristly hair atop their low-browed heads. They had only rudimentary societal development but had been known to carry large objects for use as bludgeons that, coupled with their great strength and a mouthful of hideous fangs, made of them a most formidable opponent.

The last rays of daylight were rapidly waning when Carthoris settled to the sward, shadows swiftly eradicating any remaining light that darkness might hold sway for the night. The two men, taking different directions, walked among the ruins to limber up prior to yet another long leg of their journey. Then, without warning, the very thing they endeavored to prevent occurred. As Dat Voga passed the darkened entry of a low building, he heard a low grunt followed by a resonating growl, the depth and volume of which he felt must have been heard halfway to Helium.

The young padwar considered himself a brave man, having faced many dangers in his short life. The first time he encountered an example of this, the most horrid denizen of his world, he succeeded in getting his blade into its heart and then sending a bullet between its eyes, thereby miraculously surviving the encounter. But in that situation, he had ample warning, giving him time to prepare his defense.

This attack, however, occurred so abruptly he was unable to completely draw his sword before the beast leaped on top of him, its fangs seeking his flesh. So quickly did the enormous creature pinion him to the ground that he thought his brief career as ambassador to a foreign city was over before it began. But he had not reckoned on Carthoris, whose wanderings had not taken him far.

Having heard the growl, the latter had already turned and started trotting in his friend's direction when he saw the beast launch itself from the narrow entrance to one of the buildings, its great girth tearing loose some of the smaller stonework as it exploded from the darkened interior. The beast must have turned sideways when it originally entered the building, for the width across its shoulders dwarfed the dimensions of the opening.

The humongous monster pinned its relatively tiny prey to the ground beneath its great bulk, the man's hand having just closed upon the hilt of his sword before he was overcome by the weight of the grotesque body. The ferocity of the attack caused Carthoris to fear he might only arrive in time to avenge his friend's death, for he saw not how anyone could survive it.

The beast's head snapped viciously toward the fallen man, its savage roars filling the dimly lighted surroundings. Simultaneously, powerful limbs raked wicked talons across the moss-covered ground in the behemoth's efforts to disembowel the man. It was the very proximity of the creature that hampered its own efforts, with the result that it merely sent great clods of ochre moss and dust into the air.

Distantly, Carthoris heard the howls of others of its kind, responding to the cries of their fellow. Running forward into close quarters, Carthoris, fearful of harming his comrade by swinging his sword in a beheading motion, instead viciously drove his arm forward as if hurling a spear, the sword entering the side of the thing's skull and cleanly punching its way out the other side.

A sudden wrench by the fatally wounded beast twisted the sword violently. Determined, Carthoris held on, finding himself jerked completely off his feet by his giant opponent's immense strength. Never losing his grip on his sword, the beast tossed the Prince of Helium back and forth, his arms feeling as if they would be wrenched from their sockets by the powerful death throes of the gigantic ape.

What were in fact mere moments seemed to last forever. The creature, in its efforts to throw off the thing clinging to its gory head, caused itself a wound the size of which might have allowed Carthoris to pass his entire arm through it. At last, the great beast fell dead.

Dazed, Carthoris stumbled to his feet and retrieved his blood-smeared sword from his victim. He realized the courtyard would soon be filled with the things. The screams of the approaching apes grew louder, a terrible din as they took shortcuts through the vacant buildings of the eons-abandoned, ape-haunted city. Walls were caved in with their great bulks and doorways burst open, and over all reigned the cacophony of their hideous barks, growls, and roars.

Carthoris ran to Dat Voga to find the young padwar miraculously alive and coming to his feet. Grabbing the dazed man by his harness, he dragged him at a run beside him. Stunned by the exchange, Dat Voga struggled to free his sword from its scabbard.

Carthoris cautioned, "Forget it; we've got to get airborne. It sounds like the entire horde is coming!"

Chapter Four

On to Ptarsas

Dat Voga cursed the fact that they had ever landed in this haunted place rather than somewhere further out in the desert, realizing that due to their lack of caution utter ruin now menaced their mission. He envisioned the assembly back in Helium expectantly awaiting news. Eventually they would send search vessels; possibly they would never find their bones in this dead city after the apes dismembered them in their savage fight over their various portions.

After he regained his senses, he realized that fortune alone had saved him, for the beast had fallen atop him before it could latch onto his neck and shoulders with its snapping jaws. He had not suffered so much as a scratch from the ordeal but for mild abrasions where he had fallen to the ground with the great weight of the ponderous ape on top of him.

Looking over his shoulder as he ran, Dat Voga saw two dozen of the ghostly white creatures leaping the low walls, clambering over taller portions, and jumping from nearby rooftops to land inside the courtyard.

Realizing they could never get the vessel into the air in time to escape the oncoming horde, he drew his sword. Calling to his prince to get the ship off the ground, he spun about and charged toward the creatures to buy Carthoris some time.

Pulling his radium pistol from his belt, he paused to send a fusillade of rapidly fired rounds into the oncoming mass. He saw the side of one's skull blasted out, blood and brains exploding into the face of another who loped alongside it. This one immediately stopped and attacked its fellow who died on its feet from Dat Voga's round. He took out two more in rapid succession, blasting holes in their upper body and leaving one without the use of a mid-limb forearm below its elbow when a round utterly ruined the joint and left the limb dangling.

Dat Voga crammed his pistol into its holster as the beasts closed on him. Running diagonally toward the lumbering apes, he opened the gut cavity of one, its entrails spilling out in a gush over the now bloodied and trampled ochre moss. He followed by nearly severing the leg off another. The beast crumpled to the ground where it howled hideously, thrashing and biting at its own ghastly wound.

He found himself in the thick of it then. The apes snapped at him with their great jaws and swung massive hairy, clawed fists at his face. Others lashed at him with clubs or bars of iron as they attempted to smash him. The handsome young noble's recent rigorous training presided over by John Carter fortunately had focused on scenarios where the fight involved one against many.

So now, amid this mad, tangled mass of bodies, Dat Voga pirouetted and wove his way through his enemy, his sword never moving without slicing or penetrating flesh, his movements graceful in comparison to the clumsy, yet powerful, attacks of the great white apes. His blade appeared to weave a blurred net of steel around him, leaving a horrid, repulsive mess of gutted, limbless, and headless monsters in his wake.

* * *

Carthoris, although thinking his friend's efforts futile given the numbers of the creatures bounding into the clearing, never hesitated as he leaped aboard and started up the flier. Upon takeoff he turned the craft's nose toward the inner courtyard. He had every intention of following through with the younger man's rash plan. And who knew? It just might succeed.

As he approached, he had heard Dat Voga's pistol fall silent. When he brought the ship about, he felt a shock of stunned disbelief. Bodies littered the ground of the courtyard, rendering it a scene of utter carnage. Careening toward his friend, he bounced the bottom of the skiff off the head of an unfortunate ape that lay twitching and dying in his wake.

Several of the apes had ceased attacking the human and were rending the corpses of their fellows. Dat Voga desperately fenced with a determined ape that wielded an iron bar as deftly as if it weighed no more than a malagor feather. The padwar used the ape's own bulk against it to maneuver himself to its rear so he might get at it with the point of his sword. The coarse, white hide of the beast became darkened with gore. The color of the dark ichor was not distinguishable in the rapidly dwindling light, but Carthoris knew what stained its hide.

The radium motors of Barsoomian fliers are nearly silent, so Carthoris called out to warn his friend of his approach. "Dat Voga—jump!"

The padwar took one more determined swing, opening a sideways gash in the lower lip of the enraged ape below its gum line, causing it to recoil in retreat. Gathering himself, he leaped for the bottom of the skiff passing over his head. He believed he was too late and had missed his one chance at salvation even as Carthoris clutched his outstretched hand from a position leaning over the gunwale. Dat Voga felt his body wrenched powerfully upward and over the side of the craft. The padwar fell to the decking as Carthoris rushed back to the controls.

From the floor of the flier, Dat Voga instinctively sought

a deck ring for his harness. He half expected eight or ten apes to flow over the sides in pursuit, so he took a firmer grip on his blade. He glanced at Carthoris. The prince, half-crouched at the controls, had not bothered to resume his seat.

Carthoris grinned over one shoulder as he directed the craft with a practiced hand over low roofs and ancient walls toward the former sea wall and the open desert.

"My first thought," he said, "was to drop the mooring cable for you, but I was afraid you might not see it in the dark. And anyway, it would have left you dangling like bait for your friends back there." He barked out a laugh at his grim joke.

"Very solicitous of you." Dat Voga grinned.

"So, I dropped the ship's elevation within arm's reach of you and locked the controls. Jesting aside, I'm happy you made it! Gods—what remarkable swordsmanship. My father would've been thrilled if he'd witnessed the manner in which you comported yourself—"

A vicious wrench from below, followed by a steep list toward the stern, interrupted them. The nose of the craft shot skyward, sending Dat Voga sprawling backward where he came to an abrupt stop against the gunnery bench. Carthoris was hanging from the controls, his sandaled feet unable to gain purchase on the smooth, sloped decking. Desperately, he sought to regain control of the vessel. With the bow in the air, he was flying blind, leaving them in imminent peril of careening into whatever wall or building happened across their path.

Scrambling for a foothold, Dat Voga at last clutched the backrest of a nearby seat and pulled himself upward, whereupon he turned to find himself staring into the hideous, blood-smeared face of the ape with which he had just grappled, and from whose clutches he had thought himself safe.

Seeing the author of its hurts near at hand, the ape voiced a hideous roar, most of which blasted the padwar in the face. The putrid spray, filled with saliva, phlegm, and blood, splattered his eyes and assaulted his olfactory senses, its venomous spittle burning his orbs and the ear-ringing roar nearly deafening him at this close proximity.

The ape's lower lip, which he had sliced wide open as his parting shot before leaping for the ship, now dangled by a thread. The beast had nearly ripped it off in its great rage and herculean efforts to get at the hated man-thing who was the author of its injuries.

Rather than watch its quarry escape, the fury-fueled ape had given chase to the fleeing vessel. It caught up to them as they crossed a low wall and had leaped for the rear of the small ship, with blind luck guiding its hands to the gun mount at the stern. The weight of the creature had pulled the stern downward, pointing the bow into the sky.

Miraculously, it missed getting its lower abdomen into the propellers. Had it done so it possibly would have killed itself and destroyed the blades, necessitating lengthy repairs; should the need arise, they had the required tools and spare parts aboard. For now, the steep angle of the ship prevented the creature from being carved to pieces by the whirling blades.

Releasing its hold with one hand, the ape sought to clutch the man that it might drag him toward its gaping, fang-filled jaws. It grunted with its efforts, its eyes staring with cold intelligence into the padwar's own while Dat Voga struggled to prevent being catapulted into its reach.

The two continued thus—the ape trying to clamber over the gunwale, the padwar trying to regain his footing. While attempting to secure purchase on the bottom of the slippery hull, the beast's foot encountered a whirling blade with a loud clang, resulting in yet another tremendous roar and a renewal of its exertions to clamber aboard.

At last, Dat Voga found purchase and braced himself against the gunner's bench. Keeping one hand upon the seat he brought his sword down, neatly severing the creature's hand at the wrist. With a bloodcurdling, humanlike scream it fell, losing several fingers off one of its remaining hands in the whirling blades as it attempted to save itself.

The vessel had now crossed out over the sea wall in the direction of the dried-up floor of the evaporated Throxeus, so that the creature's fall was not a short one. At their low elevation over the city, a fall would have been nothing to the monstrous bull ape. Instead, the unfortunate beast plummeted to the slope leading into the dead sea basin.

No gentle incline this, but more nearly a vertical cliff—a steep, rocky shore once submerged beneath the tumultuous waves of the sea. After traveling end over end and bouncing from one jagged rock to another, the enormous, lifeless body came to rest just outside the city the hulking brute had haunted its entire life.

With the weight gone, Carthoris immediately righted the ship. After tending to his controls, he turned to see how Dat Voga was faring just in time to witness the padwar use his sword to pry off the hideous, hairy ornament yet clutching the gun mount and then hear the man sigh heavily in relief as the severed limb disappeared in the darkness. For at that exact moment the sun dipped below the horizon, blanketing this hemisphere of the planet in night.

His gruesome task done, Dat Voga turned back to face the Prince of Helium. "My prince, I believe my curiosity regarding ancient Xanator has been thoroughly quenched. What say you we fly nonstop for Ptarsas?"

Carthoris, taking in his bedraggled, out-of-breath but otherwise none-the-worse-for-wear friend in the low luminescence cast by the controls, threw back his head and laughed. He laughed so hard his sides hurt. Dat Voga, dusting himself and picking pieces of moss from his hair and harness, joined him.

"Well said! We'll do exactly that!" Shooting up to five thousand sofads, Carthoris reset their course and opened the throttle—destination Ptarsas. From then on, they did their sightseeing from two haads above the ground.

* * *

As they flew on, the youthful ambassador often contemplated their upcoming visit to these historical cities. Dat Voga wondered why they knew so little about them. Why had the Ptarsans not sought them out? Eventually he posed the question to Carthoris. The Prince of Helium sat in silence for a while, considering the other's question.

"I have to believe," he replied eventually, "that these people, if they still exist, are happy in their isolation. It's reasonable to believe they have fliers. If that turns out to be the case, then obviously they could've flown anywhere they wished. The possibility also exists that, in the remote past, they harbored resentment against the world after trade ceased and they were abandoned to their fates. Maybe they don't want to find anyone—maybe they wish to be left alone?

"Thousands of years ago, when all travel was accomplished by sea, the trade routes were the only way to reach these countries. Between the times of the oceans' depletion and the invention of flight, I believe it required too much effort to venture there. Other than the mountain ranges we've read about in ancient manuscripts that were reputedly filled with stratums of quality radium, there would've been little else, I'm afraid, to draw visitors to such a remote area.

"Today, Dat Voga, we of Helium reach out to others, not solely for what we stand to gain in trade, but in simple friendship. As you know, we believe if our races are to survive, we shall do so with the aid and support of friends and allies. On their own, our societies would certainly perish; they would descend into an inexorable vortex of extinction that, once begun, would stand no chance of being stopped."

The night sky, typical of most Barsoomian nights, shined clear and cold. Carthoris sat at the helm of the skiff. It had been a long day and so, rolling up in his silks and furs and securing himself to a deck ring, Dat Voga wooed Morpheus, although, of course, he had never heard of that salient shape changer of Jasoomian mythology.

Chapter Five

The Forgotten City

THE NEXT DAY FOUND CARTHORIS and Dat Voga within sight of foothills of the Ptarsan Range they sought. They were in the vicinity they believed the city to lie but were unsure of its precise location. They thought the original city lay on the western side of the range.

Being uncertain, they maintained their altitude at a height from which they could scan both sides of the mountainous ridge for signs of civilization. They thought it possible the people of Ptarsas may have retreated over the range during the thousands of years since the seas receded. For a flight path they simply followed the meandering range.

They were surprised to find snow among the peaks, while upon the foothills of the lower elevations on the western side they spotted what appeared to be sompus forests. These were sparse, but forests nonetheless.

Trees such as these were rare, being a much sought-after commodity. Nothing fabricated of wood could in good conscience ever be destroyed. Old objects were always repurposed, whenever possible, into new articles once they began to exhibit excessive signs of wear.

But not only did *their* eyes scan these snowy vistas. The eyes of others followed their progress from outposts deftly hidden among the snowcapped peaks and craggy cliffs.

As they examined the forests, the Heliumites determined that they were no accident of nature, and so they decreased their altitude, dropping below the summit upon the western side of the peaks to move in for a closer look. The evidence of cultivation demanded further investigation. But soon they became aware that they were not alone.

Two fliers, one upon either side, had joined them, both remaining slightly to their rear. They first became aware of the other airships when their own vessel automatically increased its velocity in response to the promptings of the destination control compass, the instrument having detected the proximity of the ships behind them. At the first sign of their acceleration, a voice hailed them in a tongue that was familiar and yet possessed a strange accent.

"Attention foreign vessel! Do not attempt to flee! We have you under our guns and you are within range. Follow us without deviation or we'll blow you out of the sky!" The commanding voice issued from a loudspeaker.

Carthoris disengaged the automatic compass for it was clear that their ship's increasing speed had been viewed as a sign of flight by the alien vessels. The perfectly functioning compass had accelerated their velocity to prevent what it deemed to be an imminent collision. Their speed now began to decrease, and the two vessels shot forward within hailing distance.

Dat Voga had spun around at the hail. Behind them he saw two very foreign-looking craft of highly antiquated design. Neither resembled any vessel with which he was familiar. Realizing the possibility that these people were of Ptarsas, he glanced at Carthoris.

The Prince of Helium smiled reassuringly at the younger man. "This is why we're here, ambassador. Answer his hail."

Taking a deep breath, the youthful ambassador faced the ship that hailed them. Gunners were visible, crouching in the bow behind cannons. From below the keel of the ship protruded a spherical turret containing two more guns, enabling them to fire upon enemies below them. These were trained upon the Heliumites. A man stood amidships, likely an officer, his hands gripping the wind visor. It was he who challenged them.

"We come in peace!" Dat Voga called out to the ship. "We seek audience with the Jeddak of Ptarsas with whom we would speak regarding trade and other matters." He then waited to see the effect of his words.

"You will follow us," the other replied. "It shall be determined by someone other than me if you will speak with Ptar Ras, as that is not for me to decide. I shall take the lead; you will follow with my wing behind you. Our guns will remain trained upon you—so, no tricks!"

The man motioned to his pilot who gunned the throttle, executing a smooth maneuver that resulted in his assuming the lead position, with Carthoris behind, and the third ship bringing up the rear. As the speaker's flier passed over their skiff, the spherical turret revolved as its gunner kept them in his sights. Once the lead ship pulled ahead of them, the Heliumites saw that its stern was as formidably armed as her bow, with two gunners facing them. Settling into the seat beside Carthoris, Dat Voga glanced at his prince with a wry smile.

"Well, we're not off to the start I'd hoped for," he admitted.

Carthoris nodded but remained silent. He did not wish to jump to conclusions. He would wait and see how this developed once they arrived at their destination.

"I wonder exactly with whom we've made contact, and where they're taking us. That officer never mentioned Ptarsas, and we don't even know whether or not Ptar Ras is the name of the jeddak," the padwar mused.

Without waiting for Carthoris to reply, the young man leaped to his feet. He could see the gunners on the ship ahead of them taking a firmer grip on their weapons and watching his every move. Only twenty-five sofads separated them from the lead ship, and the Heliumites did not know their escort's wireless frequency, so the padwar shouted from the bow to indicate he wished to parley once more.

"Would you tell us from which country you hail, and where exactly you are leading us?" he called across the short distance between the vessels.

The warriors in the stern of the lead ship turned to converse with their officer. After a brief discussion, one yelled back, "You are in the country of Ptar Ras, Jeddak of Ptarsas; we are taking you to the city of Ptarsas."

The leisurely pace of their escort eased the nerves of the two Heliumites, who had been cruising slowly as they scanned the terrain prior to the sudden appearance of other fliers. This fact, combined with the archaic design of the strange ships, led Dat Voga and his companion to speculate that the newcomers' top speed might be far slower than that of the ship from Helium, which, when pressed, could accelerate to several hundred haads per zode.

Shortly, the two Heliumites discerned a city ahead of them. They were surprised at how much it reminded them of one of the ancient piles such as Xanator or Thark. The buildings were nowhere near as tall as the structures of most modern and post-cataclysmic cities, although not even all of these boasted the sky-kissing buildings of Helium, which sometimes reached over three haads in height.

Surrounding the city they saw the familiar sea wall, which would have been formidable indeed to a land-bound force of the ancients. This outer wall was approximately a hundred sofads in height. The wall enclosed a wide area filled with buildings that appeared to date from the precataclysmic period. Beyond this perimeter, they saw a much shorter inner wall that rose to about half the height of the outlying sea wall. Behind this shorter, inner wall lay a sprawling city whose architecture was obviously of newer construction.

The ships began to descend, sailing over cultivated fields

and forests, and finally coming to a halt about a haad from the outer wall as two heavily armed and armored ships lifted from their stations to meet them.

Both Heliumites had noticed gun emplacements upon the walls, artfully concealed so as to not detract from the beauty of the architecture, which would make a hostile landing by air extremely hazardous. They paused their flier in midair while the lead ship carried on a conversation with the Wall Guards. Finally, the officer who had escorted them from the mountain peaks approached the stern of his vessel, where the Heliumites awaited to hear what disposition these people would make of them.

"Follow these ships, and do exactly as you are told, and all shall go well with you. If you attempt to deviate, you will be fired upon." He smiled, and added, "Do not fear, we are a friendly people. If your intentions are honorable you will have nothing to fear from us. Kaor, until we meet again!"

As the man turned to resume his forward position on the vessel Dat Voga called out to him. "Warrior, what is your name?"

The officer paused and turned. "Padwar Doss Varr, First Officer of the Ptarsan Range Guard. And you?"

"I am Dat Voga," replied the young padwar, "and this is Carthoris. We are ambassadors from Helium."

At that the officer looked surprised. "Helium? Why—we thought that country had turned to dust eons ago! I cannot wait to hear more about this. But for now, farewell; I must return to the peaks!"

With that he spun about and issued orders to his men. Their former escort came about and, at a leisurely speed that placed the men of Helium at ease, flew back the way they had come toward their alpine post.

Now, in a similar fashion, they were escorted into Ptarsan airspace, this time by a flier of the Wall Guard. An anxious Dat Voga strained his eyes forward in excitement as they approached the rim of the mighty sea barrier.

Carthoris noted and smiled at the younger man's enthusiastic curiosity. Yet he also felt a burgeoning excitement in his belly. This was the spice of life he lived for. He had inherited his love of travel from his sire, John Carter. Both men always yearned to see new sights and meet new people, finding it lent value and meaning to their lives.

The Heliumites now looked on in amazement at the remains of the original city over which they slowly passed. This sector was not filled with the accumulation of ages as typically found in these ancient piles, which drew green hordes and great white apes as iron to lodestone. The streets were clear of any debris, the roofs were whole and of sound construction, and the buildings appeared as habitable as they might have been thousands of years ago.

Trees dotted the squares, and they saw other mysterious foliage in gardens and mazes of intricate design. The two men, hailing as they did from the arid environs surrounding the twin cities of Greater and Lesser Helium, found these features especially beautiful and captivating. Ptarsas held more the appearance of a newly constructed city awaiting occupancy rather than one that had been long abandoned.

"Amazing!" Dat Voga burst out in youthful exuberance. "I've never seen a people who have maintained their precataclysmic city in such a state."

"Nor I," agreed Carthoris, equally amazed. "It appears that as their population shrank during the upheavals, they consolidated behind a new defensive wall, thereby maximizing the effectiveness of their dwindling martial forces. It seems they've made an unprecedented effort to maintain the original city. Look at all that foliage. Old Val Statt would have a thoat if he were here."

Dat Voga grinned but continued to stare, entranced, as they left the abandoned, prehistoric city behind and crossed over the shorter, inner wall.

The metropolis lay upon the western side of the range as they had suspected, the mountains continuing southwesterly.

The city resided on what formerly had been a wide shelf that fell off into an ochre sea bottom. The original harbors were still very much in evidence. One could make out the unmistakable and sad growth of the city down the steep embankment of the continental shelf into the depths of the sea basin where the marinas of the ancients followed the dwindling waters.

Both men roved their eyes as they took in the sights of this living, populated metropolis, which, so far as they knew, had never been visited by any modern culture.

"Gods, but Val Statt would die!" cried an exuberant Dat Voga at last, unable to contain himself.

Carthoris flashed his companion a smile.

They felt as if they had traveled into the distant past, so archaic had the city appeared. Contrasting with this notion, however, were modern conveyances such as ground hoverers and fliers, the former being the low-altitude vehicles of the pre-flier era, used for transportation down the city's streets and broad avenues.

The hoverers were designed with an open-topped body equipped with a small radium motor for propulsion. Buoyancy tanks concealed within the body contained just enough of the eighth ray of Barsoom to maintain an altitude of two to three sofads off the ground. Although the vehicles were antiques, they appeared to be well maintained and meticulously kept.

Unlike the buildings of the city's outer perimeter, those of the inner section were clean and new in appearance, and had the same design as buildings from a hundred thousand years ago, the architects having borrowed from the original archetypes, evoking the bygone era. New additions had taken this into consideration, with the entire ensemble shining forth with an essence of smooth harmony rather than the eclectic appearance one might expect of an ancient city kept alive, maintained, and expanded upon over the passing millennia.

This inner section of Ptarsas teemed with activity, its citizenry being much in evidence. Only a few pedestrians glanced overhead to observe the ships flying over them, indicating that the conception of air travel was certainly not new to them. Their houses were beautiful and quaint, many having gardens and floral paths about them. Overall, the city impressed them greatly with its quiet loveliness.

Soon larger, statelier buildings came into view, which they guessed to be governmental buildings or museums or institutions of learning. These were constructed of a uniform, white marble, clearly utilizing this specific variety of stone to set them apart aesthetically from the domestic and commercial buildings.

The streets of the city were paved in an outmoded fashion, using small circular stones, the interstices of which were filled with an enduring sealant in a contrasting shade. More modern cities utilized an amalgamate material that could be applied more quickly than this time-consuming stonework of a bygone age.

For all its antiquated elements, the city felt as fresh as a breath of clean air to the Heliumites. Thus far it had turned out to be not at all what they had expected. They were thoroughly enjoying the vistas passing below them to such an extent that it seemed all too soon before they arrived at their destination—a hangar deck atop an edifice adjoining a great domed palace.

Following the lead ship, they landed, Carthoris bringing his skiff to rest alongside their escort. As they were powering down it became apparent that a wireless communiqué had been sent ahead of their arrival to summon a detachment to the hangar. An assembly of stern-faced warriors had already convened on the landing platform; with them stood two officers. This detachment met Carthoris and the padwar as they disembarked from their flier.

Chapter Six

Zat Simpus

As the men from Helium stepped from their flier to the landing platform, they observed that they were not the only guests being escorted into the hangar. Further down the landing stage a heavily armed and armored ship had just landed.

This craft's escort touched down only long enough for an officer of the Wall Guard to disembark and speak briefly with an official awaiting him, whereupon he reboarded his craft. The patrol then took to the air and disappeared from view as it headed toward the outer wall.

Soon an officer approached and spoke with the commander of the Wall Guard who had guided Dat Voga and Carthoris here from the perimeter. After a brief exchange, this sharp-eyed officer walked up to the two men from Helium. His demeanor was perfunctory and businesslike, but his face had a wholesome appearance that reminded Dat Voga of an officer he knew stationed at the royal hangars in Helium. The two men smiled as he approached and waited patiently for him to speak.

The officer opened with a benign, "Kaor! I am Ran Tasis, a padwar of the Royal Guard. It has been reported that you were spotted traveling along the Ptarsan Range with the look of those seeking . . . something."

He smiled. "At the risk of sounding conceited, we assumed

you might be seeking us. First Officer Doss Varr intercepted you because on the course you were following, as I am sure you're now aware, you would have eventually arrived here on your own. If you would, please state the reason for your coming to Ptarsas."

Carthoris glanced at Dat Voga. The padwar took this as an invitation to answer the man's inquiry. "Kaor, Padwar Ran Tasis," Dat Voga began. "We have indeed been searching for Ptarsas. We are here as ambassadors from Helium, a mission we hope will be beneficial not only to Ptarsas and our own nation, but to all the peoples of Barsoom."

The officer, a man slightly older than the youthful ambassador, smiled. "A worthy endeavor, by the sound of it! But I am not the one who will decide whether your mission to save the world is of note or not. With whom had you thought to speak in Ptarsas?"

Dat Voga replied, "Our mission is of such urgency that it is with your jeddak we must speak."

By now, the occupants of the other flier had disembarked. Escorted by the Royal Guard, they approached the Heliumites on their way to an exit stair, an unusual architecture feature, as it predated the common use of ramps on Barsoom. The stair descended into the edifice upon which they had landed, which comprised a portion of the royal annex that connected to the palace.

Just as the other visitors had passed by them, Ran Tasis said, "Come, I shall take you to rooms where you may refresh yourselves. Later, you will be summoned to the Council of Ptarsas, before whom you will make your case. The council will decide whether your mission merits an audience with Ptar Ras, Jeddak of Ptarsas."

They turned to fall in behind the party from the other vessel, who were proceeding along the causeway leading to the hangar exit. As Dat Voga stepped behind one of the new arrivals, he felt something tug lightly beneath his foot. Glancing at the floor, the padwar noticed that the man ahead of him wore a lengthy garment depending from his shoulders that dragged along the floor behind him. It was this trailing garment upon which he inadvertently trod.

This resulted in the unfortunate, albeit comedic episode in which the fellow in front of him was nearly precipitated to the floor, an epic catastrophe that was narrowly avoided thanks to Dat Voga's quick reflexes as he swiftly lifted his foot. The man recovered and turned hastily to look behind him.

"My apologies, friend; I didn't see your train," the padwar said apologetically. He tried not to smile as he could easily see where the other would find no humor in the incident. An expression of bridlement spread across the fellow's haughty face.

"That is not a train, *friend*, but the robe of the Prince of Banaal—a mark of distinction you would do well to remember in the future!" The man's tone was mean and condescending, the sneer he inserted when he said *friend* unmistakable.

"It is also apparently the mark of a cad," interjected Carthoris. He took a step nearer his friend.

Dat Voga made no further reply. Instead, he folded his arms and waited to see what action the stranger would take; an anticipatory half-smile now playing upon his lips. It had been an accident for which he had apologized. To him, that was enough.

The prince's not-unhandsome face turned almost purple in instant rage. Dat Voga noted the man's slightly pudgy figure, his muscles nowhere near as toned as those of the athletic Heliumites. His form appeared much softer—especially about the midriff, as if he were given more to eating and drinking than to the care of his physique.

The man stood glaring at Carthoris, his rage plainly mounting for all to see, but what the outcome of their confrontation might have been they would never know, for it was then that Padwar Ran Tasis interrupted.

"I apologize, Prince Zat Simpus, but I must get these two men to quarters. If you would excuse us."

The padwar deftly directed the two around the other group, but not before Carthoris noted a smile pass between Ran Tasis and the officer of the Royal Guard who was escorting the empurpled and surly prince. That worthy, sputtering curses beneath his breath as they preceded him down the stairs, took a turn down the passageway that blessedly cut off his further vituperations. The Heliumites had apparently earned his instant and undying enmity.

Dat Voga and Carthoris shared a little look of surprise as they approached the stair. As far as they were aware, that mode of transition from one level to another had been replaced by ramps eons ago in every known city on Barsoom, from Zodanga to Duhor and from Thark to Okar. These leftovers from the distant past could only be attributed to the affinity these people had for maintaining their modern additions in harmony with the more ancient portions of their city. As they proceeded, the two men, unused to climbing down steps, had to carefully watch their feet for fear of precipitating a fall, an happenstance that would not have been very flattering for visiting dignitaries.

After they had left the hazards of the stairway behind, Ran Tasis led them along a veritable maze of corridors, eventually coming to an imposing door. Here he ordered two of his men to remain outside, then opened the door and, motioning his guests to follow, proceeded into the room beyond. Once they were inside, he turned to the two men with an embarrassed smile.

"My apologies," he began, ruefully. "Zat Simpus is the spoiled son of Simpus Fonn, Jed of Banaal. He's not well liked in Ptarsas, being, as you so aptly put it, a cad and also somewhat of a boor, if I may be excused for the redundancy. It is typical of him to exhibit the level of refinement one might expect from the east end of a westbound thoat. But he is a voracious suitor of the youngest daughter of the jeddak, so we of the Royal Guard have become accustomed to his uncharming visits.

"We must regularly endure his arrogance," Ran Tasis went on, "since he may well be jeddak one day. He can be a powerful enemy and so is not one to provoke lightly. There is no telling in what manner he may strike back at you, but you can depend on his attempting to redress his perceived wrong. By the way, what with all the excitement of discovering we entertained visitors from Helium, and with Zat Simpus fuming and saber rattling, I neglected to ask you your names?"

"I am Padwar Dat Voga, and this is Carthoris—Prince of Helium, the son of John Carter, Warlord of Barsoom."

At hearing the title of Carthoris, Ran Tasis looked at the prince and smiled broadly. "That will make it even more interesting. My friend, it is obvious you are of noble descent. For, while Zat Simpus is quick to bandy his title about, either as a threat or to open doors that might otherwise be closed to him, you mentioned not a word of yours during your encounter with the prince. I salute you. And now, what word am I to carry to the council?"

Dat Voga briefed the man on the reasons for their visit, as well as their official titles. Ran Tasis seemed pleased. "I assume that you bear an official seal and documentation from your government to confirm your claims?"

They assured him they did.

"Then I shall carry word of your arrival to the council and return once a decision has been made. Rest assured: the worst that will happen to unwelcome strangers here is eviction from the country; while the Banaalians are cads, we of Ptarsas are not. In the meantime, I shall send for refreshments."

Ran Tasis left, leaving a detail of two warriors outside their door. True to his word, within a short time, food and refreshments, together with wash basins to freshen up, arrived. The two men were famished and ready for a meal.

Dat Voga recalled their earlier conversation after they had fled Xanator. "My Prince, it appears you hit the thoat right between the eyes. The Ptarsans and Banaalians are apparently maintaining a self-imposed isolation."

Carthoris nodded. "Yes, exactly what I was thinking. The thing we must find out, then, is why? I hope these people are not so reclusive that they won't entertain an agreement, but such may well be the case. We'll see."

Later, having eaten, laved, and changed their negligible clothing and harness into something more presentable, they stood upon a veranda overlooking a portion of the city and parts of the royal gardens. In the distance they beheld a magnificent view of the snowcapped peaks of the Ptarsan Range. Dat Voga was reminded of his last night at home as he stood with friends overlooking the nighttime sky over Helium.

A soft courtesy knock announced a visitor; Ran Tasis opened the door and entered their chambers with a smile on his affable face. "I trust the refreshments were satisfactory?"

They assured him they were.

"Then if you're ready, you may follow me, as the council wishes to see you immediately. I must say, it isn't every day that visitors from mythical Helium arrive on our shores, and the rumors of your arrival are flying throughout the city. The members of the council are anxious to meet you, but are, as you may understand, cautious as well. We do not typically entertain visitors here—from Helium, or elsewhere for that matter."

The two ambassadors were indeed ready to face the council. Both men felt their real journey began here, in speaking with the Ptarsan officials and the jeddak, and so they fell in behind Ran Tasis without delay. Soon they were traversing a veritable maze of corridors and halls, resplendent in their decor and artwork, as were most public buildings and palaces of Barsoom.

They could tell immediately when they transitioned from the hangar and Royal Guard complex into the palace proper. For one, they began passing through many more checkpoints where they were made to declare their identities, their attestations being corroborated by Ran Tasis.

As they continued on, they also began to see a change in the dress of the people they met in the halls and walking among the various rooms through which they passed. There was a greater sense of opulence, all tastefully executed. It became evident that the city of Ptarsas, far from being the destitute, poor, struggling nation they had believed it to be, held unimaginable wealth.

Soon the assertion to which Ran Tasis had alluded was borne out in truth; rumors of their arrival had indeed proceeded them. Everywhere they went, people stopped talking to stare at them, their excited whispers following them down the halls as they made their way to the chamber of the council. Many times, the men heard the name Helium uttered in hushed tones as they passed among curious onlookers.

At last they arrived at the conference room where they were to meet with the council. Ran Tasis bid them wait in an antechamber while he entered to verify the body was ready for the visiting emissaries, returning shortly and motioning them to follow.

Passing through a doorway upon whose great hinges hung a carved door made from a species of tree unknown to them, they found themselves in a large room covered in heavy, wooden panels inset with landscape paintings revealing the quality of a master's hand. The room was softly lit, utilizing methods of distributing the light that were both natural, via openings on two exterior walls, and artificial, by means of radium bulbs recessed in the ceiling. These sources of light blended and diffused to eliminate shadows, with the obvious goal of not overwhelming the eye or washing out the artwork.

Throughout the room were other decorative elements accented in gold, platinum, and other precious materials that caught the light in a pleasing manner. The whole ensemble amounted to perhaps one of the most classically beautiful rooms either of the two men from Helium had ever entered.

As they continued to take in the opulence of the ornate chamber, their gazes stopped in surprise upon a table of such ponderous dimensions that a small forest might have been leveled in its construction. Its component parts were immense, the top being nearly a sofad in thickness, while the whole was intricately carved with a multitude of soft, curving lines.

They recognized a jeddak's ransom in the wood contained in the table alone, but besides this there were also matching chairs to the number of twenty-six. In addition, satellite chairs and smaller round tables were set at various points about the chamber in case the number of individuals was greater than what the main table would seat, for Ran Tasis had told them earlier that the place where the jeddak's council met doubled as a conference room where various military officials held meetings with their staff.

However, those now seated at the table numbered ten, not twenty-six, all of whom regarded their visitors with gazes of suspicion mixed with curiosity. Ran Tasis indicated for his guests to take two empty seats near the head of the table.

Chapter Seven

In the Council of Ptarsas

As the Heliumites took their seats, the voice of Ran Tasis rang out clearly. "For the Council for the Acquisition of Radium, I give you Padwar Dat Voga of the Helium Navy, Ambassador of Helium to Ptarsas and Zoquan, with Prince Carthoris of Helium, Plenipotentiary."

A great many whisperings and mutterings could be heard around the table. As soon as the two men were seated a councilor at the head of the table stood, an austere looking man, with the demeanor of one who would brook no nonsense. Uncharacteristically of most Barsoomians, the man sported a tightly trimmed beard that was as brilliantly black as were his eyes. He stood without speaking, gazing at the two strangers.

Before he could utter a word, a side door opened and a latecomer entered who took a seat at the far end of the table. After a brief nod to the late-running councilman, the man who had risen spoke.

"I am Garr Karosa, Chairman of the Council of Ptarsas. You will forgive me if I stare, gentlemen, as I look upon you as though you were specters. You see, it has been thousands of years, to the best of my knowledge, since a Heliumite visited inside these walls.

"As to your country, I must say, our most erudite historians believed your city had turned to dust eons ago. Still, it should not surprise us to find out otherwise since we have been isolated from the rest of Barsoom, in great part by choice, for thousands of years. Excepting, of course, our dealings with the cities of Zoquan and Banaal with whom we sometimes have commerce, and at other times war.

"Ran Tasis informed us of your explanation for this remarkable visit. But now, if you would, please enlighten us in detail as to your motives for coming here. Should you convince us of the merits of your case you may well win the ear of the jeddak, as you desire."

Dat Voga glanced at Carthoris; the prince encouraged him with a smile and a nod. The young ambassador stood, greeting the assembly with a friendly, "Kaor," and one of his disarming smiles that so dazzled the hearts of maidens and had earned him many lifelong friendships. It was with this precise moment in mind that he had been chosen for this position.

The nervous young man now recalled the past to the Council of Ptarsas in a manner that would have made old Val Statt smile with pride. He painted a picture of the ancient trade and commerce that existed aforetimes between Ptarsas and the other nations of Barsoom who had once relied so heavily on their rich lodes of ore.

He described the recession of the seas, the descension of society into chaos, much of which these two remote cities, along with Banaal—a small, less prosperous city in the vicinity—had been insulated from due to their inaccessibility. He went on to describe the new spacecraft they wished to build, and the reasons, detailing their requirements for greater quantities of radium. In short, he covered everything discussed at the summit prior to the undertaking, leaving out nothing.

"When we planned this venture, we had no idea in what state we would find your cities. Many savants propounded the idea that your nations were long extinct; others that you would have long since fallen into poverty and lawlessness. We guessed that, if your societies survived, you would probably grasp the hand of Helium as might a beggar an extended coin."

He glanced about the room, his eyes taking in the tasteful opulence of his surroundings.

"Such is certainly not the case. And for that we thank our ancestors. Your society has not only survived; it has flourished. We earnestly hope you will consider a trade agreement with us. We believe it will require the channeled efforts of all nations for our project to be successful, and it is for the salvation of all that we struggle toward the goal. And now, I will entertain any questions you might have."

As he finished, he caught the eye of the prince, who flashed him a smile. When he resumed his seat beside him, Carthoris whispered, "Well spoken, Ambassador Voga."

His speech must have made an impression on the assembled council. They all began speaking at once, their spokesman finally taking his feet again to ask them for composure. "Let us not bombard our guests like common rabble! Each will be given an opportunity to voice his concerns. Now, who would be first?"

The tardy attendee stood before any could raise a hand. The chairman nodded and yielded the floor. "Men of Helium! It is indeed a wonder for two such as yourselves to arrive here—ghosts as it were, as Garr Karosa so aptly put it. You admitted it yourself; we have flourished in our isolation. Crime? It's nonexistent. War? Well, we skirmish from time to time with our neighbors. Man must always play at war; I think you would agree.

"But we of Ptarsas do not fight for power or riches—at least, not the riches for which the rest of the world would conquer their neighbors. You've no doubt seen evidence of the wealth we mine from our mountains—it abounds within this very room. Have we any need, then, for the lucre of your city? No, we fight for survival. And survive we have—without any intercession from Helium!

"We've become masters of irrigation and horticulture over the millennia. You doubtless noticed the forests we have cultivated. I'm confident their like exists nowhere else upon the surface of Barsoom. Extinct! Gone—many of the varieties you will see here. It is these riches we do not wish to see plundered, and our way of life that we strive so valiantly to protect.

"You will have noted that we patrol our mountain ranges and our approaches vigilantly, nor are our walls naked. We protect our own, men of Helium. Why then, I ask you, would we wish to risk all of this by allowing foreign invaders to enter our walls as banths in thoat skins, as it were?"

Dat Voga slowly resumed his feet. He did so slowly in order that his response would seem neither a counterattack on the man, nor the rapid defense of one trying to sell questionable goods, but rather as one with the poise of confidence, one who speaks the truth without guile.

"It is true that you could remain behind your mountain range, maintaining an aloof border between yourselves and the rest of the world. Doing thus, yes, you could keep criminals out, thereby maintaining the shielded atmosphere to which it's obvious you've become accustomed.

"Yet think on this: already have you enjoyed the fruits of labors not your own of the very air you breathe, the same air that makes possible your fantastic forests and your incredible gardens. This air exists thanks to the efforts of the Orovar engineers who began the construction of the plant that oxygenates the thin atmosphere of our world, and of the engineers of Helium and her allies who completed it. This facility we have maintained for millennia that it might sustain life upon the surface of this, our fast-dying world.

"You might recall when this plant failed a few decades past. I'd guess you were gasping for breath without a clue as to why. That is, you were gasping for breath until the father of this man seated here, Carthoris of Helium—the same Helium you say you have done just fine without—until John Carter cast the telepathic key that allowed our engineers inside to repair it, thus saving your beautiful forests, not to mention your lives.

"We fight against invaders and assassins at every turn, and so yes, we would give much to have your envious peace and security. This place is a veritable Garden of Issus! It is stunning and beautiful, what you have here.

"But while you've gardened, we've reached out to the green man, our age-old enemy with whom, at long last, we've made inroads of friendship. We've fought tyranny where we've found it and brought peace and prosperity to nations that have not known those priceless qualities for centuries. And we did so, not for what we could gain from them, but for what we could give to them.

"Helium! How she shines and towers over all nations in her glory, her structures, her rich knowledge, her technological advancements! Yet even she cannot save a world by herself. She has a long list of allies ready to lend whatever it takes—I speak of Tjanath, Gathol, Hastor, Ptarth, Thark, and others. Each has something to contribute, but none has what you possess—the absolute richest deposits of the purest radium on the planet."

An animated Dat Voga had paced about the room as he spoke. Now he returned to stand behind his seat.

"We will certainly find other sources of this ore, sources yet unknown. But it will take years of prospecting—years that we are fast running short on. While you dwell on this, consider these last words. If we fail, your mountain ranges and your walls will not be high enough to save you. Doubt it not—destruction will be visited upon you as surely as Thuria will continue her orbit in the sky as she looks down on your moldering bones and your dying trees. I have spoken."

The Heliumite could not be sure how this oratory would

be received, but he saw approval in Carthoris' expression as he took his seat. The slightly older and wiser Prince of Helium knew that, at times, stern words shot straight from the hip were the best way to drive politics and other silliness aside and get to the heart of an issue.

Certainly, the Ptarsan had voiced serious concerns, those the Heliumites had already considered in the short time they had been here. The isolation in which these people lived was an insulating barrier. Obviously, it would be difficult to convince them to open their gates to thousands of people from foreign lands.

The late arriving councilman rose and advanced to the podium from which Dat Voga had given his delivery to the assembly. Gar Karosa came to his feet. "Dat Voga, Prince Carthoris, I give you Ptar Ras—Jeddak of Ptarsas."

The Heliumites were surprised. Supposedly this council had been convened to evaluate the merit of their visit that they might decide on whether to involve the jeddak. Yet he attended the meeting himself, masquerading as a late-arriving member of the council! Never having met the man, they had been easily deceived.

Ptar Ras, Jeddak of Ptarsas, smiled at the visitors. "Men of Helium, welcome. I apologize for my subterfuge. Your words were well spoken, Ambassador Voga, and I agree with nearly all you said. I hope you understand, I needed to hear how you of Helium truly perceive things. During the years I've governed, I have found that, when goaded, a man is more likely to speak from the heart; that in anger, his words, however biting, will have the ring of candor and sincerity.

"I deem it time we of Ptarsas resumed being the nation of commerce and trade we once were. As to Zoquan, we cannot speak for its jeddak, but we shall have an ambassador accompany you there after everything is finalized here. I have always believed in my heart that the loss of trade is what catapulted our countries into the constant state of warring and bickering that has existed all these years. In earlier times, we were friends and allies.

"I have a great hope that your arrival will usher in a new era of prosperity and peace between we of Ptarsas and Zoquan. Now, as formality requires it, would all members of the council in favor of an alliance between the countries of Ptarsas and Helium raise your right arm."

The members of the assembly not only raised their arms, but sprang to their feet, overcome by the moment. Each in turn approached to take the right shoulder of the men from Helium, each feeling in his heart that an exciting new era dawned for Ptarsas.

After the clamor died down Ptar Ras spoke again. "We have a gala planned for tonight; everyone in the nobility is invited, as well as many outstanding citizens of note. Among the guests shall be those who are associated with our mining industry, as we still maintain many of the ancient mines. They will be able to add valuable information about the excavations and answer any questions you might have.

"Also, you will meet many who are involved in trade and commerce with Zoquan and Banaal; they, too, can add enlightenment relative to this enterprise. I would be honored if both of you would consider being my guests tonight. I know you have but just arrived, yet I can't help but feel you will be glad that you did so."

Carthoris nodded. "Yes, of course. It is most fortuitous, then, that we arrived when we did. This will be a fantastic opportunity to shed light on aspects of the project that we've had to wait until we spoke with you to understand."

Ran Tasis approached and stood beside the Heliumites. "If you wish, I will come by your quarters at the sixth zode and escort you to the Great Hall myself."

Chapter Eight

A Slave and a Princess

Tahn Dih, princess of Ptarsas, the youngest daughter of Ptar Ras, watched as an armored courser, escorted by fliers of the Wall Guard, slid slowly over the royal gardens toward a hangar atop a tower not too distant from where she sat with her attendant beside a pebbled garden path that glittered with many precious stones.

The girl's lithe body, draped more in dangling jewels than silken coverings, had paused in its natural animation at sight of the craft; paused, that is, but for the rapid rise and fall of her breasts, and the flaring of her fair nostrils. From her widow's peak of raven colored hair to her dainty feet, her entire body had become in an instant as tense as a Lotharian's bow drawn to the snapping point.

In an instant, however, she composed herself, and from the look of boredom that then descended upon the girl's face, one might deduce the sight to be as common as a passing cloud, which would have been far rarer than a flier over her father's palace since on Barsoom clouds are a remarkable and rare phenomenon. Although the triviality of the sight might explain her expression of ennui, it would not, however, account for the wrinkle of disdain briefly announced on her small, upturned nose—an expression momentarily marring an otherwise perfect feature.

The cause of this disdain might be credited to her recognition of the insignia on the flier's bow and its name: the *Cunning*. The combination of these two facts meant that her evening must now be spent evading undesired and clumsy comments, together with the many importunities for her hand in marriage that were sure to accompany any encounter with the chief occupant of that flier. For he could be none other than Zat Simpus, only son of Simpus Fonn, Jed of Banaal, a smallish city two hundred haads northeast of Ptarsas.

"Oh, *wonderful*." The muttered comment was almost, but not quite, inaudible. The girl's mood instantly became rife with resentment.

She allowed her gaze to wander over the beauties of the garden until her eyes rested upon her sole companion, her personal attendant and best friend, Thuria of Zoquan, thus named by her father after Barsoom's nearer moon. At present, she occupied the same carved sorapus bench as her disconsolate mistress.

Although technically a slave after her capture as a young girl, she had been offered her freedom many times by the princess who looked upon her as confidant and tender-hearted friend more so than a servant. Thuria met Tahn Dih's gaze, her expression reflecting her own quickly rising ire. She, too, recognized the vessel. Having been raised around noble folk most of her young life, she saw in the person of the churlish prince nothing of value or principal that would measure up to the standards she held for the future betrothed of her mistress.

Thuria was from nearby Zoquan, a city with whom Ptarsus had warred and quarreled off and on since the seas receded and both nations found themselves cut off from the rest of the world. Watching the craft disappear into the hangar, Thuria's stormy eyes flashed in anger as she envisioned the miserable evening confronting her princess. What would have certainly unfolded as a pleasant time had now been irrevocably wrecked.

That night, the princess was expected to attend a gala that the jeddak had planned. Other members of the nobility would be present as well as visiting dignitaries from Zoquan, and representatives from outlying districts where many rural citizens of both nations lived. Centuries ago, with the drying up of trade, the people of Ptarsas and Zoquan had become perforce nations of horticulturists, reviving many species of growing things that were now extinct elsewhere on Barsoom. What might be considered a lavish waste of wood in other cities was viewed here as simply making good use of what had once more become a common construction material.

Thuria knew with certainty the Prince of Banaal would not fail to attend tonight's gala since the presence of the princess would be obligatory. While the prince was not one to miss an opportunity to go to any event where free food and drink were in the offing, he would make it a point to be there this evening where his status as a visiting foreign dignitary would offer unfettered access to the princess.

"Mistress, let us feign ill this evening and remain within your apartments until Zat Simpus takes his leave," she exclaimed. "That ill-bred lout deserves no courtesy from you, arriving thus unannounced! Surely your father won't insist on your presence?"

Tahn Dih's eyes smiled impishly at the suggestion. "Thuria, you are devilish, my sweet friend! But no, the burden of my station demands my attendance. And too, we have other guests tonight who will make it worth the desultory conversation that must ever accompany association with the drab Prince of Banaal. I intend tonight to finally make myself clear to this simpleton that I am not for him, and hopefully this will be the last time we are burdened with his presence."

Thuria looked into the eyes of her friend for what would have been an uncomfortably long time were they not as close as they were. She sighed in resignation. "Well, I hope so, for the man frightens me. I've seen an expression in his eyes before when he thought no one was looking that reminded me of a banth, a look like he could kill without compunction. I don't trust him."

Tahn Dih met the eyes of her best friend, her expression determined. "Nor I, Thuria, and I could never spend my life with a man who engendered such a feeling in my heart."

With that pronouncement, the two stood. Walking among the blooms of sorapus, gloresta, and Hands of Issus, they soon threw off the pall of gloom the arrival of Zat Simpus had produced. Chatting gaily, for nothing can forever dampen the spirit of youth, they disappeared around a bend in the path while Thuria's namesake sailed swiftly across the daytime sky in mad flight about a dying world.

As the two girls disappeared behind the lush and aromatic blooms of a pimalia, yet another vessel appeared in the skies over the royal gardens of Ptar Ras and glided toward the hangar deck nestled in the towers of the palace. Escorted by fliers of the Wall Guard, the strangely configured craft would have seemed unlike any aircraft the girls were familiar with, had they seen it. Its bow displayed not the insignia of any one country, but rather many countries, an oddity without parallel quite possibly in all the annals of history.

Chapter Nine

A Fete in Ptarsas

Carthoris and Dat Voga had gladly accepted the offer of Ran Tasis to be their guide that evening. After what seemed only a moment of respite, he rapped on the door to their rooms situated in an annex of the palace to escort them to the Great Hall of Ptarsas.

Traversing many stately and beautiful hallways within the palace they arrived at the entrance to the Great Hall. Large and magnificent wooden doors were cast open; from this entry the sounds of music, tinkling laughter and joviality drifted. A detachment of the Royal Guard was arrayed along the approach, each warrior standing at attention.

Partygoers were filing in to mingle with those already there, adding to a kaleidoscope of sound and color. Ran Tasis bid them pause just inside the room as a warrior stepped to a position beyond them to announce their arrival, as these were important guests of the jeddak.

As Tahn Dih wished Thuria to accompany her to the gala, the two maidens began their preparations early. They did so in order that Thuria might assist the princess with her bath and coiffure while still retaining adequate time for her own preparations. The princess offered to obtain a servant from her mother's retinue to attend them, but Thuria demurred. She did not wish anyone else to touch the princess' hair.

This level of care and consummate attention exemplified Thuria's character and endeared her to her friend.

Tonight's festivities should prove to be interesting, for there had been received in court that very day two visitors from mythical Helium. The princess and her attendant were excited to meet them since no one alive had ever met anyone from that city, but also because the reasons for their visit were cloaked in mystery. Tahn Dih had been unable to get any details from her mother, who assured her she knew nothing—her father was keeping it a secret, wishing to announce their visit that evening in fanfare fashion.

The armored courser of Zat Simpus that the princess observed passing over the gardens earlier that day crossed her mind, and she frowned. "It is as though he has premonitions when events of this nature are scheduled in the kingdom of Ptar Ras," she proclaimed, "for the timing of his arrival is always so inconvenient and intrusive as to be impossible to be accomplished through sheer serendipity!"

She knew her parents wished to see her mated to someone who was her equal in station, and it just so happened that the prince filled all the prerequisites—except in regard to personality. But she understood their reasoning: it would be an advantageous alliance with another city that could prove beneficial to all.

She also knew she would as lief slide a dagger into her heart before allowing that ulsio to touch her, let alone share a matrimonial dais with him. Surely her parents would never force her to mate with someone she despised so heartily? Recalling the gala, the princess realized she needed to focus on getting ready and to cease allowing thoughts of Zat Simpus ruin her mood.

At last, Thuria finished readying the princess and began her own preparations. Her fingers were deft at coifing hair, being so adroit that she could do so as readily to herself as to others. In short order she had bathed, fixed her hair, and begun trying on several of the princess's harnesses, as

Tahn Dih had insisted. Finally, the young girl selected an accoutrement that caused the princess to literally laugh aloud with gaiety, clapping her hands when she saw her friend in it.

"Why Thuria, it is obvious that harness was intended for you! Those colors look amazing!"

The harness did indeed flatter the girl. Thuria's skin consisted of a softer reddish hue than was common, more like a blush, so that the deep jades, soft creams, and pastels of the harness, which both concealed and accentuated her girlish figure, made her appear as beautiful and regal as the princess herself. Her hair she had pulled up and over to one side, creating a curtain depending over one side of her face while offering an exquisite view of her profile, as contrasted against her raven locks upon the other.

At last the time arrived for them to leave for the banquet. Living in the palace, they would not be entering from the same direction as other guests. Tahn Dih had been informed that her mother the jeddara had already left with her father, so the two girls walked alone, chatting gaily at the happy prospect of seeing handsome men and beautiful women enjoying themselves. Thuria was both nervous and excited, and she found herself anxiously squeezing the princess' hand as they made their way to the Grand Ball Room of Ptarsas.

The room had been made resplendent, with variegated hues that would defy the imagination of anyone not from that world. Warriors of the Royal Guard stood at attention throughout the halls and chambers, arresting in their black dress leathers trimmed in pure white gold. Soft music drifted on the air from nowhere in particular, for the musicians were concealed in alcoves with drawn, semitransparent tapestries through which they could view the proceedings without distracting the guests.

The walks and ramps inclining from one level to another were carpeted in sanguine and purple. The formal dress of the nobles and attendant military functionaries all added

Tonight's festivities should prove to be interesting.

to a mosaic of living color, with the dancers lending a veritable medley of motion.

From below many guests noticed the Princess of Ptarsas, standing with another woman her equal in beauty and poise where they had paused upon a balcony overlooking the Great Hall. As the two eye-catching belles allowed their gazes to travel over the scene of gaiety, an announcer at the main entrance caught their attention as he raised his voice to proclaim the arrival of important guests.

"His eminence, Prince Carthoris of Helium, son of John Carter, Prince of Helium and Warlord of Barsoom, with Dat Voga, Ambassador of Helium to Ptarsas," he announced over the din of merry making, nodding to the two men.

The Heliumites! Tahn Dih watched as these men were greeted by emissaries of her father. At the start of the pronouncement, Ptar Ras began moving through the crowded floor to greet these important visitors himself. Both girls were galvanized with excitement to see these two representatives from a city they had only read about in history lessons.

The Heliumites were both immaculately groomed and possessed exquisite figures. Perhaps their home city lent them an exotic air, but they were indeed impressive as the guests, including the two on the balcony above, took them in.

Each possessed a lean, muscular build with the thick, black hair characteristic of Barsoomians. Their skins were red, although Carthoris had a lighter shading. They were both tall, and each wore a simple yet elegant harness that seemed as though it could easily translate from the Great Hall of Ptarsas to the gunnery deck of one of Helium's naval ships. Each wore a sword and matching dagger.

"How striking!" The exclamation escaped Thuria's mouth before she realized she had spoken aloud.

The girls were impressed with the visitors, although they presented quite a spectacle themselves as they stood at the apex of the Grand Stair. Tahn Dih flashed Thuria a grin. "Come on, Thuria!" And they descended the stair.

At the bottom of the steps stood a brace of Royal Guards who stole surreptitious glances at the two beauties as they passed between them; each warrior nodded his head deferentially while keeping his eyes also upon the guests. After they passed, one of the warriors stepped forward and, removing a dagger from its scabbard, struck a bronze gong with the pommel to announce the Princess of Ptarsas, whereupon he immediately returned to his post.

Hearing this gong, which is sounded upon the arrival of any member of the royal family at events such as this in Ptarsas, Tahn Dih's father immediately turned to face the Grand Stair. The sound of the gong had a distinctive quality, with the ability to be heard even over the din of music and merry making. He saw his daughter with Thuria and motioned them to him.

The crowd parted to allow the two girls passage that they might make their way to the side of the jeddak where he stood with the Heliumites and a handful of members of the royal court. As they crossed the room the girls were frequently intercepted by friends and admirers. Many of these were surprised when they recognized Tahn Dih's slave. Tonight, the beauty of the servant girl rivaled that of the princess herself.

Ptar Ras extended his arm, guiding Tahn Dih to his right side with an arm about her shoulder, and Thuria to his left, with an arm draped similarly about her slim frame, to all appearances as much his daughter as the princess.

"Prince Carthoris, Ambassador Voga," he said, "allow me to introduce my beloved daughter, Princess Tahn Dih, and her best friend, Thuria of Zoquan. Thuria doubles as Tahn Dih's personal attendant, although we have for years now attempted to make her stand among us as an equal."

The two men from Helium could see the look of pride upon the face of Ptar Ras. They bowed to each girl in turn, taking one of their hands briefly in theirs in a stately manner to indicate their pleasure in meeting them.

Chapter Ten

The Dance of Ptarsas

The girls, with a show of excitement the two ambassadors found charming, began to eagerly question them about their city, and what brought them to this out-of-the-way place, and about their family, and what they did in Helium.

They were delighted by their interest and answered many questions about themselves and life beyond the Ptarsan Range. They acquainted them in brief with the reasons for their visit but left out any details Ptar Ras did not wish discussed in this public forum. The jeddak wished to make a proclamation himself, since news of this import occurred but rarely in this far-flung metropolis.

The two men were not left alone for a moment, for this city was starved for news of the outside world. They found the citizens and nobility of Ptarsas to be both charming and curious, their inquisitive natures indicative of native intelligence.

Judging from the exotic plants and trees they had noted, they began to suspect that these people might be foremost in all Barsoom in the fields of floriculture and hydroponics, having taken the science to the extreme end of the spectrum in their efforts to revive and propagate rare varieties.

The Great Hall, too, roused their admiration for the society that produced it, with its tasteful decor and wonderfully archaic appearance, coupled with the artful use of natural lighting. Arrangements of flowering trees and green growing things throughout further augmented the ambiance of the hall. For the first time they saw ivy clinging to walls where it made its way up toward skylights above. It was, to these men of the desert, a wonder.

The people surrounding them were gaily caparisoned, for they were in the habit of wearing more clothing than these desert dwellers, although their basic dress still consisted of a harness and belt, with the women also wearing stylized breastplates of precious metals.

The young ambassador commented to Carthoris that he felt as though he had been whisked away to times past, the gala having an enchanting, surrealistic aura. The girls had taken possession of the Heliumites, and proceeded to drag them from one group to another, introducing them to their friends and showing them the exquisite artwork and statuary that abounded.

At one point they approached a group they had yet to greet, and Tahn Dih recognized an acquaintance. She stopped and touched the woman upon the shoulder to introduce her to their guests.

"Flavia," began the princess, "You must meet—" She stopped short. As Flavia turned, smiling as she recognized the voice of her friend, a man with whom she had been conversing stepped to one side from behind the girl where he had been hidden from view. It was Zat Simpus.

The man sneered when he recognized the Heliumites, recalling them from the incident upon the landing stage. Refusing to look at them, he spoke to Tahn Dih. "Good evening, my princess, I've been looking for you."

Dat Voga sensed the man had just unflinchingly lied.

"You really must be careful of the company you keep,"

he continued smoothly. "I ran into these ill-bred louts earlier at the landing stage; I found them disrespectful and presumptuous."

At his words, Tahn Dih stiffened, her lip unconsciously assuming a snarl of repulsion. "Zat Simpus, there is but one disrespectful, presumptuous, ill-bred lout in this room and it is neither of these two from Helium. Do not presume to call me your princess. I am not your princess, nor shall I ever be. I intend to speak with my father about this—I do not wish to see you again."

The prince snarled. "We shall see about that. I came here intending to ask your father for permission to make you my mate. I see it is fortunate I arrived when I did!" He glanced angrily at the visiting dignitaries who, up to this point, had remained out of the conversation.

"Fortune had nothing to do with it," Tahn Dih snapped. "I believe you to have an informant here, and I intend to speak to my father about that as well!"

Zat Simpus stepped in close to the Heliumites, who had surreptitiously arrayed themselves between the man and the two women as the conversation became heated.

"All of this is *your* fault," he spat at them. "You would do well to return to whatever ulsio hole you crawled out of and forget about Ptarsas. While you're at it, you need to learn to mind your business when in the company of your betters."

The man's breath was overwhelming, reminding Carthoris of a war thoat with a bad tooth he and his father had once doctored; apparently, the man had been heavily into drink. The Prince of Helium had taken about all this man's attitude he could stomach, yet he hated to interject himself into the local politics. As a stranger and a foreigner, he was on precarious ground, and Zat Simpus knew this. Just then, they began to hear the strains of an engaging and grand sounding piece of music.

Tahn Dih, stepping to a position with her back to the Banaalian, touched Carthoris lightly upon the arm. "It is the Dance of Ptarsas," she began, changing the topic. "I do not suppose you and Dat Voga could be tempted to escort myself and Thuria? I know you are unfamiliar with the dance, but it is remarkably similar to the Dance of Barsoom, albeit sans instruments, the music being provided by the alcove players."

Carthoris, never taking his eyes from Zat Simpus, proffered a short bow to the lady as he replied, "Ambassador Voga and I would be honored to learn the dance of your fair city, my lady."

Zat Simpus, enflamed and humiliated at this rebuff, grabbed Tahn Dih by her upper arm with a foul oath and jerked her savagely away from Carthoris, beside whom she was standing. His clumsy effort nearly ripped her upper harness away. The fabric, torn at the intersection of a strap and buckle, dangled from her breastplate.

"This dance has always been mine!" he roared. "I will not allow the arrival of these oafs to change that!"

Carthoris considered himself a calm man, but more warrior than diplomat. He recalled the tenderness Ptar Ras displayed to these girls when he introduced them earlier. Without further thought, he hissed, "You calot!" And then the son of John Carter smacked Zat Simpus soundly across the side of his face with the flat of his open palm, as his father was inclined to do with scoundrels.

It was a head-ringing, staggering blow. The blood fled from the face of Zat Simpus, leaving a scarlet handprint across his cheek. Inebriated, the man stumbled backward, knocking two guests from their feet in his flailing attempts to regain his equilibrium. Failing, he smashed into a table of food and drinks. A tremendous crash ensued as everything on the tabletop fell upon the personage of the prince.

The Heliumites arrayed themselves between the enraged man and the girls. The prince's retainers appeared and began extricating the inebriated man from the mess he lay in. Two of them faced the ambassadors aggressively, their fists clutching the hilts of their short swords. Struggling to his feet and cursing all the while, Simpus drew a breath to release more hate-filled billingsgate at the men of Helium.

"That is enough!" The bellow, interrupting whatever Zat Simpus was about to say, could be heard from one end of the hall to the other. Ptar Ras had arrived.

He had heard the altercation and headed in that direction with members of the Royal Guard in tow. He took in the scene instantly. The men of Helium were standing in postures of pure kinetic energy, facing the Banaalian prince. Thuria tried to comfort the princess as tears streamed down the stricken girl's face.

Ptar Ras realized that Tahn Dih had understated her reasons for dislike and distrust of this man. She had been attempting to arrive at a diplomatic solution without pointing an accusing finger and causing an international ruckus. It was now beyond any such niceties. The music, laughter, and conversation died as a stunned audience watched the sordid spectacle play out.

"Zat Simpus." Ptar Ras pronounced the name as if it were a thoat dropping. A sneer of disgust was on his face. "I see that my daughter has been remiss in applying a fitting description to your personality, a disposition you are apparently quite adroit at disguising. I find it no wonder now that she voiced dissent whenever the subject of a possible alliance between our families came up in conversation.

"Now I see what a despicable piece of vermin you are, and I thank my ancestors my eyes have been opened at last. And to think that you aspired to the hand of my daughter—you, who are not fit to clean the cage of her sorak! You will leave this city without delay.

"I shall be sending a delegate to the court of your father posthaste with a letter describing the actual account of events, as I am sure the version he hears from your filthy lips shall be far from accurate. Now go. And Zat Simpus—you are *not* welcome to return!"

His retainers and bodyguards literally dragged the

screaming and threatening prince from the Great Hall, prodded on by the Royal Guards. Zat Simpus had been feted in Ptarsas for the last time. The Banaalian prince finally ceased struggling and shrugged off his men, seeming to wish to walk on his own. Pausing near the entry, with the eyes of everyone in the room on him, he yelled, "You will all pay!"

With that parting shot, he exited to be escorted directly to the royal hangars, under guard, where the warriors of Ptar Ras stood waiting until they sailed. An armed escort vessel hovered nearby to ensure they left Ptarsan airspace.

In the Great Hall, the jeddak instructed servants to clean up the spills, and the musicians to begin playing. Everyone returned to the festivities, although there were many conversations and much speculation about what had occurred.

Ptar Ras escorted his visitors and the two girls up the Grand Stair, a short distance down the hall and onto a balcony overlooking the royal gardens. He listened calmly as each told of the events that ended with the altercation.

"Ptar Ras," Carthoris said finally, addressing the jeddak, "I hope my actions have not caused you grief; if such is the case, I apologize. But you should understand that I could not stand idly by as he manhandled your daughter."

Ptar Ras glanced at Tahn Dih and smiled before facing Carthoris. "Any blow struck in the defense of my daughter I view as a blow struck in her honor. No, Carthoris, Prince of Helium, I thank you for that blow! Had you not struck it, I should have struck it myself and then had to fight a war because of it. Even now, that may not be averted; we shall see. Now, come. Let us return to my guests."

Tahn Dih hugged her father. "We shall follow shortly, Father. For the moment, I prefer the fresh night air and the smell of the blooms in the gardens." Ptar Ras returned to his guests, leaving them under the stars upon the balcony.

After he left, Tahn Dih alternately cried and fumed,

while Thuria attempted to repair her harness. It would have to be replaced. One of them indicated the flier of Zat Simpus as it rose from the nearby hangar and headed north, followed closely by an escort of the Wall Guard.

The girls left for the princess's rooms to change her attire, leaving the Heliumites upon the balcony. Carthoris turned to Dat Voga with a wry smile. "So, do you miss your laboratory yet?"

Dat Voga returned the smile with one of his own, and then both men had a hearty laugh, releasing pent-up energy. They returned to the Great Hall, but the princess and Thuria did not, leaving the men despising Zat Simpus for ruining the evening for these good people.

Chapter Eleven

Explorations

ALTHOUGH THE INCIDENT at the gala cast a pall of gloom over their introduction to Ptarsan society, the dignitaries from Helium were assured they should not have acted otherwise. Many told Carthoris they were grateful for his intervention, and none sought to castigate them for their actions.

In fact, for them to have acted any differently would have belied their very natures, running contrary to all they had been taught since they broke their shells. To succor those in need, to respect women and treat them accordingly, to comport themselves with honor—those qualities were as ingrained in their characters as sincerity and self-preservation.

The treatment Zat Simpus had accorded the princess they considered the basest form of human behavior—behavior they found intolerable. They found out shortly after the incident that the Ptarsans viewed it similarly; any diplomatic troubles from the Banaalians over the confrontation were simply inevitable.

Relations between their two countries had been strained for years. Commerce with the Banaalians had been on a steady decline, while interactions with their jed were typically as icy and rude as his son was arrogant and boorish. The relations of the two cities had been friendlier in the past, but ever since the usurper Simpus Fonn had taken power, it was as though a narcissistic thug held the reins to the city, his decisions benefiting none but himself and his unctuous son.

On their second day in Ptarsas, the trade agreement talks began in earnest and negotiations progressed splendidly. Dat Voga and Carthoris spent a good deal of time cloistered in meetings with Ptar Ras and his advisors, as well as the scientific and engineering community, in discussions about the proposed mining operations.

The Ptarsans were hopeful the new trade would prove lucrative to their city, as well as to Zoquan, envisioning a future in which exciting technology advances from their newfound allies enriched their nations. Ptar Ras mentioned many times that he hoped it might even go so far as to aid in the healing of old wounds between the two cultures which, in aforetimes, enjoyed friendship and burgeoning trade. This point seemed especially important to him.

"Our histories are rich with tales of the storied past telling of the great friendship that existed ages agone between Ptarsas and the people of Zoquan," he recounted. "It is written that in olden times we of Ptarsas considered Zoquan our right arm. No enemy came against either city without also facing our combined military might. There are murals in the old structures depicting quays filled to bursting, ships overflowing our wharves with merchandise from afar, with the peoples of Ptarsas and Zoquan working side by side to unload stores of goods.

"And the galas that were held several times a year—Great Issus, but they would have been something to see, judging by the descriptions we have from times gone by. Our young men sought their mates in Zoquan, and they in turn sought theirs here. This intermating kept our cities close. But during the cataclysms our cities began to struggle to survive. Both nations began about the same time to study the science of engineering food to provide for our people.

"The first documented strife between us occurred over a piece of land barely large enough to have placed this palace upon; yet we both desired it for plantation. In a single day, the forces contending for that ground irrigated it with the blood of ten thousand men. After the engagement, both cities, bitter at the obscene losses, shunned that tract of land. Today it is stark and barren—our skills have been denied it. The only fertilization it will ever receive was that of the blood spilled there that dark day."

The days were long while they discussed matters, addressed concerns, and worked out details of engineering and trade issues. But work did not consume their every waking moment. As energetic as were the Ptarsans about the opportunities Helium was bringing to their shores, they gave their guests time for leisure as well, seeming eager for them to see the sights of their city and the natural beauty of the region.

The ambassadors were taken on lighthearted excursions with the sons of Ptar Ras and were often accompanied by Tahn Dih and Thuria. Ran Tasis, the padwar of the Royal Guard with whom they had become friends, would also join them. They enjoyed the company of the Ptarsans, whom they found to be intelligent and adventurous, and eagerly looked forward to seeing interesting sites in the countryside and curious remains from the city's past.

Carthoris and Dat Voga particularly enjoyed walking among the ruins of ancient Ptarsas, the portions of the city that were abandoned when the people had retreated behind the shorter sea wall as the population dwindled and the former sea front area became uninhabited.

These ancient ruins were in unbelievably good condition and the youths enjoyed the excursions where they could appreciate the beauties of yore without fear of white apes or green men, for none of these were found here. Carthoris guessed the proximity of the ruins to the occupied city acted as a deterrent to squatters and roving beasts, leaving these early remnants in exquisite shape. For the lower orders, as well as the green men, have no appreciation for art or architecture, and destroy or deface it as it suits them.

Both Heliumites agreed these were the most pristine and complete ruins of any dead city they had visited and could not wait to inform the Society of History back in Helium of their discovery. Val Statt particularly would find this an archaeological opportunity like no other. They walked among these structures one late afternoon and had still not tired of their explorations. Ran Tasis suggested they walk out upon one of the ancient piers to its end far out in the dead seabed.

Now, these horrendously long piers exist in all the ancient ruins anyone had ever seen, but Dat Voga could not recall ever having started on the shore and walking along a pier to its extremity. On an adventurous whim, they determined to do so.

It lent an eerie feeling as they would come to the end of a section and be forced to descend to a lower level, at which point they would be on a newer section, which would then continue on for some distance. The drops were often a hundred or more sofads down, indicative of the declining sea levels. They continued in this manner for several haads until they had walked straight out into the moss-covered dead sea bottom of what was once the Throxeus.

At the end of the pier, they noticed that the quality of the remains, although they were the latest construction, were not in as good condition as earlier sections. Dat Voga said it might indicate the hopeless despair of the builders, that they had grown less meticulous as the situation became more desperate. Carthoris observed that this final section had been the last to be exposed to the hammering effects of the ocean, with the earlier sections having possibly been repaired prior to new additions.

Be that as it may, they sat on the end of the pier and spoke quietly, watching the sun dip toward the desert horizon.

Dat Voga felt a melancholy settle upon him as he thought of those halcyon days. He sat quietly while the others talked, absorbed in his own thoughts. Thuria glanced at the usually cheery young ambassador to find his face long and thoughtful.

Surprised, she commented, "Why, Dat Voga, is anything amiss? Are you ill?"

Her question startled him from his dark thoughts. "Nothing so serious as that. I guess I let the gloom of the past get to me. But we can't change it, can we? All we can do is bear its burden and try to alleviate suffering where we find it today. For a moment, I mourned the people of the past and I wished that I could change this."

He gestured at the ochre seabed and the near colorless sunset, an inky black sky following on its heels in typical Barsoomian fashion.

Thuria laid a consoling hand on Dat Voga's arm. "As do I, my friend."

The warmth of her hand upon his flesh caused him to glance quickly at the girl, but she was herself, as he had been but a moment ago, gazing wistfully out over the mossy plains. And then she removed her hand and stood with the others. Dat Voga was the last to come to his feet.

Lighting the pocket torches the Heliumites kept in their possibles pouches, they made their way back toward the deserted parts of the city and thence toward the sea walls, topped by their vigilant sentinels.

They also enjoyed the wonders of the occupied city which they happily discovered to be rich in music and food and dance, pleasures they had not looked to see again until such time as they returned to Helium. They delighted in wandering about the incredible orchards, forests, and gardens of these ingenious people.

The two men from Helium could not but wonder what made these people so phenomenal in the field of horticulture. Modern cities used canals to irrigate their groves, but this was to a much lesser extent, as they were limited to varieties resilient enough to have survived to the present day.

But the Ptarsans and the folk of Zoquan could identify trace elements of extinct plants in deep substrates in which they dug. Using their miraculous science, they were then able to resurrect these, causing them to flourish and grow. They had propagated them to such an extent that they now possessed entire groves of fruit- and flower-bearing trees, plants, shrubs, flowers, and vines that had been extinct elsewhere for eons.

In addition to the canals with which they were familiar, the Ptarsans constructed aqueducts into the mountain reaches where snow was melted and channeled to the lowlands. These sources were connected to underground branches that watered their orchards and brought fresh, cold water into the city.

They were astonished also to find flying insects flitting among the flowering trees from bloom to bloom, such as had not been seen since before the seas evaporated. The Ptarsans had recovered nearly intact specimens frozen in time in underlying layers of sediment and used the same mysterious science and arts to revive them and cause them to flourish, as well.

"We've found that these creatures are necessary for the survival of the plants," Ran Tasis explained. "You see, they carry seed from one plant to another, enabling the process of fruition."

To this Dat Voga replied, "We use other methods for this propagation. Much of it is manual labor performed by farmers in our canal regions. We've also designed several varieties which are asexual, requiring no fertilization."

Ran Tasis nodded. "We have varieties of these as well. Through research, we found that the artificial means of fertilizing these plants isn't as successful as this natural means. It took quite a bit of effort and years of experimentation before we successfully recreated these creatures.

"Some we recreated only to discover that they were not what we thought, being merely pests. It took years to exterminate them. Once, we released a species that caused rampant disease. Another time, the creatures attacked us in swarms, stinging and causing horrific suffering. It was a learning process."

They had walked the length of a grove sporting different varieties of plants and then climbed a small hill to a quaint park with shelters, tables, and benches. Ran Tasis had directed that many specimens of fruits and various potable concoctions be laid out for their repast after their long tour of the groves, botanical labs, and gardens.

Carthoris, overlooking the area they had toured and admiring the many forests in the distance along the foothills of the mountain range, commented, "One can easily see why your people have chosen to remain here, aloof and apart, for so many centuries. It's wonderful.

"Moreover, I can see that your city has much more to offer the world than radium. Cities will offer fortunes for your gardening skills and plant specimens. Their like is not equaled anywhere in the world."

On another occasion, as the ambassadors, along with Ran Tasis, Tahn Dih, and Thuria, prepared to embark in Carthoris' flier to take in some natural formations in the vicinity, Carthoris noticed a person skulking in a doorway near the hangar. The man was watching them intently, with more than just passing curiosity. The fellow paid particular attention to the girls, failing to note Carthoris looking at him. Without appearing to have noticed him, Carthoris whispered what he saw to Tahn Dih and Ran Tasis, who were standing nearby.

Tahn Dih pretended to give an order to a guard. Turning, she said loudly enough to be overheard by the eavesdropper, "I believe I left it over there." She then turned suddenly and looked in the direction indicated by Carthoris, the direction in which she now pointed.

As she looked in that direction she saw, briefly, the man's face which froze in surprise at his sudden discovery. In that moment, he spun and dashed into a corridor. But the one quick glimpse was enough for the princess, her ruse having caused the fellow to pause long enough for her to recognize him. She turned to Ran Tasis.

"That is the man I mentioned to my father whom I believed to be an informant of Zat Simpus. I thought he was evicted along with the prince. He's no Ptarsan. I've seen him in the court of Simpus Fonn on two occasions!"

Ran Tasis ran for the corridor, followed closely by Dat Voga, Carthoris, and the guard whom Tahn Dih employed in her ruse to catch a glimpse of the Banaalian spy. They returned shortly, Dat Voga shaking his head.

"The corridor has many branches, and we weren't sure into which one he darted. The guard who accompanied us is taking word to his commander, who will inform the jeddak. The fellow is obviously up to no good. It appears he is following your movements. I would guess he intends to report back to Zat Simpus, but I fail to see where it will do him any good. Any attempt to enter Ptarsan airspace and he will be seen by your scouts."

The thrill seekers did not allow the occurrence to alter their plans, however, and continued their pursuits. The Heliumites had been at Ptarsas for approximately a month, during which time they had finalized and worked through many tedious details.

Chapter Twelve

A Surprisal

Much to the delight of Carthoris, his friend was demonstrating himself to be quite the statesman. One instant he would listen to the young physicist explain a complex theorem to a scientist involving radium engine design, and the next he would field questions relative to mining or the city's imports and exports.

The Ptarsans extolled Dat Voga's virtues to Carthoris. It was their custom to pass complements to a confidante of one with whom they were impressed, and to then trust the well-intentioned comments to find their way to the ear for which they were intended. Carthoris passed on their praise to his friend, who was relieved to hear they thought so highly of his work. Dat Voga was beginning to feel it might be possible after all to accomplish his assignment. A man of science and the sword, it had taken time for him to feel a measure of self-assurance in his new role.

The two diplomats spent their final week in Ptarsas preparing for the approaching journey to Zoquan, where they received much assistance and advice from their new friends. While an agreement with Ptarsas would go far toward meeting the requirements of the new spacecraft, they now viewed this also as an opportunity to reach out to Zoquan and salve ancient wounds, hopefully ending eons of senseless strife between two peoples who once shared mutual friendship and respect.

Having spent a great deal of their free time in the company of Tahn Dih and Thuria, the ambassadors had become fast friends with both girls, whiling away many engaging zodes in their company. The watcher Carthoris had spotted had disappeared, causing them to suspect the princess' movements had been monitored by the Banaalian prince. Although warriors of Ptar Ras combed the city, no sign of him surfaced.

The Heliumites finished readying their six-man flier in preparation for the journey to Zoquan, where they hoped to begin the next phase of trade agreements. They were anxious to meet with the people of Zoquan, having in their possession copies of the documents detailing their treaties with Ptarsas. Also, they carried letters of introduction from Ptar Ras in which he extended a warm invitation to the Jeddak of Zoquan to visit, the latter to be delivered by Voss Borgas, the newly appointed ambassador to Zoquan.

As they prepared to depart, Thuria rushed onto the landing platform. She had received permission to accompany the Heliumites to visit her family. Although she enjoyed her life in Ptarsas, where she had unwittingly played the part of peace advocate and unofficial diplomat, she missed her father, Darfa Quan, and her brother, Quan Cluros.

Jeddak Ptar Ras would readily admit that after she entered the lives of the Ptarsas royal family and they had all fallen in love with the sincere, gentle-hearted girl, he no longer had the heart to fight with her country. He said it felt as though he warred with his own people whenever forced to do so. He often invited Thuria's father to the palace, where he enjoyed the stately man's keen wit and intelligent conversation.

Thuria saw the visit of the Heliumites to her native country as a godsend and wished to take advantage of the opportunity. For their part, the two men were thrilled to have her bright spirit for company and so all boarded the flier, with Carthoris at the helm.

Now, the Heliumites had heard mentioned a certain place of note they had become keen to visit but had not yet an opportunity to do so—a mighty sea trench that lay out in the desert. It was known by different appellations, with the Ptarsans calling it the Trench of Ptarsas while the Zoquans referred to it as the Zoquan Gorge, for this prominent fissure lay halfway between those nations. By either name, it was an impressive geological formation.

The girls had told them how interesting the landmark was to explore in a flier. Twice, outings were planned to visit it, but each time some occasion arose, causing a postponement. Then, as the time approached that they would travel to Zoquan, Carthoris suggested they defer the visit and include the fissure in their journey since, as they had been told, it lay en route.

The gorge had once been a split in the sea floor, laying approximately fifty haads from Ptarsas out in the dead sea bottom. A million years ago, when the seas still lapped the shores, the canyon would have been an abyss unknown to the ancients plying the waves above it, plunging as it did several haads below the surface of the prehistoric sea into the substrata of the planet's crust.

They found the approach to be rocky, barren, and sun-scorched, consisting more of dust and cracked soil than ochre moss. The area, often referred to as The Barrens, was so dry that even the omnipresent moss struggled to survive there. As they sailed over this desolation, a ship arose from behind a rocky outcropping after they passed. The vessel climbed until it was above and behind the ship of Helium, which continued flying just above the rim of the ravine.

Carthoris had temporarily disengaged the destination control compass while they explored, so the vessel was able to position itself behind them without their being warned by the compass of its approach. And being distracted by the colossal rent in the planet, none aboard noticed the presence of the craft behind them.

Here the abyss narrowed to a width of some half a haad, while in depth it plummeted five to eight haads, the bottom veiled in darkness as the very closeness of the walls obscured much of the light, yet not so much that the immensity of its depth could not be appreciated. The Heliumites were absorbed by the magnificent spectacle. On a sudden whim, Dat Voga suggested they drop the vessel into the canyon for a better view. Carthoris smiled and agreed.

"Hold on!" he called out adventurously. He put the ship into a dive and angled their flight path toward the rim. Used to the great stretches of low hills and monotonous, featureless desert, the Heliumites were relishing the spectacle unfolding below their plane.

As they dropped below the former seabed into the rift, they were surprised by the staccato crack of gunfire from their rear. Carthoris frowned. Moments later they heard the sounds of impacts and saw the explosions of radium projectiles upon the surface of the nearby cliffs. They were under fire!

Carthoris wasted no time seeking the source of the gunfire but sent the vessel into a steep dive. Having seen no one else, there could be no doubt at whom the shots had been intended. Over one shoulder he ordered the occupants to get their heads down and buckle their harnesses to deck rings if they had not already done so. Thuria had no such fastenings on her raiment and could only clutch a seat as she crouched in the floor, where she kept her head below the gunwales and tried to avoid being tossed from the rapidly descending craft.

Dat Voga touched a hidden mechanism, releasing one of the back rests on the port side. Hinged along its bottom, it folded over to reveal a hidden compartment. From this he withdrew a heavy rifle. With a practiced hand he swung about and attached it to the mount located at the rear of the vessel, the very one to which a white ape had once clung as they fled the ruins of Xanator.

With a fluidity earned by practice and drill, he slid aside a panel on the rear gunwale below the weapon, revealing a cache of magazines; selecting one, he attached it to the cannon. Although specializing in physics, and a member of Helium's nobility, Dat Voga was first and foremost a warrior, as are all the men of Helium. As such, he practiced with martial weapons continually.

With the loaded gun in its cradle, Dat Voga scoured the sky for their attackers and was rewarded with the first glimpse of a heavily armored vessel. Peering intensely, he spotted Banaalian hieroglyphs inscribed upon the bow. Though he was unable to read the language, he had become familiar enough with the characters to know that their meaning conveyed the ship's name: the *Cunning*. The next words of Voss Borgas, the Ptarsan ambassador, confirmed his deduction.

"By Issus, if that's not the ship of Zat Simpus, my first ancestor was a tree!" exclaimed Voss.

"I suspected as much," Dat Voga affirmed.

Momentarily disconcerted by the steep dive of the smaller vessel, the Banaalian courser, a ten-man craft, quickly emulated the dive of her prey. Dat immediately opened fire, but the small-caliber gun had little effect against the heavily armored courser.

Clinging closely to their ship from behind, the *Cunning* unleashed a hail of heavy fire from forward gun pods and keel batteries. Each projectile contained a larger amount of the same radium powder used in exploding bullets. Upon striking a hard surface, the projectile would burst, thereby exposing the explosive powder to sunlight, causing it to detonate.

These explosions pockmarked the vertical face of the gorge, with occasionally one detonating upon the bottom of the chasm where the morning sunlight was beginning to reach. The rounds only narrowly missed the diplomatic vessel as she spun and dove under the expert guidance of Carthoris.

What was intended to be a deadly ambuscade now turned into a running pursuit. The fortuitous dive Carthoris had made had stolen from the Banaalians their chance of a speedy victory. If he had not acquiesced to Dat Voga's whimsical suggestion when he did, they might have been shot down at the first burst of explosive bullets and fallen, a flaming wreck, into the cavernous depths of the trench.

Dat Voga was doing his best with the mounted rifle. But the Banaalian courser was able to stay above and behind them, thereby exposing only her heavily armored hull upon which the small caliber projectiles, designed to penetrate flesh and thin metal, produced little effect.

Banaalian gunners sit in projections along both sides of their courser, the vessel having been designed primarily for firing on targets below, giving the crew an advantageous position from which to mount a surprise attack.

This approach went against the grain of the Heliumites, who were accustomed to bombing the decks of an enemy and then dropping aboard using tackle. It was a style of fighting John Carter said reminded him of the pirates of the high seas of Jasoom whenever he would reminisce about his former life on Earth.

The Heliumites considered the idea of sneaking up on a foe in a vessel specifically designed for ambush a cowardly act. The Banaalians obviously had little stomach for a straight-on fight. Judging from their tactic, they preferred to take their enemies out like airborne assassins.

With the throttle held wide open, Carthoris threw his stalwart craft into a zigzag course as he eluded enemy fire. In times like this, traveling at such a tremendous velocity, his expert skill became apparent. Only an accomplished aviator could maneuver at these speeds without throwing the craft out of control. His mouth wore a slight smile, and his touch was feather-light on the control grip as his steady, concentrated gaze scanned the rapidly varying scenery through the windscreen.

The Banaalian pilot cursed as the craft drew away. The six-man flier he pursued was quicker and more agile and the additional weight of his own craft was a hindrance in a chase of this sort. The positions of its armament were also disadvantageous in a nearly vertical descent. Still, he continued his deadly pursuit.

The stony sides of the gorge flashed by in a blur. Below, the way became even narrower and the further they descended, the closer those sides became, giving them less room to maneuver.

Rocky projections now extended outward from the cliff face; these Carthoris approached until, at the last moment, he would dive below them, hoping to force his attacker up to a higher altitude, too high for their fire to be effectual while he put more distance between them.

But he really needed to climb above their fire to escape, a maneuver the Banaalian vessel continually thwarted, it being to their advantage to keep above their prey. To give them credit, the Banaalians were adept at getting their target where they wanted it—below and forward of their ship.

Eventually the inevitable occurred—Carthoris ran out of room and nearly collided with the rocky floor. His flier scraped the bottom, but he managed to get the nose up and the race continued. Now they were chased along the bottom. Carthoris whipped his craft in one direction then another as he sought to avoid the *Cunning*'s fire.

He dodged around rocky debris, taking the flier over boulders and around heaps of rubble, a maneuver that further forced him to expose their ship to gunfire. All about them flew fragments of stone, blasted into the air by exploding bullets.

Carthoris guided their ship under a large segment of cliff that had been shorn away, the enormous slab having fallen against the opposite side. They darted into an opening that was barely larger than their vessel, and Carthoris hoped it would not narrow to the size of an ulsio hole before they emerged. The courser was pressing them hotly, however, and their bullets followed them deep into the void and spattered across the surface of the rocky incline.

Shooting out the other side, Carthoris attempted to dart upward, hoping the Banaalians had lost sight of them. No such luck; they were again forced to the bottom while the courser's pilot began pulling his vessel into a better position for their keel batteries.

Carthoris kept close to the scaly sides and rocky debris, the flier darting dangerously close to obstacles that might shelter them from the cannon fire or smash them to bits. It was just as he was attempting one such maneuver that scores of rounds struck the engine compartment and ballast tanks of their flier.

The lightweight craft, not designed for such combat, lurched heavily. Smoke and flames gushed from her perforated sides. Out of control and rocketing toward the trench floor, Carthoris aimed the vessel as best he might for a clearing where there were no large boulders. He called out to the others to brace for impact.

Dat Voga relinquished his grip on the rifle and grabbed Thuria about the waist to prevent her being hurled from the ship. Carthoris managed to pull the nose of the flier up an instant before they slammed into the ground, avoiding a total nosedive.

The impact resulted in a concussion that sent the ship into a slide. The flier's metal screeched in protest as the gunwales and hull took the brunt of the force. The crash had left a long trail of debris behind them by the time they came to rest in a cloud of dust and smoke.

Chapter Thirteen

Clash in the Abyss

INSIDE THE *CUNNING*, his expression determined, Zat Simpus yelled, "Report!"

The pilot excitedly cried into his monogog, a device of a bygone age used for piping vocals in these old ships: "She's down, sir!"

Zat Simpus, licking his too-thin lips, nodded eagerly. "Bring us about and prepare to examine the wreckage. I want to make sure of them. I'll show those calots!"

The Banaalian courser zoomed overhead, slowing all the while, while her air brakes, a leftover of ancient Banaalian technology of yore, screamed like a dying soul as the pilot sought to slow the ship and turn her about to make another pass.

Aboard the downed flier, Carthoris lay over the controls, stunned. Clouds of dust, kicked up by their slide on the rocky floor of the trench, filled the air. Upon impact, he alone had occupied the cockpit, the others having been seated in the rear passenger area. They were all tethered to deck rings except for Thuria, whom he had last seen clinging to a seat.

When the ship struck, Carthoris had suffered a head-ringing blow, his brow slamming into the console despite his best efforts to brace himself. Now he snapped his eyes open as he came to, a sinking feeling lurching in the pit of his stomach.

Shaking his head to clear it, he began unbuckling from the deck rings that he might extricate himself from the wreckage. The ship was a total loss, having been ripped nearly in two and suffering untold damage to the hull. Both propellers had been stripped away.

"My prince!" Dat Voga shouted. "They return!"

Carthoris looked up in time to see the Banaalian courser flash by overhead, indistinct within the cloud of dust and smoke stirred up by the crash. Dat Voga, tethered to the deck at the stern of the vessel, had been cushioned by a padded seat rest that softened the impact for himself and the girl. Letting go of Thuria, he retook his position at the stern gun.

Taking quick stock of their condition, Carthoris saw that he and the padwar were fine, and that Thuria, although shaken, seemed sound and coherent. Carthoris felt a flood of relief that the spirited and likable girl had not been cast from the vessel. Not knowing Dat Voga had clutched her before they struck, he was amazed she had survived without a stitch of restraint. However, Voss Borgas, the Ptarsas ambassador, lay as though dead, tangled in the wreckage of the ship.

Dat Voga opened fire upon the returning courser, able now to take careful aim at their view ports. It would have been futile to waste rounds on the heavily armored hull.

He now noticed something he had been unable to note during the initial onslaught. The gun pods on the sides of the courser, while offering excellent concealment and protection during an attack in which the courser was above and behind the enemy, left the courser's gunners slightly exposed when they were on an even keel, as they were now. Apparently, they did not expect to find any survivors in the downed ship. As such, the courser came in low rather than taking a position of greater altitude from which to mount a fresh attack.

His burst of fire killed three warriors along the starboard bow, as well as a navigator in the cabin when several shots careened through a view port and exploded in the interior. The detonation within the confined space nearly ripped the man in half, covering the pilot, who had also been injured in the blast, in his comrade's gore.

Now the morning sunlight, peering over the edge of the cliffs, began to detonate unexploded radium capsules as it touched them, the solar rays being the catalyst that ignited the compound. Wounded from the barrage that had killed his navigator, the Banaalian pilot desperately tugged on his control stick, pulling the front of the craft into the air and exposing their armored undercarriage.

Slamming gears, he reversed the craft, her nose in the air and her engines and propellers complaining loudly at the shift in gearing. The keel batteries opened fire. The suddenness of the maneuver, however, undermined the gunners' aim. None of their shots hit their target, although the exploding capsules sent fragments of splintered stone flying in all directions and added to the dust hanging in the still air.

On the downed vessel, the discharging rounds roared all around them. Bits of rock showered them, and smoke stung their eyes. During all of this, Carthoris crouched low, attempting to keep his head below the gunwale as he made his way to the side of Ambassador Borgas to seek signs of life. Surprisingly, he discovered a pulse. He unbuckled the Ptarsan, pulling mangled wreckage from around his body to extricate him.

Thuria, seeing his efforts and realizing the ambassador lived, crawled over to help. Together, they dragged the unconscious man toward the gash in the side of the skiff. Fortunately, this was on the opposite side from the enemy. Carthoris yelled over the staccato reports for the padwar to lay down concentrated fire until they could get the ambassador out, and for him to then join them in finding cover.

Dat Voga did as he was directed, sighting down the telescopic sight and spraying the visible side of the courser with a hail of bullets, causing the Banaalians to keep their heads down. And they were wise to do so since through his telescopic sight he could pick out individual rivets along their hull, making the task of putting a bullet between a pair of eyes all too easy.

In a matter of moments, Carthoris called for him to join them. Reluctant to abandon his gun, the young scientist slapped a quick release on the gun mount and wrenched the lightweight cannon from its mooring. Withdrawing a leather satchel of ammunition from beneath the gunnery bench, he slung that over a shoulder and took the rifle with him. Backing away, he laid down a constant stream of fire at the Banaalians who had maneuvered their craft partially behind an outcropping.

Dat Voga heard indistinct shouts from the courser. Taking off at a low run and firing occasionally in their direction, he ran from rock to rock. These were plentiful here after eons of erosion and collapses. He followed the sound of Carthoris' voice and found them at a low, dark opening at the foot of the cliff. It offered a place of retreat, so they wasted no time scrambling within.

Carthoris drew his radium pistol from its holster and took a couple carefully aimed shots. The wreck of their ship had become engulfed in flames, adding smoke to the haze of dust in the air, so that they could barely make out the enemy's vessel. Carthoris scored a hit; a warrior from the Banaalian camp screamed and slumped at his post. The Banaalian courser retreated and landed out of sight behind a bend in the winding gorge.

Aboard the *Cunning*, Zat Simpus, standing within an armored console where he would be safe from enemy fire, watched the battle from the forward keel batteries. The man's rage knew no bounds. He screamed at his warriors, applying all manner of censure and insults.

The men took the abuse mutely but wore dark scowls on their faces. Even rogues could admire courage and hold cowardice in disdain. And who enjoyed hearing one's family insulted back to their first ancestor?

"You're fools! Stupid, ignorant fools," the prince fumed. His somewhat handsome face was twisted and marred by insensate rage. "Your orders were simple! All you had to do was shoot them out of the sky. But you could not accomplish even this simple task!"

The officer on deck, one Gaff Vlor, stood at a portside forward battery. A much older man than the prince, he had been in the service of the military of Banaal for longer than Simpus Fonn the usurper had been jed.

"My prince," the man said through clenched teeth. It was obvious he was exerting considerable effort in keeping his tone respectful. "Their craft is faster and more maneuverable than ours. That pilot reacted so quickly he must have the reflexes of a banth. That tail gunner, too, is no novice—which is obvious as we have five dead! Now, what are your orders?"

Zat Simpus looked at the dead and wounded on their ship. He did not care one bit for the tone of his First Officer, but cowardice made him fear to remonstrate him, knowing him to be correct. His throat felt constricted as he realized what it had cost thus far to salve his wounded pride. These deaths would have to be explained, no doubt about that. It would be preferable if the entire crew disappeared, and the blame somehow shifted to Ptarsas or Zoquan.

One thing was certain: no one aboard the Heliumites' vessel could remain alive to carry tales that would prove difficult for his father to explain. Ptar Ras would send inquiries to the court of Simpus Fonn. The crew of the *Cunning* had no idea how many exactly were on the ship they had shot down, nor how many they had killed. They must be destroyed at all costs, now.

Recalling the effrontery that the Heliumites had placed upon him, his face flushed anew, and his eyes narrowed to angry slits. They had ruined his plans to seduce the daughter of Ptar Ras and derailed his plot to become Jeddak of Ptarsas. His father would be furious. Holding the reins of both Banaal and Ptarsas would have been a major shift in the powers of the region; Zoquan would have fallen in short order.

"We track them down and kill them," he growled. "Now!" he roared impatiently, sensing unwillingness on the part of Gaff Vlor.

Glumly, the remaining warriors extricated themselves from their snug gunnery positions, grabbed compact rifles from a rack and buckled on gun belts holding pouches of cartridges and holstered pistols.

The few that carried them left their swords, as the Jed of Banaal favored vanquishing his enemies from afar from positions of advantage. As such, he had forced his military to adopt these tactics with the result that many no longer even carried blades, a fact that burdened Banaal's army with a stigma of cowardice insofar as their neighbors were concerned. In Banaal, the sword had been relegated to a badge of office.

Gaff Vlor, however, after stepping from the ship, reattached a slender sword to his harness, his contempt and refutation of the House of Fonn's preferences obvious. Loosening a radium revolver in its holster, he issued his prince's commands to the men. "Let us finish this ugly business, then."

Chapter Fourteen

The Cave

AFOOT, THE BANAALIANS MARCHED UP the gorge toward the downed flier. His eyes wild and thinking furiously, Zat Simpus knew he could leave no survivors. He could not risk anyone later revealing his perfidy.

First Officer Gaff Vlor took the lead, and the remaining men fell in. With Zat Simpus trailing, they began working their way across the rock-strewn floor of the abyss, taking advantage of outcroppings and debris mounds for cover, not knowing the location of the enemy. Gaff would readily admit he expected a bullet in his forehead at any moment from the sharpshooter who had so handily slain his men.

Wasting no time, Carthoris and the others scrambled into the dark opening at the foot of the cliff and found themselves in the interior of a large cavern. He and Dat Voga took out their radium torches, since the further they ventured within, the darker it became. The diffused light from the canyon faded quickly inside the deep recess.

The flooring started out level with a low ceiling causing them to crouch, but after a few sofads it inclined upward. The further they climbed, the higher the ceiling became. At fifty sofads they found themselves in a cavern with a high, vaulted roof from which depended stalactites of prodigious dimensions. Being inclined, the floor was free of any corresponding stalagmites, and worn smooth by the passage of water in a distant age.

Near the top of the incline, the sloping floor flattened out in a plateau. On this high ground they paused and set up a defensive position should the enemy venture within their retreat. It soon became obvious that such would be the case. They heard the clank of accoutrements; Zat Simpus had also discovered the entry to the cavern.

Carthoris lay the Ptarsan ambassador behind a rock where he would be out of the field of fire. Using a practiced hand, he examined the man's body, discovering a wound from which a bullet must be extracted. By its location, he judged it a flesh wound from which the man might recover. Gaff's unconsciousness, he guessed, was caused by a heavy gash across his temple from which blood yet oozed—a wound sustained in the crash, not from the bullet.

But Carthoris had neither the time nor the instruments to remove the projectile. To attempt to do so here, with an enemy approaching, might result in his untimely demise if there were any mishap. Sliding over to Thuria, he described the man's wounds and asked her to do what she could to make him comfortable, and then he joined Dat Voga.

The padwar crouched with his rifle behind a boulder, ready to strafe whoever walked into his field of fire. Carthoris drew his pistol, checked its settings, and then followed Dat's example, staring into the darkness where they had entered the cavern. He entertained no illusions of engaging these men in honorable swordplay—men who preferred snuffing out their victims from behind.

They did not wait long. The foremost warriors were already within the room before the Heliumites noted their presence, the intruders made practically invisible in the shadows of the grotto. The sound of a sandal scuffing against stone alerted the two men and they began firing.

It was well they did. The light cast from their weapons illuminated six men sneaking up the incline—five surviving crew of the *Cunning* and Zat Simpus. At the first burst of fire a warrior fell screaming, while the remainder made it to cover.

The Heliumites now found themselves in a standoff, with each side firing and then moving to a new location. When a weapon was discharged, the muzzle blast gave away the shooter's position, causing him to quickly abandon his post for another as his previous location became instantly riddled with fire.

After suffering a burst from a Banaalian rifle, a stalactite broke from the ceiling of the cavern and smashed onto the sloping surface with a tremendous crash. Fracturing on impact, great pieces of rock skittered downward, nearly taking out a crewman of the *Cunning* who desperately leaped from its path.

Thuria ran to Carthoris' side during a lull. Everyone's ears were ringing from the cacophony and din of battle. "Carthoris," the girl cried. "I removed the projectile from Voss Borgas! Can you use it?" In her bloody fingers the girl clutched the little cylinder in which the radium powder resides within a Barsoomian projectile.

She told Carthoris the mad scheme had come to her as she gently probed the man's wound with a hair needle from her coiffure. She had been surprised to find the bullet lodged only a short distance within the wound. She extracted it and discovered the radium cylinder had become loose and easily removed.

That she had accomplished this in the pitch blackness of a buried chamber located within the wall of an enormous ravine that was carved deep into the floor of a dead sea, all during a pitched battle, was incredible. The girl's ingenuity and grit amazed Carthoris, and once again the intelligence of her forgotten people impressed him. And now she had given him the germ of an idea.

He took the cylinder and, withdrawing his hand torch, deftly attached the radium capsule to it by its clip, which is used to fasten the light to one's harness when it is necessary to have both hands free. He set the tiny torch to be turned on with the signaling button, a small momentary switch on the light's end that is used for signaling. Lastly, he slid the intensity lever to the *Daylight* setting.

Finishing these preparations, he squeezed the girl on the shoulder. "Pray this works, Thuria!"

He only had one chance of success. With nothing to lose except his light—and maybe their lives, he thought wryly—he tossed it toward an area where he believed some crewmen were lurking. The hand torch would have to land precisely on its bottom and flash on for the plan to work—that, and the tiny radium cylinder must remain in the clip during its flight.

His first ancestor was with him. There was a brief flash of light as the torch landed on its signal button, followed by a concatenation as the brief flash of daytime brilliance ignited the sensitive radium in the capsule. This in turn set off other unexploded radium cylinders nearby, causing a cascade of detonations in which dozens were detonated.

Two additional stalactites were dislodged that hit the rocky slope with thunderous crashes, releasing fragments of stone that slid at enormous speed and force down the slope. Carthoris wondered if the entire ceiling of the grotto might not collapse and kill them all. Soon the only sound in the cavern was the roar of silence—he could hear nothing but the terrific ringing in his ears from explosions and gunfire.

There was no hint of movement from the men Carthoris had targeted; they had been slain outright. In the brief flash before the capsule had detonated, he had seen two warriors with surprised looks on their faces from the unexpected illumination at their feet.

After the explosions, Zat Simpus, his ears ringing and his face pockmarked from shrapnel, snapped. In boundless rage, and screaming curses from foam-flecked lips, he fired rapidly and randomly up the slope. Ricochets caromed off the walls and floor of the chamber and from the sides of the remaining stalactites.

The men and the girl at the top of the incline crouched, hoping a stray projectile would not hit them or the ambassador, whom Thuria had stabilized by binding his wounds with a strip of cloth torn from her filmy top.

Without anyone previously noticing, the band of defenders at the top of the slope began to have feelings of lethargy, as though they had quaffed a huge draught of a potent soporific. One instant they were alert, but the next they could barely hold their eyes open. They realized some form of odorless gas had been introduced into the cavern and it was rapidly overpowering each of them.

Knowing that if they succumbed to the effects they would be slain where they lay by Zat Simpus, they struggled to combat the effects. They covered their mouths with their hands; Thuria removed her gauzy top from about her shoulders and used it as a filter. They retreated toward the rear of the cave but found the plateau on which they crouched ended at a blank, stone wall.

They were trapped. They could hear Zat Simpus cursing as he climbed, slipping on loosened rock. They dared not use their remaining torch for fear of igniting unexploded radium pellets and drawing the fire of an enemy who might not have been affected. They began sinking unconscious to the floor.

The Banaalians remained conscious longer because of their positions downhill. But shortly after the four above them succumbed, they too fell prey to the odorless gas. The din of weapon's fire at last fell silent. A pall of smoke and dust hung in the air from the short and violent fracas.

A sliver of light appeared in the upper reaches of the cavern where Carthoris and his band had sought sanctuary. Evidently, an opening did exist there—one they had missed in their haste. It was visible now, illuminated as though by a handheld torch.

In the irregularly shaped opening, the figure of a man stood, cast in silhouette. He shined his light about the chamber, viewing the carnage. A muffled report from down the incline indicated the presence of radium. The sound of a metallic *snick* followed as the figure adjusted a filter on his light source, a filter that did not act upon the exposed radium strewn about the cavern from the gun battle.

Upon his face was a mask to obviate the powerful vapors within the chamber. He finished surveying the scene and then bent over and picked up the body that lay closest to the doorway. It was that of Voss Borgas, the ambassador. With little to no effort, he tossed the limp form over a shoulder and exited.

Had there been anyone to observe, they would have seen the light from the mysterious figure's hand torch traveling down an incline diminishing in brightness until it disappeared around a bend. Pitch-black darkness descended on the cavern, a blackness that can only be realized within the bowels of a planet.

Chapter Fifteen

Dat Voga Awakens

DAT VOGA WAS DREAMING A DREAM that, by any account, would have been considered odd. In the visions of his mind, he was a banth in a cage in a zoological garden he had visited often as a child. Restless, he paced his enclosure, tirelessly looking for a way out. He was confused as to how he had come to be caged, for he could recall nothing leading up to his arrival.

Beginning to feel annoyed, a thunderous roar built within him. He inhaled a huge breath of air and was on the cusp of releasing it in a bellow of endless frustration and rage and . . . he opened his eyes. No longer was he a banth; nor did he stand in the sunlight in the zoological gardens in Lesser Helium. Slowly he exhaled the breath he had taken as he awoke from his dream. Confused, he took in his surroundings.

He was the sole occupant of a small cell of roughly six cubic sofads of seamless, stone construction. This cell was not upon floor level, but rather about head height above it One end consisted of solid glass through which he could see and, he assumed, be monitored. He had been divested of the entirety of his belongings—his weapons and pouch were all missing.

The room outside the glass, consisting of both natural and artificial formations, was evenly lit by radium bulbs of a type in common use across most of Barsoom. It was obvious this had once been a natural cavern of immense proportions. To level any irregularities, a smooth, composite flooring had been poured.

The fixtures were of antiquated design and looked to have been remodeled over a span of several centuries, some areas having been refabricated from immense timbers of obvious Ptarsan origin, while other areas had been constructed of aluminum steel. But also visible were materials he found undefinable within the scope of his experience. This perplexed him, because he had spent a great deal of time in laboratories classifying materials and could identify many from appearance alone.

He recognized a great disparity in the construction methods, with none of the styles overflowing with panache. Any form of artistic fragility had been sacrificed for robust simplicity. Columns of immense stalactites depended to the floor, these being left in place for whatever structural support they might offer and, he assumed, to minimize labor, which would have increased tenfold had their removal been deemed necessary.

The whole assumed an eclectic accord through disharmony, and the equipment and furnishings exuded the sense of having been built by persons with a consummate focus on utility. It was apparent to the padwar that every aspect of the room had been designed with a strict adherence to function over form, the equipment having been arranged as an extreme model of efficiency.

He recognized much of the apparatus, but just as many pieces remained unidentified, possibly having been designed for unique applications with which he was not conversant. These were mysterious and he could not guess what they might be for. He noted with surprise that many pieces were of an antiquated nature, utilizing outmoded dials and switches dating back centuries.

A plethora of chemical paraphernalia, including vials,

burners, microscopes, and certain other pieces were certainly known to him. It took little in the way of guesswork to figure out he had awakened in a laboratory in which a number of researchers studied many facets of science and physics concurrently, possibly working toward a common goal in team-like fashion. He could only wonder what that goal might be.

Having observed what he might from his vantage point, the prisoner attempted tapping on the glass wall of his prison cell, this resulting in only a muted sound. The sound carried further than he guessed, however, because through a doorway a man instantly appeared.

The stranger paused at the entry of a tunnel and turned his head without hesitation in the direction of Dat Voga, indicating he was in possession of an uncommonly keen sense of hearing, for the sound must have been very faint. The rapidity with which he appeared and his aggressive stance carried the suggestion of a predator, like a great spider shooting out of its hole after someone has toyed with the entrance to its lair.

At first glance he could ascertain nothing definite about the man's age. On one hand, he had much of the appearance of youth. On the other, there were also present the unmistakable lines of maturity. In stature, his figure was immense and powerful looking, much more so than average, and his skin was of a lighter shade of red than commonly encountered, possibly from spending long periods of time underground.

His hair was slightly unkempt and looked as though it were shorn only as necessity dictated. It currently hung to his shoulders, with the front cut in a simple bang and the whole girt with a leather band about his brow, a custom prevalent in past centuries, but now seldom encountered. The contours of his face were exaggerated, the cheekbones high, the angles about the orbitals pronounced, lending an exotic air. The lines of his mouth were haughty but well shaped, speaking of high descent; he had a strong chin and a hairless face.

Overall, he seemed a powerful man in his mid-thirties, insofar as one is able to judge a man's age on Barsoom where one lives to be a thousand. The man's eyes held a quality that spoke of the ages. Even if one lived his full measure, his eyes would not have the essence of experience as did these. They were cold and calculating, but also gave the impression of boredom, as if there were nothing in the known universe they had not gazed upon many times.

As a navy man, Dat Voga had spent a great deal of time abroad, and considered himself quite familiar with the physiological idiosyncrasies of differing locales. But the padwar could not determine this man's national origin, the subtleties of his aspect being wholly unrecognizable as belonging to any of the peoples with which he was acquainted.

Seeing the Heliumite crouching at the glass, the stranger strode to his cell, his motions fluid and with no sign of wasted movement. At first, his face appeared expressionless, but by the time he advanced closer, it had subtly changed.

Now Dat Voga thought he detected a hint of annoyance. As he approached, he saw him scan the adjacent wall, causing the padwar to suspect his was not the only prison upon that wall. The man stopped before Dat's cell.

The man made an adjustment out of view, his arm then relaxing to its former position at his side. All his motions were abbreviated and with a sense of the mechanical, although he looked of flesh and blood.

The man had to look upward to meet the eyes of the Heliumite, who crouched at about shoulder height to the newcomer. "You are the first to awaken," he said. "Now, tell me. Why were you in my upper cavern?"

Chapter Sixteen

Daxxus Nahl

If the man's appearance had not revealed his age, neither did the timbre of his voice. The padwar found his tone to be stilted and direct, as if he were not in the habit of conversation.

What might have gone unnoticed by another he observed with great interest, namely that the voice did not sound muted after passing through the solid glass of his cell. This the young scientist found mystifying since neither did the voice carry the artificial sound of speech mimicked by electrical means. Instead, it sounded as natural as though there was no thick, solid barrier between them.

Briefly, the young padwar forgot he was this man's captive, finding himself fascinated by the unknown means by which his voice was conveyed so clearly through such a thick, glass wall. Once again, he rapped on it with the knuckles of one hand; it was as solid as ever.

However, it was not the auditory enigma alone that started Dat Voga on this strange tangent. He was having trouble focusing. He blinked, trying to clear a fog from his mind that he guessed to be the lingering effects of the sleeping gas used to render them unconscious.

"If you don't mind saying, how is it I can hear your voice so clearly through this glass?" His voice sounded hoarse and raspy.

"You did not answer my question," the other countered. "You and your companions have arrived at a most unpropitious time upon the doorstep of my humble abode. An untutored barbarian, you can have no conception of the enormity, the complexity, of the nature of the work you have interrupted with your petty warmongering. Now, what were you and the others doing in my upper cavern?"

The man stared at him indifferently, his gaze as cold as the starry, nighttime sky. He reminded the padwar of someone trying to make up his mind as to whether he would catch an insect and release it, or to crush it and dispose of its remains.

Dat Voga was beginning to understand that they had been captured by those who did not wish their pursuits made public, and who took umbrage at any interruption. Mentally, but with difficulty, he cursed Zat Simpus. His mind yet reeling from the gas, it was with difficulty that he focused on anything at all.

To allow himself time to think, he slurred, "Who are you? Where am I? And where are my companions?" His throat felt horridly dry, possibly another side effect of the anesthesia. The man looked Dat Voga in the eyes for an exceptionally long time.

"Surprising. Although fighting simply to focus, your eyes indicate you to be a man of some intellect, perhaps more so than I initially guessed. Certainly more than some who've ended their miserable existence in these cells. I'll fetch you water. It will help with the dryness and facilitate the dispersion of the anesthetics from your system."

He turned to go, but then paused and faced his prisoner. "It's been a very long time since I spoke with anyone who had any measure of intelligence."

His captor's casual comment about prisoners ending their days in the cells did much to jar the dregs of the drug from the padwar's head. Feeling his pulse quicken, he glanced around his stony cell. It seemed impregnable.

Striding to a nearby counter, the man selected a vessel. This he set into an appliance from which dangled a rod. He pressed a button, causing a cloudy mist to form about the rod, whereupon water commenced running in a cascade down its length to pour in a steady stream into the waiting cup. The padwar had not mentioned his thirst, but this man would obviously understand the effects of the gas he had administered. He continued to watch in amazement as the vessel filled.

The man returned, touched a switch, and then reached up to where a corner of the thick glass mysteriously disappeared. He sat the vessel inside and then touched the button again, whereupon the glass reappeared. The man's eyes never left the face of his captive, and his mouth was slightly twisted to one side with amusement at the look on Dat Voga's face.

Again, the padwar found himself astonished. The glass in that corner had disappeared at the touch of a button! He rationalized that invisibility could not account for the fact that the man had passed his hand through the space previously occupied by solid material; invisible objects were still solids, for all their transparency.

Nor would invisibility impress him as much as one might think. When Tan Hadron of Hastor returned from his wild adventures, he had brought with him knowledge of an invisibility compound created by one Phor Tak, an inventor who had dedicated his life to the destruction of an enemy.

The stranger studied Dat Voga's reaction. "You seem surprised at something so simple; perhaps you are not as remarkable as I first thought."

The comment reminded him again of Phor Tak. For years after Tan Hadron returned, the mightiest minds of Helium bent themselves to understanding the clever invisibility compound. After countless failures, their efforts were rewarded. It had been a simple thing, and only discovered by the merest of accidents. Yet, simple or not, Helium's greatest minds paid homage to Phor Tak, the man who had conceived it.

Dat Voga looked closely at the glass as he sipped the water, which tasted pure and cool. He continued to study the corner where the glass disappeared. Now he discerned a barely visible wire—the precise shape and size the opening had taken.

When he replied it was with all the confidence he could muster. "You passed a specialized frequency along that wire, causing the material it surrounds to vibrate at a specific atomic incidence, thereby immobilizing the glass at that location. The remainder of the surrounding glass you've obviously insulated from the frequency, while turning off the pulser allows the vibrating atoms to return to their native state. Fairly basic, in my opinion, and certainly not as impressive as Phor Tak's compound."

In actuality, it was a wild guess based on a technical theory he heard propounded once while he was a student at the academy, as preposterous theories often are. He had never known of its being successfully accomplished, this being the first time he had learned of someone trying.

"A lucky guess, obviously." The man's tone had darkened somewhat, having lost a layer of its former tonelessness.

Dat Voga was feeling refreshed after the water and was reminded of the enigmatic manner in which the man had produced it. He did not wish to anger their host. Hoping to mollify him, he added, "However, you did succeed in mystifying me with the method you used to fill this vessel. It looked as though water formed out of thin air from that device. If so, that's a feat the countries of Barsoom would give much to learn."

The man's face darkened. "Nothing I create is for the benefit of Barsoom. However, you do raise an interesting point. Were you to leave, you would certainly be unable to keep something with such obvious ramifications to yourself. And that device is the least I have accomplished here."

This was not the direction Dat Voga wished the conversation to take. He had already sensed this man would not succumb to feelings of compassion. He did not seem the type on which flattery, self-effacement, or threats would have any effect; Dat Voga wondered if he had any sensibilities at all to which he might appeal.

"We were only in your cavern due to a caprice of fate. Our ship was attacked by Banaalians, and our pilot dropped into the gorge to elude them. After a lengthy chase, they shot us down. We fought our way to a cave opening, where we had retreated to make our stand. We're here by accident, not from any intention to interfere."

"Banaalians are ignorant, although they do make for good test subjects. But, it really doesn't matter. You are here."

Dat Voga had the thought that if he could get the man to talk about himself, it might open a window of opportunity to convince him to let them leave. "What is your name, if you don't mind my asking? And, if not for Barsoom, then for whom do you labor?"

The man looked at his prisoner with interest at the first question. "My name? I've not heard my name spoken in centuries. Since you asked, and because it would be novel to hear it again, I shall tell you that it is Daxxus Nahl. And I work for no one but myself."

Dat Voga wondered, where were the man's coworkers who labored here, those who might hopefully be more tightly wound. Another might listen to pleas for freedom for himself and his friends and intercede on their behalf with this Daxxus Nahl. "Surely you are not alone here? Where are your fellows?"

"Whom are you referring to?" Daxxus Nahl appeared mystified by the question.

With the sweep of an arm, the prisoner indicated the array of equipment and machines about the enormous room. "Why, those who work in concert with you to staff this enormous laboratory, of course! I myself am a scientist, so I recognize much of this apparatus. I see stations utilized in several fields of study—electrical, seismological, geological, structural. Where are the scientists who operate this equipment, the chemists who heat those beakers?"

Daxxus Nahl glanced at the laboratory behind him. "I understand why you might be confused. This laboratory is designed to perform all the functions you mentioned, plus many more about which, in your infinite ignorance, you can have no idea. As astounding as it may seem to one of the upper world, I work here alone. I built everything you see.

"While you must remain clueless as to its purpose, much of the equipment is of my own invention. The same can be said of many of the materials used in the construction of this facility, materials that did not exist, but for which I had a need. I spent centuries attaining the necessary knowledge to allow myself the independence of working here alone, unencumbered by those with small minds and narrow views."

As the man spoke, Dat Voga began to have a sinking feeling. This man alone was in control of their future, and apparently there was no higher power to whom they might appeal. What was worse, no one in the outside world knew where they were, or that they were in the hands of an unstable eccentric.

"Listen to me, we had no intentions to intrude upon you, for we had no idea of your existence before awakening here. We intended you no harm. What are your plans for us?"

Daxxus Nahl did not hesitate. "Your intentions are of no interest to me. Insofar as my plans for you and your companions—why, you must be destroyed, of course. All of you."

Chapter Seventeen

Captives

Upon hearing the impending doom in store for them, Dat Voga tried reasoning with the man. On this point, however, he was immovable. The nonchalance with which he delivered the sentence displayed a callousness the padwar guessed carried with it a resolve to follow through on his threats, the statement having been dropped with no more show of emotion than were one to announce, "I'm taking the calot for a walk."

But being accustomed to a life of uncertainty and danger, the proclamation failed to siphon all hope from Dat Voga's breast. The padwar suspected something of this sort might come to pass. The man had acted brusque and inhospitable, as if burdened with uninvited guests.

An occurrence in Dat Voga's youth had long ago led him to the realization that when you find yourself in the power of others, they invariably presume your destiny is in the palm of their hands. In their arrogance, they can never imagine any outcome besides what they intend.

This was not the first time he had found himself a prisoner, nor was it the first time someone had threatened to end his life. As a naive recruit, having but recently joined the navy, he had been captured by a small band of green men. The incident had occurred in a remote region where he had been stationed near a canal farm.

Being a city dweller, Dat Voga had been interested in an outpost far from the city to which he was accustomed. While patrolling one night, he had strayed too far from the plantation and lost his way among the groves. He had been warned by his superiors of the dangers of straying at night—of hunting banths, and the green men with whom his people were perpetually at war.

Taken unawares and carried away, he had been trussed up by his captors and left just outside the flickering light of a campfire, in the heat of which they basked and made preparations for their evening meal. While he awaited being dragged before their fire for a night of torture, he lay there contemplating his hopeless circumstances and berating himself for not listening to his dwar.

His spirits had sunk low indeed when he happened to discover a bit of broken blade that had lain undisturbed in the ochre moss of the dead sea bottom—undisturbed, that is, until his questing fingers discovered its hiding place. Quietly, he used its edge to sever the bonds about his feet, whereat he slunk into the darkness, his hands yet bound, while his erstwhile captors ate and drank, vying with one another in their declarations of the hideous tortures to which they would put their young captive.

As he made his way with all stealth from that place, he continued to hear their voices, mingled with the coughing grunt of a hunting banth coming down into the valley from distant hills. The sounds of banth and brigand soon faded as he made his way on foot in what he hoped to be the direction of the canal, and his fellows.

Upon his return he found himself upbraided for putting himself in danger and congratulated on his good fortune in having escaped unscathed. His dwar and his fellow warriors, relieved, laughed and clapped him on his back, for they were overjoyed to see this popular youngster returned to them, one whom they had given up for lost.

The bit of blade, a fragment from the tip of a sword the

length of his index finger, he kept, wrapping it in thoat leather and placing it in his pouch as a reminder to never give up hope. At times reflective, the padwar would remove the piece of blade, rubbing its smooth surface between thumb and fingers. He wondered to whom it had belonged, and how the unknown warrior had fared in the struggle in which this bit of blade was lost to him only to lead to Dat Voga's salvation.

Finding himself again at the mercy of one who threatened his life, he decided he would defer lying down and dying until that dark moment arrived. In the meantime, he would work to find a manner of escape for himself and his friends.

No amount of negotiating would sway Daxxus Nahl in his resolve. Each time Dat Voga mentioned the subject of release, the mysterious man insisted he had seen too much to go free, that keeping his existence and the location of this underground facility secret was paramount. Occasionally, the man would fly into fits of rage at mention of their release, and at other times he would drop inscrutable comments, making the padwar wonder as to his stability.

"Dat Voga, if all works according to my plan, you will never have to fret over the amount of time you will have spent in this cell. For this will all pass away, making way for a new world. All that we of modern-day Barsoom have known since we broke our shells will cease to be as if it'd never been."

However, Daxxus Nahl did not seem to be in a hurry to carry out his threat, with day after day passing uneventfully for the padwar, who was plagued by both boredom and loneliness. Daxxus Nahl would bring provisions once a day, and sometimes allowed himself to be drawn into conversation. Dat Voga concluded that the deranged scientist, on occasion, welcomed the opportunity to speak with a peer.

The young padwar decided that sitting idly in a cell

awaiting his fate was not helping his escape efforts, so he tried a different tact, provoking the man into revealing an indication of his intentions. At all times inscrutable, Daxxus Nahl coolly informed him that he had experiments in mind for which live test subjects were necessary, during the course of which it would be of no great loss if they perished, since those he had in mind were already slated for destruction anyway.

Dat Voga refused to allow this pronouncement to discourage him from inquiring as to his companions' welfare and whether it would be permissible to see them. He finally learned they were imprisoned in cells identical to the one in which he was imprisoned, along the same wall, but that he did not need to overly concern himself about them; which, of course, is exactly what he did.

What with the cells being soundproof until Daxxus Nahl adjusted a dial making them otherwise, and the padwar not being able to see anything other than what was directly across from him, he could see neither his companions nor his enemies, the Banaalians. Time crept by slowly.

After spending what he guessed to be weeks as a prisoner, another concern loomed for the Heliumite. At the summit, after it had been decided to send the two ambassadors to establish relations with Ptarsas, a timetable had been set, giving what the council deemed a generous window for Carthoris and Dat Voga to complete their goals, at which point they were to report back to Helium. If they were not yet finished, but were safe, one of them would return and carry word to the council that all was well.

If this time passed and they had no word from the ambassadors, then the navy of Helium would sail to their succor, following the course plotted by Carthoris. For it would have to be assumed they had either run into trouble en route, or their reception at Ptarsas had not gone as hoped.

Dat Voga wished to avert any tragedy. He could envision the might of Helium's navy arriving at Ptarsas, demanding to know what had become of their young men. Ptarsas would most likely have sent her own ships to Zoquan to learn the fate of the Heliumites, Voss Borgas, and Thuria—the latter being so ensconced in the royalty as to be practically considered family.

Finally, upon hearing that Thuria, daughter of Darfa Quan, ambassador of Zoquan to Ptarsas, had gone missing,the people of Zoquan would demand explanation from Ptar Ras as to why she had been placed in jeopardy, perhaps even suggesting culpability on the part of the Ptarsans.

It might already be too late to avert conflict. By this time, Ptar Ras would have sent an inquiry to Zoquan, as he would have expected their return by now. Their armies might have already engaged, since their current, tenuous relations tended to create an easily ignitable state.

Dat Voga sighed. There was nothing he could do about it. And he had had such high hopes of restoring a measure of success to both nations and playing a part in the healing of old wounds!

Chapter Eighteen

A Deal with Daxxus

THE DWELLERS OF THE CELLS were forced to sit idly, their quarters too cramped for much movement. The Heliumites, accustomed to leading active lives, were particularly maddened by the inactivity. The same could be said of Gaff Vlor, First Officer of the *Cunning*, who also led a life typical of a fighting man. They each did what they might by way of exercise in their tiny spaces.

Daxxus Nahl, for the most part, ignored his prisoners. Although he continued to bring them sufficient food and water for their needs, he refused to be drawn into conversation with them, the sole exception being Dat Voga, who had impressed him with his answer to the riddle of the disappearing glass.

Daxxus Nahl had not revealed to his captive just how astonished he had been at the rapidity with which Dat Voga had solved what, in his mind, should have been an unsolvable challenge. It had been Daxxus Nahl's belief that he alone had cracked this particular conundrum. Although taken aback, he had cloaked his surprise.

The prisoners were confined in a portion of the lab in which their captor performed much of the work that kept him so absorbed. Although often in their presence, he largely disregarded them except to see to their basic needs. Designed with optimal efficiency in mind, their cages were self-cleaning, with a small area in the rear dedicated as a privy. The scientist provided no sleeping silks and furs, so the inhabitants found they must sleep upon the bare floors.

Through the clear glass fronts of their cells, they had an excellent view of the laboratory, a view for which they were thankful since watching the movements of Daxxus Nahl afforded them their only entertainment in an otherwise desultory existence.

During their wakeful moments, they watched him weave his way between pieces of equipment as he adjusted settings, twisted dials, pulled knobs, pressed buttons, and flicked switches. Much of the equipment was of an electrical nature, if the various cables, insulators, and other miscellany were any indication.

From his cell, Dat Voga could see a series of twelve enormous insulators protruding upward from the floor at roughly fifteen degrees from the perpendicular to a height of twenty sofads. On these were mounted ovoid globes of a material possibly of Daxxus Nahl's own invention.

At first glance these insulators appeared identical, but to the trained eye subtle differences became apparent in both composition and construction. Cables ran to them from openings in the floor, while further cables depended from the ceiling, which he estimated to be, at its highest point, two hundred sofads.

Any stalactites above the insulators had been removed to prevent them from falling upon the massive array of equipment below. Beneath the natural ceiling of the grotto, perched above the suspended lighting, hung layers of metal netting attached to the ceiling and walls. These were present to catch any falling rock.

The watchers in the cells naturally had no idea what the madman was attempting to accomplish. At one point, a nebulous, glowing sphere of energy hovered above the insulators, seventy or eighty sofads above the floor. The formation of the sphere was tenuous at best. It appeared briefly and then vanished. A detectable hum, audible even in the cells, was apparent prior to and after its appearance. With its disappearance the hum faded away as well.

His spectators watched the scientist hasten between stations, his quick movements precise, but harried. After one such test, his face flushed with anger. But he did not give way to emotion for long. His face smoothed to the quasi-calm it habitually wore with perhaps a hint of introspection—as though he sought to discover the reason for some failure. He went on with his work, laboring late into what would be the night had the sky been visible in this underground world.

The day after this obviously failed attempt, as Daxxus Nahl approached Dat Voga's cell with his daily provisions, the prisoner made a suggestion, hoping against hope his captor would acquiesce. Before the man finished passing a day's worth of food and water into the cell through the access window, Dat Voga called out to him. "Daxxus Nahl!"

The unpredictable scientist responded with a frown of annoyance and a tone filled with irritation. "Be quick, Dat Voga. I've no time for your pathetic requests for release. I'm on the cusp of success in a project the import of which you cannot fathom. Bear in mind that it's none of my doing that caused you to encroach so closely upon my abode as to require my interference; you can thank yourselves as to that!"

The ambassador to Ptarsas, seeing his captor was in a foul mood, spoke with haste. "Very well. I would entreat you in this manner: allow my companions to go free and I'll stay here as your prisoner, assisting you in your work until its completion. Later, you may do with me as you see fit."

Daxxus Nahl paused as though contemplating the suggestion, before dismissing it. "I'm afraid the work I carry on here must remain clandestine. You might find yourself faced with a moral dilemma where you'd be tempted to thwart me. You're endowed of uncommon intelligence, Dat Voga, I'll grant you that. And you may yet prove of value to me in an experiment where I require a living test subject. No, the work I do must be accomplished alone—and in secrecy."

Dat Voga was persistent. Before Daxxus Nahl could turn the dial that would effectively silence him until the next feeding, he spoke again. "No matter what your goal ultimately is, it appears from my observations that you require an assistant. No matter how efficiently you work, you can't be everywhere at once. And no matter how I feel about your fiendish scheme, which must be diabolical indeed to go to such lengths to maintain secrecy, I swear by my first ancestor to work toward its successful completion—only let my companions go free and unharmed."

Daxxus Nahl regarded him with the oddest look the padwar had ever seen. "You say this now, but I wonder: would you feel the same were you to know to the full my intentions? You have no idea, Heliumite, the depths of depravity to which desperation can drag a man."

Daxxus Nahl stretched his hand forth to touch the dial that would effectively seal the glass medium and end the exchange. He paused. His gaze still on the dial, until he suddenly turned his head to face the young man.

"The prisoners remain for the time being in case you later decide you cannot remain true to our agreement. I accept your offer, Dat Voga, since it furthers my goals. As you pointed out, it becomes problematic to perform all the necessary tasks when time is of the essence. Lest you think to escape, you should know the only approach to the upper cavern is sealed. The mechanism is telepathically controlled, and only I know the sequence to unlock it."

The scientist touched a control causing the entire glass front of the cell to disappear—except for the small corner through which he passed provisions; that remained. Weak and sore from long inactivity, he painfully lowered himself from his cell to the floor. He felt stiff after his long incarceration, but otherwise was in good shape for a newly released prisoner.

"Do you see this device, Dat Voga?" Daxxus Nahl asked after he had exited his cell. He held up a shiny implement about the size of a writing pen. "With this I can disintegrate you into your base atoms. I offer this as a friendly warning. Now, follow me." Glancing behind him, he saw for the first time the glass-fronted cells, saw Carthoris and Thuria and noted the location of the Banaalians. The former leaped to their feet with initial excitement as they saw him but could do nothing beyond following him with their eyes. He smiled reassuringly at his friends.

He glanced at the controls on the cells as he passed, barely recognizing the antique hieroglyphs. They were close enough to the modern Ptarsan language for him to roughly translate, having learned much of it over the past weeks spent in Ptarsas. He recognized the word *Purge* on each control plate and wondered about its purpose, speculating that it might trigger a sterilization procedure to prepare a cell for occupancy.

For weeks he had felt a growing concern regarding Daxxus Nahl's experiment. He had no idea what its ultimate goal might be but knew enough from the man's comments to guess that the outcome would affect the entire world. As far as Daxxus Nahl knew, Dat Voga had offered himself as a sacrifice in order to gain his friends' release. But he suspected that much more than *their* few lives were at stake.

Despite what he had told Daxxus Nahl, the youthful ambassador had no intentions of forfeiting his honor and integrity to save his and his friends' hides. As much as he hated the thought of anything happening to Carthoris, or sweet Thuria, he would sacrifice them all—including himself—if he felt it necessary in order to save Barsoom from this crazed madman.

Chapter Nineteen

Laboratory Coadjutor

The padwar's duties as assistant to Daxxus Nahl consisted principally in doing exactly as the scientist commanded. He found out quickly that questioning an order was not well received. Daxxus Nahl wanted to keep everything about his project to himself, so he chiefly used his assistant to perform operations he found difficult to do alone when it was necessary to make simultaneous adjustments.

Not once did he ever divulge what he was trying to achieve. He constantly threatened the padwar and his friends with destruction should Dat Voga miss any cue, delay an instant, or stumble in his assigned operations. But Dat Voga was a quick study. In short order, he discovered some details, even if Daxxus Nahl did not wish him to, and thereby, thanks to his education in science and his understanding of natural forces, understood much more than had been revealed to him.

For instance, although the scientist would not divulge his power source, Dat Voga recognized characteristics of the incoming modulations. He deduced that the power source was a combination of magnetic fluctuations and gravitational forces, combined with an unknown field of enormous potential.

All three were artfully joined into a single, unified power

source—or at least, that was the intention. The signature of the newly arrived at signal Daxxus Nahl was trying to stabilize he found intriguing because of the presence of this unknown field. The three forces, significantly intense after amplification, had to be dealt with carefully while being transformed into a single, usable force.

The combined field was highly erratic, however, and quickly became unbalanced, this instability being the center of Daxxus Nahl's power problems. The field would increase in rate, shortening the cycles until the transformation process destabilized and refused to remain synchronized.

Once desynchronization began, partially unmodified waves were then being transmitted which caused an overload in the system, triggering an automatic shutdown to prevent damage to the power array and metering equipment. Yet Daxxus Nahl insisted this specific, modified power source was vital to the project.

Although not relishing the idea of raising the ire of his new master, he decided to have a word with him after a particularly grueling and frustrating day that ended in yet another automatic shutdown of the system after all attempts to stabilize the field failed.

Daxxus Nahl was staring fixedly upon a dial at his station, his face glowering. The man claimed to be uncontrolled and unfettered by trivial human emotions, but in working close at hand with him Dat Voga discovered the scientist was not as nearly in charge of himself as he claimed, especially as regards to his temper, which seemed to always lurk just below the surface.

"Daxxus Nahl," he said calmly, "having studied the readouts at my post the last few days, I've deduced that you're trying to yoke the planet's gravitational field to the magnetic field, I'm guessing to create a new type of energy source. You might be interested to hear that I focused on energies at the academy. The identities of these individual fields are quite unmistakable." He did not mention the third field he had noted on his apparatus, as he wished to see how the scientist would react to this information first.

Daxxus Nahl eyed him for a long time. "I hope you realize you can never leave my employ, Dat Voga—you are far too discerning, and you understand far too much."

The padwar could not be too sure of that, but to prevent a scene, he agreed. "I realize that. Such was the case before I offered my assistance which, you may recall, was to aid you that I might secure the release of my companions. So far you haven't allowed me to be of any real value in this undertaking. A great white ape could be trained to tweak a knob on command.

"By revealing to you my deductions, I'd hoped to illustrate my true value. I can help you if you just let me. Your own keen intellect would develop solutions eventually. But with my aid these problems could be solved more expeditiously. My friends, however, are still your prisoners. You could release at least one of them on my recognizance."

Daxxus Nahl permitted himself a small but insincere smile that touched only one side of his mouth, and his eyes not at all. "We shall work tomorrow on this problem of my power source, and then we shall see," he replied noncommittally.

Another duty Dat Voga had assumed as coadjutor was the provisioning of the prisoners, a task Daxxus Nahl had been all too willing to relinquish. The padwar was forbidden to converse with them, but often managed to whisper a word or two of encouragement to Carthoris, Thuria, and Voss Borgas.

To the Banaalians, although they alternately interrogated him and cursed him when he brought their daily provisions, he remained mute. He would utter neither reassurance nor criticism, the latter of which would have been much deserved.

The morning after his conversation with the stubborn scientist, Dat Voga attended to his duties as related to the prisoners as usual. At Thuria's cell, he touched the dial that modified the vibratory rate of the corner so he could pass through her day's rations. As usual, he also dialed the sound inhibitor to *Off.* This enabled him to speak through the glass medium as if the glass were not there, another of Daxxus Nahl's ingenious inventions that caused Dat Voga no little wonder at the abilities of the arcane scientist. This morning, Thuria was particularly anxious to see him.

"Dat Voga." She spoke in a hushed whisper, her voice betraying her obvious excitement.

Noting her alarm, he glanced about to take stock of the whereabouts of their jailer, who he noted with satisfaction was preoccupied across the laboratory. "Thuria, what is it?" he whispered.

"After you were sent to your quarters last night," she replied. "Daxxus Nahl came before my cell. He never spoke a word, he just stood in front of the glass and stared at me as if I were an animal in a menagerie. At first, he stared into my eyes, but eventually gaze raked me from head to foot. He frightens me. I fear he may come for me!"

This unwelcome news alarmed Dat Voga. Although he had never regarded himself as anything other than Thuria's friend and protector, a man would have to be blind to not have noticed the girl's burgeoning beauty. To keep her safe, they must escape soon, or he would have to kill Daxxus Nahl.

He saw Daxxus Nahl out of the corner of his eye. Ever suspicious, the man watched the two of them from the power array, waiting for his assistant to begin the day's testing. Apparently, the man had observed him speaking with Thuria.

Dat Voga realized it was within the realm of possibility that the scientist, with his acute hearing, had overheard their conversation, even at that distance. The knowledge made him cautious of saying anything too specific to the girl. "Courage—you still live!" he whispered.

As he spoke, he also made some slight noise with his supply trays to overshadow his words of encouragement. He finished and approached the primary power control station to which he was assigned.

The scientist remarked, "You're not supposed to be conversing with the prisoners, and yet I just now observed you whispering to that Ptarsan girl. What did you say to her?"

"She is afraid, Daxxus Nahl, being uncertain of the future. I told her you were considering her release. And just so you know, the girl is from Zoquan—not Ptarsas."

Daxxus Nahl stared at him with an implacable gaze. He could deduce nothing that passed through the mind behind that inscrutable stare. As far as telepathy was concerned, Dat Voga had never been able to read so much as a passing thought in the mind of the scientist; and while he did not believe the man was able to read his mind, either, he had perceived several attempts by Daxxus Nahl to do so.

Even now he felt a delicate probing which he successfully blocked, albeit with effort. It would not do to have his captor know he was thinking of an object lying nearby that would be useful if the situation called for the abrupt wrecking of the madman's skull.

The probing stopped as suddenly as it began. Daxxus Nahl continued his stare for a moment longer as if he now sought to read the truth in Dat Voga's eyes. He abruptly turned toward the power apparatus and began preparations for testing.

"You have a very strong mind, Dat Voga," he said, with his back to the Heliumite. "And a strong will."

Continuing as if nothing had happened, he said, "I've been thinking about what you said, and have decided that it would be advantageous, since you're monitoring the power source, to know more about what you're dealing with. Perhaps you will stumble on something I've missed, as unlikely as that is. So, the requirement for my power source is that it produces a harmonious wave of ten million cycles per tal, with a maximum amplitude of ten planetary spherons."

Dat Voga refocused on the present, clearing his mind of murderous thoughts. "Planetary spherons?" he asked, confused. The term was unknown to him. Could it refer to the mysterious third modulation he had noticed at his monitoring station?

Daxxus Nahl looked sharply at him. "Ah, yes! You're unfamiliar as yet with my third power source. Come, Dat Voga, and let me show you something the existence of which the greatest minds of Barsoom have no idea—a discovery that led me to the conclusion that it is indeed possible to—" Daxxus Nahl stopped himself short.

He then continued, "Well, there is no need to go into *that*! But come, and I'll show you this discovery of mine. You will have the high honor of being the first man, after myself, to learn of its existence, although you cannot possibly guess to what use I intend to put it."

The sudden turn to transparency stunned Dat Voga, but he attributed it to deranged genius assuming that none of the prisoners would ever escape the grotto. Daxxus Nahl led the way toward a doorway, which he opened and proceeded through, motioning Dat Voga to follow.

As he stepped into the passage, Dat Voga saw a hieroglyph over the door labeling the passage *Tunnel One*. From their cells, the prisoners watched the door slowly close behind the two men.

Chapter Twenty

The Spheron Harvester

Dat Voga followed the scientist, conceiving and discarding one idea after another about how to free his companions. He considered slaying Daxxus Nahl to prevent the completion of the deranged man's plans since, per his own words, the consummation of his goal was inimical to the entire population.

However, he intuitively felt that to end Daxxus Nahl's life without answers would be to deprive Barsoom of—something; he just had no idea what. The scientist had dropped only the vaguest of hints about what he hoped to accomplish, but the possibilities of this new power source were significant, leaving Dat Voga with a feeling of deep foreboding.

The padwar wished he might achieve the salvation of his companions while remaining behind to find out what the madman hoped to accomplish with this intricate laboratory. The scientist in him was intrigued by the new technology to which he had been exposed as Daxxus Nahl's assistant.

Whether it was fate or chance that brought him here, he knew not. Maybe the shades of his ancestors had guided him. However it had occurred, he was in a position to achieve something possibly more significant than their mission's initial goal. He recalled the strange premonitions of the night before they winged their way to Xanator. His instincts had not misled him—something portentous was on the horizon.

The access to Tunnel One closed behind them with a soft *click*, the doorway opening onto a stone ramp that led downward to another grotto below the cavern in which the laboratory sat. The padwar saw conduits coming down through the ceiling and surmised these were the same ones protruding from the floor of the lab. They ran across the floor before the two men and disappeared in the darkness. Daxxus Nahl led on.

Daxxus Nahl's coadjutor soon noticed a natural phosphorescence emanating from the stone walls and floor of the grotto, but it was not of sufficient brilliance to illumine their path, which led over the edge of a rocky escarpment into black, vertical deeps. The two retrieved their pocket torches to aid in their descent. The distance to the bottom Dat Voga did not know, but he could not see the far side of the chasm, and darkness obscured its bottom.

Daxxus Nahl commented, "We could have used equilibrimotors for our descent, but I find this climb exhilarating!"

Dat Voga did not reply. They descended what he guessed to be thousands of sofads when they arrived at a wide shelf that extended for half a haad before dropping off into an abyss. On this rocky ledge rested a large piece of equipment from which emanated a quiet hum. Above was only blackness, the light of his torch dissipating before it could find the roof of the cavity.

As they approached, the machine loomed over them. Up close, the thing took on immense proportions. In typical Daxxus Nahl fashion, it was imposing and enigmatic. The scientist eyed him as the padwar stared at the monstrosity.

"I see I have you guessing this time, Dat Voga! But I shan't hold it against you. Had you guessed the intention of this device I would swear you were endowed with omnipotent powers of deduction. Rest assured, the equivalent of this mechanism exists nowhere else upon Barsoom, nor upon any other planet for that matter, and has no counterpart in the galaxy from which you might draw comparison.

"This discovery, young Dat Voga, is of one of those naturally occurring forces that one does not suspect the existence of and seek after. Rather, a breakthrough of this nature occurs when one is looking for something altogether different, only to come face-to-face with the unknown. And although one doesn't at first comprehend it, one senses its significance."

The madman's eyes took on the glazed stare of one mesmerized, who spoke aloud to himself as though oblivious of sharing dark secrets with another.

"This experience happened another time, when I discovered the essence of life, and I was able to synthesize and recreate it, or at least, to prolong it. But any attempt I made to resuscitate the dead met with abject failure." His voice had become hoarse and his tone bitter.

"What are you talking about, Daxxus Nahl?"

The scientist's eyes refocused glaringly on the young man beside him, as if he had become angry at some passing thought; but he refused to divulge the source of his wrath.

"I'm going to tell you something you might find shocking, young Dat Voga, since there is no likelihood of your recounting it to anyone else. I am over twenty-five hundred years old. There is no need to go into the details of my discovery of the formula; maybe one day I'll tell you my incredible story of love. Yes, I was capable of love once—I saw the look of shock pass across your brow just now.

"In any event, I was eight hundred when I made the discovery, and was beginning to feel the ravages of age. The first year after taking the serum, I discovered it had some unforeseen side effects. My body began to change, and the acuity of my senses is now far beyond what can be achieved through evolvement or medical enhancement. I've had no ailments for over seventeen hundred years. In my youth I was never so powerful as I am today.

"Even my appearance remains unchanged since that miraculous transformation. But I assure you there have been appreciable changes, such as the fact that my knowledge increases exponentially, year after year, causing me to create the strange inventions that no doubt fill your mind with wonder."

The scientist gestured toward his machine, humming away on the wide shelf, haads below the upper crust. "*This* is a direct result of the discovery I hinted at earlier. I had come here to take measurements of the magnetic field using a new measuring device I invented. I recorded field patterns and found myself surprised by the results.

"After years of testing, I proved to myself my findings: I'd discovered an undreamed-of field, generated at the planet's core, that blended its modulations within the magnetic and gravitational fields. I gave this new field the appellation of Soom Spheron, which is also the name I gave to the measurement of its mean amplitude. Mastering this field is essential to creating the power source I require, which in turn is crucial to the success of my entire venture.

"It took me hundreds of years to invent, build, and perfect this machine. I built it here, far below my laboratory in this vast hollow, for the harnessing of this power is filled with the unknown and the risks were significant. Here it shall sit forever, quietly harnessing the Soom Spheron field from the planet and, after purifying the signal, sending it to the power array in the laboratory.

"You see, it is unusable in its native state, or at least I have found it to be, and therefore needs be purified, much as one would a fine metal. By default, it is harmonized with the other fields. To produce my power requirements, they must be separated, remodulated, and then recoalesced in a unique way such that their harmonics match flawlessly."

Daxxus Nahl finished his shocking revelation. Leaving Dat Voga speechless, the scientist turned and retraced their path. His mind racing, the padwar stared at this fantastic apparatus, sitting far beneath the surface where it channeled a planetary field unknown to the world save for the two men on this ledge.

What were Daxxus Nahl's intentions for the new power source he was trying to perfect? Was he really twenty-five hundred years old, as he claimed, or was he delusional? And had he discovered the secret of life, an elixir he administered to himself as one might an inoculation? He wondered if he would solve any of these mysteries, and if he did so, would he escape the madman's clutches to tell of it?

Chapter Twenty-One

A Way Out?

Returning to the laboratory, Dat Voga went back to work on the power issue with a new understanding of the sources. Already he grasped its potential if they could but stabilize it. He could envision an infinite array of practical applications.

With the proper scaling, the power source could be created anywhere in the world, potentially doing away with his people's reliance on radium. The immense machine in the bowels of the planet might be reduced in scale or done away with if another solution presented itself. He rapidly lost himself in his work. This type of research is what he lived for; only work of this kind could adequately challenge one with his fertile mind.

Yet he had not given up hope of securing release for his friends, having determined that if Daxxus Nahl could not be persuaded to release them, he would risk everything that they might escape, even if it cost him his life. The question was: How? The announcement from Thuria that the madman might have designs on her burdened him with a responsibility to act.

When he had first assumed the title of coadjutor the scientist had him return to his cell each night, releasing him each morning to see to the prisoners before beginning his day. Later, Daxxus Nahl assigned him a room off the main laboratory so he could be summoned at any time should his master have need. The arrangement proved to be convenient for Daxxus Nahl, who had no fear of his assistant escaping the sealed cavern.

Daxxus Nahl had shown him the doorway leading to the cavern where they fought the Banaalians. This doorway was sealed with a telepathic lock like that utilized by the atmosphere plant. Without the proper thought sequence, the door was impassable. Daxxus Nahl assured him it was the only means of leaving these subterranean grottoes and tunnels. If his friends were to escape, then, an alternate route must be found. As to this, he had an idea.

Scattered throughout the immense redoubt, which consisted of multiple caverns with interconnecting tunnels, were aeration openings. The padwar guessed that if he could find plans to the complex, he might discover an escape path utilizing these ventilation shafts to reach the outside air.

While he considered how to proceed along these lines, Daxxus Nahl required the routing of new cabling, and delivered into his hands a set of plans for the complex. The padwar did not know how he managed to hide his elation. Daxxus Nahl assigned him the task of finding the best route for the new cable conduit, the requirement of which was based on Dat Voga's suggestion to stabilize the power field.

Several days later, Daxxus Nahl sent him on an errand into Tunnel Five, which led into an upper portion of the complex. The young man was to retrieve materials stored there required to complete a phase of the project Daxxus Nahl was very tight-lipped about. The latter mentioned that he had labored on this phase for a hundred years but disdained to reveal anything further.

Having located the items, Dat Voga investigated an air duct indicated on the plans. He suspected this particular one led outside. He found the way difficult but entered the duct, climbing and squirming until at last he saw daylight ahead. When he arrived at the opening, he found it blocked by a sturdy iron grille. He screeched the grille open on its ancient hinges and stuck his head through to find he was several hundred sofads above the ground upon the vertical face of the gorge!

The sides of the canyon at this point were smooth and the drop was sheer. He closely examined the surface below the opening, wondering if a rope could be lowered to a point at which the wall might be descended. He saw this might be feasible.

He was running short on time, not wishing to raise Daxxus Nahl's suspicions. He might have been found out already. He closed the grille and retraced his path down the ventilation shaft, which he quickly exited. After replacing the grating in the wall of the cave, he turned and picked up the box of items for which Daxxus Nahl had sent him. As he stood up with the box, there in the doorway before him stood the scientist.

He had no idea how long the man had been there, or if he had seen him reenter the cavern through the grating. He worried that the scientist, with his highly acute hearing, had heard him replace it. Hiding his concern, he raised his eyebrows in inquiry. "Did you require something else, Daxxus Nahl?"

"There you are!" Daxxus Nahl replied with seeming innocence. "You were taking overly long, so I came to see if you were having trouble finding the bronze ores and the other items. Come, Dat Voga, we have much to do." With Daxxus Nahl leading the way, they left the cavern.

Now Dat Voga had the escape route for which he had been longing. He had only to formulate his plan.

Chapter Twenty-Two

No More Waiting

ABOVE A NAVAL HANGAR IN HELIUM that towered three haads into the heavens, the swiftly falling night darkened the sky. John Carter stood by his mate, the ever-glorious Dejah Thoris, with a look of expectancy on his handsome face.

A warrior approached the Warlord and spoke briefly; Carter nodded as he replied. He had just been informed all was ready, down to the last ship. He turned to Dejah Thoris. "Are you sure you wish to go? It's likely, my princess, that we march to war."

Her exquisite face remained resolute as she nodded affirmatively. When she replied, her voice was firm and unwavering. "I'm positive, my chieftain."

In the hangar stood Helium's mighty air fleet. Fully provisioned, each vessel quartered five thousand men. In their batteries was enough firepower to wipe out a city in the form of bombs, and new torpedoes designed by Carthoris utilizing a destination control compass adapted for unmanned weaponry. On their decks were cannon for strafing walls and destroying incoming fliers.

The warriors aboard were the finest fighting force ever assembled on any world. There were various divisions among the numbers, some of which were utilized by descending en masse using boarding tackle, while others, of a new concept, would issue in a military version of the equilibrimotor—the motorized flying wing. These were intended for taking out small vessels.

John Carter was proud of this force. He had played a key role in the design of the new ships, and in the training of the men. His only son, Carthoris, together with his team, had designed much of the equipment and many of the weapons found aboard, such as the guided torpedoes. A single hit from one of these could drop an enemy ship into a moss-covered sea bottom.

At the thought of his son, his jaw tightened. They had not only allowed the amount of time agreed upon during the summit, but had extended the time frame by several weeks, although it wrung the heart of Dejah Thoris to agree to it. But John Carter had not been idle during those weeks.

Far ahead of the deadline, he had been busy planning. During the agreed-upon extension, he prayed for the safe return of Carthoris and Dat Voga, but also finalized preparations for an assault the likes of which it was doubtful had ever been seen on the face of that aging planet.

The Warlord of Barsoom and his mate strode across the hangar deck to the *Tycheus*, where Dejah Thoris preceded her husband up the ramp. Without a backward glance, the Warlord boarded his ship. Two warriors raised the boarding ramp and secured it in its place. He paused at the rail and stared briefly toward the distant horizon, toward which they would soon be sailing, while Dejah Thoris continued to the bridge.

After a few moments, he strode toward the command bridge where he found his mate. She handed him a wireless set as he entered, and then took her seat. Carter adjusted the set upon his brow and spoke into his microphone. "On the *Tycheus*, mark—allow two haads following. Moss Fet, you will bring up the rear."

Turning off the wireless, he turned to his First Officer, Dwar Brik Lakko. "Take her up, Dwar. Make it half speed until all are airborne, then go to three-quarters. You have your heading."

Below, few warriors remained on the landing platform, most of the men having returned inside after the great ship had launched. Cqsius Grimla, a warrior grown old in the service of Helium, exited the command room onto the platform, trailing Tardos Mors and Mors Kajak. The three men approached the edge of the deck, watching the *Tycheus* lift buoyantly into the air. Already, she was angling to gain her desired altitude and appearing as light on her keel as a balloon.

By Issus, what a spectacle she was! They were on a heading slightly south of west. The last angling rays of the sun were hitting aslant her hull, casting back the image of her majestic lines, the pennons of the Prince of Helium visible, as well as many mysterious shadows. Falling in behind her sailed the remaining fourteen ships, all of the same design, armed, provisioned, and crewed alike.

Within only a couple of xats to the watchers atop the hangar, the line of vessels disappeared into the twilight. Tardos Mors, Jeddak of Helium, turned and looked at his son. Their eyes locked briefly. Who knew if they would make war or not? Only their ancestors knew for sure.

Then the great jeddak placed his hand upon the shoulder of the simple warrior, Cqsius Grimla, a man as much friend as personal retainer. "Come, Cqsius! What say you we find a warmer place, and wherewith we might stave off starvation? This old jeddak could eat a thoat. Our work here is done for the moment."

With that pronouncement, the great jeddak, followed by his son and Cqsius Grimla, entered a flier bearing the insignia of the jeddak whose controls Cqsius manned to take the great lords back to the royal palace of Helium.

Chapter Twenty-Three

The Gauntlets

Over the next two sleep periods—a fitting description of the time spent within those oppressive walls, where the passage of the sun went unseen—the padwar wrote down his escape plan, together with a detailed diagram showing the route to the entrance of the ventilation shaft. It was his intention to lead the prisoners in a bid for freedom. He had smuggled supplies and hidden them just inside the entrance to the air duct, including lengths of rope to rappel down the smooth, stony wall below the opening in the face of the gorge.

He had hoped to locate the equilibrimotors Daxxus Nahl mentioned the time they visited the Spheron Harvester, when the scientist stunned him with his revelations of the newly discovered planetary field,and his elixir of longevity. But these he had been unable to find, and assumed they were secured in the scientist's quarters, or hidden elsewhere.

Before they made the attempt, Dat Voga told Carthoris of his plan in the event that something went astray. He slipped the diagram with instructions to his friend when he next delivered the prisoners' provisions. He had already spoken to the Prince of Helium in hasty whispers about Thuria's situation. With his cell being located next to hers, Carthoris confirmed that he had observed the scientist watching the girl with a lubricious gaze.

In the event Dat Voga could not accompany them, the stage was now set so that Carthoris would lead the escape if he could be freed from his cell. With two brilliant men of Helium in on the scheme, the odds were vastly increased of at least some of them escaping.

For what he guessed to be weeks, Dat Voga had importuned their captor to allow Carthoris to assist them in their efforts. He elaborated on how the prince was an inventor of note, telling the scientist of the improvements to fliers and navigational systems he had single-handedly devised, including the autopilot feature with which the ships of Helium's navy were equipped.

While Daxxus Nahl found the navigational device interesting, he remained firm that no one else was to be involved in the project. Doubtless the scientist did not wish to have to keep his eye on two potential conspirators at once. Dat Voga was disappointed he could not convince the man to release his friend, but there was nothing he could do about it.

While he worked to solve the power issue, Daxxus Nahl concurrently busied himself with the other project that he refused to discuss. The man was an enigma, often telling Dat Voga confidences that would keep him a prisoner here forever, but then on matters the younger man thought trivial, he would maintain the utmost secrecy.

One day, as the younger man bent over his desk analyzing figures from his meters, Daxxus Nahl approached him with as smug a look of self-satisfaction as the coadjutor had ever seen him exhibit. "Now see here, Dat Voga," he announced as he approached.

The padwar immediately noticed that his jailer wore a pair of unique gauntlets, manufactured from the bronze ore he had fetched from the distant storeroom the day he risked climbing into the ventilation shaft. Each gauntlet consisted of a fingerless glove that left the thumb and fingers exposed, made of a flexible, metallic fiber with the palms extended to below the wrist.

Attached to the glove were intricately constructed bronze gauntlets that enclosed the forearm nearly to the elbow and were much thicker than conventional gauntlets. He later learned they concealed machinery and circuitry. There was a mysterious lug on the inside of the right gauntlet, midway between elbow and wrist, while an indentation was present on the outside of the left gauntlet at the same distance from the wrist. Obviously, this socket would mate with the corresponding lug. What function the interlocking of these two might serve was not apparent.

The scientist studied his coadjutor for a few moments. "I see I once more have you at a disadvantage, Dat Voga. I shall enlighten you—in part, at least. These are the remote-control mechanisms for the power equipment, as well as the means by which one may—how should I put it?—*calibrate* a certain frequency I have in mind to modify," he said cryptically.

"When one is wearing these, one assumes full control of the power and modulation array. I have worked on the design and construction of these off and on for over a hundred years. And now they are finished!"

He had a strange expression on his face as he eyed his gauntlets. Then, he thrust his gaze upon Dat Voga and his lips parted, as if in contemplation of expanding on what he had just revealed. The erratic nature of the man was such that he may have, on a whim, spun about and left without saying anything further. In this instance, he continued.

"It is time to explain something further to you, Dat Voga: the goal of this project, and how I hope to accomplish it, although my reasons for doing so I shall keep to myself. After discovering the planet spheron field, I learned something equally fascinating. I found that *time*, like the gravitational and magnetic fields, is a frequency. The understanding of this astonishes me yet. This frequency fluctuates on such an infinitesimal scale that you would find it staggering. However, one need not seek out this frequency to an infinite level of accuracy, as I've deduced that one million points past the decimal should be sufficient to—*remodulate*, shall we say—to any time frame to the nearest tal."

Dat Voga started. "Time is a frequency, you say?" Daxxus Nahl, however, continued as if the padwar had not interrupted.

"After discovering the existence of the planetary spheron field, I studied it from every angle science could conjure, and applied every known physic to its properties. I even discovered an aspect of natural law that, in combination with telepathy or astral projection, might allow one to use one's mind to move oneself to any other point in the galaxy. I extrapolated, however, that it might take thousands of years to unravel the mysteries to the level needed to make it practicable."

The padwar instantly thought of John Carter and Ulysses Paxton, or Vad Varo as the latter is now known on Barsoom, both of whom had traveled from Jasoom in the manner Daxxus Nahl just described. He did not mention it, however, never knowing what kind of insensate rage into which it might throw the unstable man. But to learn that Daxxus Nahl had perhaps stumbled onto the cosmic secret that would enable travel between planets with the quickness of thought was exhilarating. It would make moot the problem of the depleted radium, by offering a way for the planet's population to flee Barsoom before its impending doom.

The scientist continued, breaking the padwar's train of thought.

"The most stunning thing I discovered was that all time coexists with merely a subtle difference in its modulation. This law appears to hold true for the entire known universe. For instance, were I to remodulate your atoms and attune them to a frequency that existed several days ago, you would immediately exist in that time frame and cease to exist in this one; it is all controlled by the universal time modulation at an infinite subatomic level.

"The problem I encountered was that an energy source powerful enough to modify the time frequency did not exist, except in a form that would destroy you. Then I had the epiphany to combine the forces you and I have been attempting to mold into a single, all-powerful field, since our bodies are already attuned to these forces as we interact with them daily.

"Once stabilized, this field will transmit the necessary power to modify the time field. The field will be created around the area to be remodulated with the object in the center of the field not coming into direct contact with its extremity. This is essential, as remodulation would leave portions of the object in both the newly attenuated time frame, and the time in which the object currently existed, which would be unfortunate. This phase of the project is at last complete. I have even preset the value in the gauntlets in preparation for their first trial. All that remains is to stabilize that field!" His voice finished loudly on a note of high excitement. The scientist paused to allow this to sink in.

The meaning of what he had just heard stunned Dat Voga. Although he knew how seriously Daxxus Nahl took himself, almost without thinking he blurted his thoughts aloud. "You don't mean you intend to travel through time! Why—it's impossible!"

Daxxus Nahl's face flushed with instant wrath, and his eyes narrowed to two narrow slits, inflamed to anger by the obvious disbelief evident in the tone of the rash, young noble from Helium. It was obvious to Dat Voga that the man forcibly suppressed the urge to strike him.

"Do not dare presume, Dat Voga, to doubt one who is as superior to you as you are to a troglodyte! Do not forget that any ulsio will do when one is required for a test subject," he spat nastily.

Daxxus Nahl did not take any form of criticism lightly. But Dat Voga was not going to simper and suck his thumb because his open and honest speech offended the scientist's finer sensibilities. Although he knew he risked provoking the man, his noble spirit demanded he make a reply. With his chin lifted, he spoke, his words clear and methodical.

"Daxxus Nahl, I attempt each day to learn from your obviously greater experience. But you should bear in mind that I have been exposed to every sort of theoretical bosh that could possibly be propounded, by a great many scientists and learned men who were as convinced of the soundness of their ideas as you are of your own.

"Further, I am unafraid to die, so your death threats have no effect on me. They more approximate the words of a common thug than the words of a supposed learned man of science. If you wish to destroy me, then, by all means—cease your prattling and have done with it. You have it in your power to do so. But know this: I will not be intimidated by your threats."

The brash young padwar then folded his arms across his chest and waited for annihilation, while Daxxus Nahl caressed the pen-ray bauble he kept inside his work pouch after he had agreed to take on the young padwar as his assistant—the slender, wand-like instrument the scientist had threatened to use if he had to destroy Dat Voga instantly.

"Very well, Dat Voga. I told you once that I perceived you to be a man of intelligence, and I believe I was correct in my surmise. Perhaps there may be a hint of cavalier recklessness there as well, but I myself am given to speak straightforwardly. You must forgive me, as I do not take criticism lightly as I am confident in my abilities.

"So, rather than disagree, we shall let scientific experimentation decide who is correct, which is exactly as it should be between peers. To give you a greater understanding of my 'theoretical bosh' as you put it, I shall give you this to experiment with, using the spheron metering with which you are now conversant. Here, this is my cipher as I have deduced it."

Daxxus Nahl took a piece of vellum and rapidly wrote a short but deceptively complex formula upon it. This he handed to the young padwar.

"If you will take a benchmark reading using the spheronic meter, and then use the cipher to forecast the next modulation at a time interval that you may select for yourself, you will be embarrassingly surprised to find the modulation exact—and that to the millionth decimal!"

With that, Daxxus Nahl, his nostrils flaring, and his eyes spitting flame, spun on his heel and left the room.

Chapter Twenty-Four

The Power Conundrum

Dat Voga, feeling he had narrowly avoided a calamity in this latest of many confrontations with his mad jailer, and being anxious to put this new information to the test, went directly to his metering station. Here stood an array of gadgetry to monitor the incoming raw fields they were trying to recoalesce into a single power source.

He began studying the piece of paper Daxxus Nahl had given him. Upon it the scientist had written only one simple calculation. This included the inverse of the square of the spheron modulation rate, an interval of time measured in tals, and a constant utilizing the square of minus one—an odd formula, indeed.

Dat Voga entered several characters into a small computation device and immediately received an answer matching the readout on his meter. The modulation of the spheron field at that precise moment matched exactly the result of his calculation after carrying it out to the required level of accuracy.

Following Daxxus Nahl's instructions, he chose five xats as the interval for his next readout, set his chronometer, reran the calculation to obtain the theoretical value of the modulation reading at that point in time—and waited.

Dat Voga guessed that the modulation of this newly

discovered planetary field would be unchanged when he measured it the next time, expecting it to match his benchmark value out to the prescribed decimal points of accuracy, without variance. He knew that if he took a reading of the magnetic field and then retook the reading five xats later, the values would be identical, yesterday, today, and tomorrow. He expected nothing less from measurements of the spheron field.

The xats slipped by slowly. Once, Daxxus Nahl appeared in the doorway of the antechamber. He observed Dat Voga bending over his bench, staring at his chronometer. The padwar turned his head and took a quick reading from his meter, beside which sat his chronometer. He felt a tightening in his chest. "Issus!" he hissed.

Dat Voga shook his head. He did not understand how, but this madman was right. How he had not noticed this subtle change in the modulation rate was beyond him. He must have been rounding it off and therefore had not noticed the minor discrepancy. He had not seen the need to take it out to this degree of accuracy.

The fact that he had just proved that the modulation rate changed exactly per the calculation and in the correct direction, which was positive since he had added five xats the second time he ran the formula, pushed aside any lingering doubts.

Recalling his benchmark reading he reversed the calculation per the formula he had by now memorized, this time substituting minus five xats for the time interval. Again, he found himself astounded. The numbers matched, to the decimal, his original benchmark value.

Being a man of science, he could only account for it by arriving at the same conclusion as Daxxus Nahl: to wit, time was a constantly remodulating frequency. And if that were the case, if that modulation could be modified, such as they did with other frequencies, then time travel *was* theoretically possible. It must be. The numbers did not lie and neither did the metering.

He could not explain the sensation, but the instant he completed the calculations and proved to himself the astounding truth, he felt something extraordinary loomed that would forever eclipse their lives. Even if he were to escape the clutches of his warden and return to the gay capitals of Barsoom, he could never return to his old life. This discovery was too momentous to continue as before. He now understood why Daxxus Nahl was so driven.

Dat Voga had always been happy in his work, popular among the warriors, the nobility, and the youth among whom he fraternized. But he knew he would be miserable after learning this revolutionary truth if he did not see this through to the end and know the outcome for himself.

He had another question he wished to know the answer to—regarding Daxxus Nahl. Was the man brilliant, mad, or both? That his mind had been affected by the solitude in which he had condemned himself to live was obvious. His heights of eccentricity and fickleness were beyond belief—making him dangerous and volatile. His temper was shocking and erratic.

There were also his fellow prisoners to consider. Could he but aid them to escape, he would be content to remain here as coadjutor, to see this through to the end and prevent Daxxus Nahl's perpetration of any act the man of Helium found intolerable. He particularly feared for Thuria. Rather than see any harm come to her, he would attack Daxxus Nahl with his bare hands if need be. The padwar racked his brain to think of a way out of his quandary.

Whatever transpired, whether the mad scientist released the prisoners, or he himself somehow helped them to escape, Daxxus Nahl was too dangerous to leave to his own devices. A sense of impending doom warned him that calamity would strike should he depart with his friends and leave the man here with this power at his insane disposal. He bent his head to his work.

He had been dwelling much of late on everything Daxxus Nahl had told him. He had so filled his head with field amplitudes that he dreamed of them when he slept. Throughout his waking zodes he pondered the unstable power field.

As such, it was little wonder the answer came to him in his dreams as he tossed upon the cold, bare sleeping platform in his chamber the night after Daxxus Nahl's staggering proclamation and their ensuing row. The revelation caused him to jolt wide awake from his restless nightmares in the little room near the laboratory.

Stepping to his station he made a quick adjustment to the spheron field, switching the input from the cable running to the mysterious machine on the plateau thousands of sofads below their feet to an unpurified influx of the field he used as a benchmark against which to monitor the modified stream. Ordinarily this adjustment would have had a calculated, deleterious impact upon the combined modulation of the three fields—an assumption based on Daxxus Nahl's beliefs in its instability and impurity, those beliefs comprising the sole foundation for the existence of his Spheron Harvester.

He threw all the switches on the raw fields, made several adjustments, and noted the results—but without throwing the final switch that would divert the combined power to the Magno-GraviSpheronic insulator array.

If he was correct in his surmise, to do so would result in a spheronic nexus the likes of which would be instantly obvious to all. He stared fixedly at his meter, thrilled at the sight of that unwavering needle that showed a purely combined power source and a perfectly seamless and harmonious amplitude. An idea born of dreams bore out in fact; he had solved the power quandary.

Daxxus Nahl would have never suspected this modification

to have the desired effect because he had already convinced himself the spheron field must be "purified" for proper use, being as he said, "unusable in its native state." Dat Voga had just proved that such was not the case at all, but rather quite the opposite. He now guessed that the device Daxxus Nahl had originally used to measure and monitor the field had been responsible for incorrectly indicating that the field required transformation.

He had seen what he wished to know. For no sound reason he could explain, he quickly reset the dials and switches on the spheron field to their original settings. His gauges and meters immediately responded with the now-familiar, unharmonious readings. He had begun powering down the fields, one by one, when Daxxus Nahl stepped to his side. The man was so quick and silent!

His appearance startled him, just as he had that time Dat Voga had exited the ventilation duct only to turn and find the man standing in the tunnel. He had been wise to act on the creeping sensation he had felt running down his spine a moment before.

Daxxus Nahl looked suspicious when he spoke. "What is it, Dat Voga? Did you discover it?" He spoke in a rush, appearing overly anxious—creepily anxious—to hear the coadjutor's reply.

Dat decided he would keep what he had learned to himself. He felt it imperative Daxxus Nahl not know he had solved the riddle of successfully modulating the triumvirate of power sources into a single, all-powerful field. He could not be sure, but he suspected that were he to make the man aware that he had solved this problem—to give him this much sought-after solution—it would sign the death warrants for himself and his fellow captives. Instead, he pretended to be frustrated, as if angered by yet another failure.

"Issus, you startled me! No, unfortunately not. I had a dream, a dream so vivid it awakened me. I thought I'd figured it out! Awakening, I felt the vision might be portentous, but that's not the case."

The scientist stared at him longer than necessary, so that the padwar began to wonder if the man doubted his reply. One could never tell how much he had seen or heard with his hypersensitive senses. He felt the probing of that cold, analytic mind.

"Very well, then, Dat Voga. Perhaps on the morrow the answer shall come. Sleep well."

The young noble of Helium acquiesced. "Yes, perhaps tomorrow. Sleep well, Daxxus Nahl."

Chapter Twenty-Five

The Experiment

The next day, trying to be as discrete as possible and summoning his most detached tone of voice, the coadjutor sought to probe the scientist for more information as to his ultimate goal. Having noted Daxxus Nahl's fascination with the gauntlets, he began there. He hoped the obvious excitement the man displayed over the completion of these would influence him to wax garrulous.

"If you explained more fully how the power source will function in conjunction with the gauntlets, it might add clarification as to the unstable power field. Also, it could be of benefit to have at least a degree of understanding of how the experiment will proceed once we discover the solution to the power failures. Anything, however trivial, might aid in controlling the sources and correcting their ambiance."

At first, he did not believe Daxxus Nahl would answer; yet finally he spoke. "The gauntlets are now complete. And as you will assist in the testing, you will eventually require a rudimentary understanding of that phase—from a power monitoring standpoint. All of this, however, hinges on our regulating the power to stabilize the nexus."

To Dat Voga's relief, the scientist went on to explain the functioning of the gauntlets, as well as the plan for the experiment. The gauntlets were the wherewithal by which the remodulator controlled the powering up of the equipment and the calibration of the Magno-GraviSpheronic nexus so that, alone and single-handed, the wearer might direct himself to another time frame by remodulating the time field once inside the nexus.

Daxxus Nahl stressed that only the time field inside the nexus would be remodulated such that, once they reached the experimentation phase, Dat Voga would be safe enough at his station when the scientist triggered the remodulation of the time field.

The nebulous sphere of energy that he and the other prisoners had witnessed many times before had been an incomplete and unstable Magno-GraviSpheronic nexus. Had it been successful, the scientist would have been able to manipulate the time vibrations by remodulating the spheron field; but it consistently collapsed too early for that.

Daxxus Nahl had modified an equilibrimotor belt that had been preset, upon activation, to attain the height of seventy-five sofads, the height to the exact center of the spherical field from the floor, where it would hang suspended above the ovoid globes atop the dozen insulators of the power array.

Dat Voga had learned that four of the insulators were dedicated to the magnetic field, four to the gravitational field, and the remaining four to the spheron field. Each field had qualities that set it apart from the others, so each set of insulator and power conductors had to be designed with each individual field's unique properties in mind.

The spatial coordinates of the destination were set in a similar fashion to a destination control compass. But while Carthoris' invention utilized a radium generator diffuser for distance calculation, the forces inside the nexus itself were used to set a center point from the planet's core using the spheron field to place one at a preset distance of five thousand sofads above Barsoom's surface.

Daxxus Nahl had decided this figure would be sufficiently high in altitude to avoid landing one inside solid rock or beneath the surface of a body of water, were such to exist. This location, which determined the final physical location of the traveler, could also be adjusted as desired, while the required modulation of one's time-destination point could be set as well at this time. After his explanation, Dat Voga remained puzzled by one item that Daxxus Nahl had not mentioned.

Still frowning as he pondered the problem, he said, "I believe I understand the phases of testing, and the procedures make sense but for one thing. Once you're in the remodulated time frequency, and the power to the nexus has been terminated on this end, how would you return to the present? Would you not be stranded in whatever time frame you found yourself? If you require all this equipment to affect the remodulation, will you not require a similar laboratory of equipment to return? Or were you not planning on returning?"

Daxxus Nahl smiled a haughty smile.

"Naturally, I planned to return! And that question, Dat Voga, is answered once again by the gauntlets. You see, they are paramount to this project. With them one adjusts the time modulation and sets the spatial destination coordinates. With them one initiates and controls the equipment. But the true beauty of their design, young Dat Voga, lies in their hidden power-storage cells, of which you know nothing, the design of which drove their size. Could I have made a device the size of a timepiece, I would have."

"They operate in a similar fashion to an electrical capacitor in that they store power. This is the only method of remodulating from a newly arrived at time frequency without having to reproduce all this equipment in another time frame where it does not exist."

"Once inside the Magno-GraviSpheronic nexus, the gauntlets store enough energy from the field to provide for a single, return nexus. The instant you interlock the gauntlets, the stored power creates the return field. This field, generated by the gauntlets, will exist long enough for the return modulation to occur per the gauntlets' time and spatial values. The store of power gone, the field will then dissipate, with the traveler having been calibrated to the new values."

At this point Daxxus Nahl crossed his arms and sat looking at him, as if to say, "See, there is nothing else that can be created to compete with this."

Dat Voga was shocked. "It's astounding! Daxxus Nahl, if you could but be persuaded to bend your enviable scientific acumen to the amelioration of humanity's ills, I can scarcely imagine what you could accomplish with the wealth and resources of the nations of Barsoom at your disposal, which they would be! Will you not join me, and come to Helium? This gorge is no place for a man to dwell, alone and isolated from all human contact and intercourse—"

A look of scorn had slowly crept up Daxxus Nahl's face. The expression of bitterness ceased any further importunities from Dat Voga.

"Do not attempt to entice me to your twin cities, Dat Voga," he said icily. "I had my fill of them fifteen hundred years before you broke your shell. At one time I thought much as you. Luckily, I saw in time the sullen ugliness that lies behind their vaunted humanity! If I could wipe them all from the surface of Barsoom in one magnificent swoop, they would be gone erenow—for the amelioration of Daxxus Nahl!"

Chapter Twenty-Six

The Magno-GraviSpheronic Nexus

His last conversation with Daxxus Nahl ended so bitterly that the padwar decided he must step up his plans to effect their escape. Hoping to discover more about his mad scheme, he had delayed for as long as he deemed safe; he had learned enough. While unsure what Daxxus Nahl hoped to accomplish if he succeeded in remodulating to a different time frame, he was certain it boded ill for all Barsoom.

In the note he had slipped to Carthoris days earlier, he had informed the Prince of Helium that he would *accidentally* drop the daily rations as a signal to be ready. He did not wish to speak aloud of their plans for fear the hypersensitive hearing of Daxxus Nahl would betray them.

The morning following the explosive exchange in which he attempted to entice the scientist to Helium, Daxxus Nahl informed him he had to make a half-day venture to check on distant equipment. He instructed Dat Voga to continue his endeavors to decipher the power problem, being yet unaware his assistant had already solved the issue.

Prior to his leaving, the scientist was disagreeable and bitter. He complained loudly and threateningly when Dat Voga dropped a tray of daily supplies for the prisoners, making a mess and having to retrieve more, which did even less to improve his mood.

Daxxus Nahl spoke little, pausing only to give his assistant orders for the time during which he would be gone. He turned to leave, but at the tunnel entrance he paused and spun on his heel. "Be prepared when I return to finalize your work on the power field, and to move the girl Thuria to my quarters. That is all."

Dat Voga's wrath instantly flared. So, it had come! "While I've only known Thuria briefly, still, I object to moving her to your quarters. I consider her under my protection, as much as that is possible."

"I think you shall find, Dat Voga, that there is a great deal that is impossible for one in your position," the scientist spat back.

Daxxus Nahl's hand toyed with the slender device in his lab apron, as if he would draw the weapon and annihilate his coadjutor. Unpredictable as always, he about-faced and stormed through the door into Tunnel Two.

The announcement came as no surprise, and only reaffirmed Dat Voga's belief that he had made the right decision to move on his plan for their escape. He could not get Thuria away quickly enough, and the timing could not have been better, for Daxxus Nahl, distracted by his rage and in haste to complete the trip to the distant equipment room, had exited and left his quarters unlocked.

Unarmed as he was, the handsome young padwar had not relished a confrontation with the lunatic, who always kept the tiny destructive ray device upon his person that he threatened was capable of vaporizing Dat Voga instantly. After the many other things he had seen during his tenure here, the Heliumite had no reason to doubt the veracity of the claim.

He stepped within Daxxus Nahl's quarters and scanned the room for the gauntlets. He knew that without them, and without the secret of the power stabilization of which only Dat Voga had knowledge, Daxxus Nahl would not be able to complete his plans before the padwar could return with an army and take this redoubt, capturing the scientist and ending whatever mad scheme he had devised.

The man had become too dangerous to remain free. He had enslaved them, threatened to use them as test subjects and now menaced Thuria's honor, as well; as far as Dat Voga was concerned, he had sealed his fate.

Dat Voga knew little about the gauntlets. Daxxus Nahl had not gone into much detail as to their use, only what he thought might aid his assistant in stabilizing the power while the scientist worked on other projects. Inside Daxxus Nahl's quarters, Dat Voga discovered the gauntlets sitting on a shelf. Nearby lay the specially modified equilibrimotor belt he had mentioned.

The padwar realized it would be useful if his hands were free for the climb up the ventilation shaft, so he slipped the equilibrimotor belt around his waist and buckled it in place. Upon a wall, he discovered a sword, something he had very much missed the weight of upon his side; this he slipped into the belt. Glancing about, hoping to find more weapons so he might arm the others, he spotted an article he was gladdened to see—his pouch.

Out of all the belongings Daxxus Nahl had confiscated, why he kept Dat Voga's personal pouch laying on a workbench in his private quarters was a mystery. Perhaps the man hoped to understand his assistant by inspecting his articles?

He felt elated to have it back, thinking of the sentimental bit of blade it contained that had saved his life years ago, a simple item that inspired a philosophy of hope within the breast of the young man that would remain with him for life. Happy with the discovery, he snatched the pouch off the bench and girt it to his harness, looking about one last time for weapons, but finding nothing.

To further free his hands he slipped the gauntlets on,

attaching the buckles to ensure a snug fit. He paused. Noticing again the lug on the inside of the right gauntlet and the obvious female connector on the outer portion of the left, he inserted the lug into its receptacle, saw that it required a quarter turn to lock, and did so to satisfy a curiosity.

He had surmised the lug to be part of the works of a mechanism. After rotating the gauntlets with the lugs interlocked, a small hidden plate on the left gauntlet slid silently into a recession, exposing a button that lay directly beneath his finger.

He had no doubt this switch would instantly calibrate the spheron field, thereby adjusting the time modulation. He performed a quarter turn to free the lugs, and was satisfied when the plate instantly slid across and covered the button; he disengaged the lugs.

He guessed the quarter-turn motion interlocked the stored power sources, closing an electrical connection. The scientist had once told him it would take the combined gauntlets to provide the required stored charge of power—in much the same manner as a capacitor—for the return Magno-GraviSpheronic nexus. He left the room.

Daxxus Nahl had left the prisoners in the keeping of Dat Voga, secure in the knowledge that without the telepathic signal they could not leave by the only exit. The scientist had no reason to fear them even if they were freed since he possessed the destructive ray device he always kept on his person.

Dat Voga would later curse himself for not remembering to bar the door to Tunnel Two. He had already freed Thuria, instructing her to wait near his metering bench, and was in the process of releasing Carthoris when Daxxus Nahl unexpectedly thrust open the door and ran forward shouting, momentarily forgetting his slender pen weapon.

However, Dat Voga did not forget the sword, the only weapon he had with which to face the enraged scientist. With one hand he held the sword at Daxxus Nahl's throat;

with the other he sought for and found the dial that vibrated the larger portion of the glass-cell front that allowed solid matter to pass through, which it promptly did in the form of Carthoris. Dat Voga pressed the sword into the hands of his prince, whom he considered the more proficient swordsman, and together they backed toward Thuria.

Daxxus Nahl exploded. "Dat Voga! Unfaithful calot! Despicable, perfidious defector—I suspected as much! That is why I only went a short distance and waited, then returned to see what manner of foul betrayal you would commit. You and your vaunted humanitarianism! Vile apostate! What other lies have you told me? You and your ilk—it is for this reason and many others that I shall wipe clean the face of Barsoom. Now die!"

Daxxus Nahl whipped the slender pen-ray device from the pouch hanging from his harness, but before he could fire his weapon, his coadjutor raised a palm toward the scientist.

"Hold, Daxxus Nahl!" he shouted. "Behold: In your haste, you would destroy the gauntlets. See here!"

Dat Voga raised his arms and for the first time Daxxus Nahl saw the extent he had been outwitted, for prominent to view upon each of Dat Voga's forearms were the gauntlets.

While his compatriot distracted the deranged scientist, whose eyes now bulged from their sockets in a face made hideous in the extremity of his rage, Carthoris struck, lunging at the man with the sword. He meant to disarm the man, and in this he succeeded. However, reflexively jerking his hand, Daxxus Nahl caused himself to lose a finger together with his weapon. The device fell clattering to the floor and fired a burst of rays upon impact—a burst that carved an enormous cavity in the wall of prison cells behind Carthoris, disintegrating portions of two unoccupied cubicles. The small weapon then skittered across the composite flooring and disappeared beneath a piece of equipment.

It could be construed to be a measurement of Daxxus

Nahl's rage that he appeared to take no notice of his missing digit, nor of the blood pouring from his wounded hand upon the smooth stone floor before the cells. The ray device lost to him, the scientist now drew his own sword to face the pent-up frustration of the Prince of Helium.

Daxxus Nahl appeared very much like a madman in that instant. His eyes were pealed back and filled with anger and lunacy in his reddened face; his injured hand flecked his body and the floor in blood while his spittle turned to foam in the corners of his mouth. Upon his head his hair stood in mad disarray.

But, mad or not, Daxxus Nahl was no mean swordsman. He pressed Carthoris mercilessly, the prince finding himself disadvantaged from having been a prisoner for many weeks with little by which to maintain his vigor.

"Blast you! Stand still, Issus take you!" The madman's rage increased in magnitudes at his seeming inability to quickly defeat even a weakened Carthoris of Helium.

"I'm not your puppet, Daxxus Nahl, nor do I obey your commands. Come and make me stand still—if you can!"

The scientist hurled a stream of venomous curses at his former assistant. The padwar was looking for a weapon so he might help Carthoris defeat the scientist, who, with the increased strength and vitality given him by the longevity serum, bid fair to overcome his friend who was weak from long incarceration. Spotting a metal tool on a table, he lunged for it when Carthoris called out to him.

"Save the girl, Dat Voga!" he cried sacrificially.

Dat Voga demurred, "But my prince—"

"There's no time. The plan! Flee!"

Carthoris slipped then in a pool of blood from Daxxus Nahl's missing digit and, hitting his head on the side of a cell, fell to the floor, stunned. With the speed of a great Barsoomian spider ambushing its prey, Daxxus Nahl pounced upon him.

Just as Dat Voga feared to see Carthoris run through

Daxxus Nahl appeared very much like a madman in that instant.

upon the monster's sword, from a pouch upon his harness Daxxus Nahl whipped a roll of roping. The material was thin and seemed to have a tacky quality that allowed it to stick to itself. This he wrapped several windings of around the stunned man's wrists and ankles. Kicking the dropped sword to one side, the immense maniac heaved himself to his feet and turned to face his erstwhile assistant.

"See now what will soon be the fate of you all!" Without further ado, the madman reached out to the nearest cell which happened to be that in which the pilot of the Banaalian vessel the *Cunning* was confined. He wrenched the dial marked by the archaic hieroglyph to *Purge* with a vicious twist.

Instantly, a blinding flash filled the cell. If the man screamed, it was not heard through the sound-deadening glass. The remains, if there were any, were immediately whipped away by a blast of cleansing fluids and heated air. The cool, glass front of the cell steamed from the heat and moisture, and then the cell appeared pristine again, leaving no evidence a man had occupied it up until a moment before.

"You may thank yourself for that man's death, Dat Voga."

Whether by accident or intent, the madman advanced and now stood between them and their path to Tunnel Five—the tunnel leading to the ventilation conduit through which the padwar hoped to make good an escape.

Dat Voga backed away, keeping himself between the enraged scientist and the girl. "It didn't have to end like this. I don't know what tragedy happened in your past to make you so filled with hate, but you should know: you won't succeed in your plans, whatever they are."

Daxxus Nahl threw back his head and laughed. "What can you know about it, you decrepit vermin? You wish to know my plans, contemptible betrayer? I told you once that if you knew my intentions, you'd be honor bound to stop me. Shortly you will all be dead and so it can make no difference. After your death, I shall carry out my plan for the destruction of the current waste of humanity.

"I know you were close to finding a solution to the power problem. I shall finish it myself! After I'm done with you, I intend to remodulate to the past, where I shall dedicate my life to preventing the depletion of the seas. I intend to return our planet to its ancient, pristine glory, wiping away the billions who should have never been spawned."

"You're crazed, Daxxus Nahl. Don't you realize that—"

"Before you say it—yes, I realize I shall cease to exist, simpleton. But then, none of this will have happened, for the course of the planet will have been irrevocably altered. It is quite easy for me to be the diabolic monster you think me to be, because soon it will come to pass that neither you nor I will have ever existed. You once claimed you were unafraid to die. I, too, am unafraid!"

The padwar saw Carthoris stir where he lay. The faces of Zat Simpus and Gaff Vlor were pressed against the glass of their cells, where they could only stand and watch helplessly. Zat Simpus was unaware of the destruction of his warrior, being able to neither see nor hear what transpired in the other cells. Had he known, it is doubtful he would have cared since the man had become a liability, with Daxxus Nahl's actions only following a path similar to that which he already had in mind.

Dat Voga continued backing away until he and Thuria were in the center of the twelve towering insulators. Without taking his eyes off Carthoris, he tapped a button on the gauntlet marked with a familiar symbol—a symbol replicated upon the controls where he had labored for weeks.

A hum became instantly perceivable. As he passed his workbench where he had finally solved the incredible riddle assigned to him by Daxxus Nahl, he made a quick adjustment on one of the dials—a tweak Daxxus Nahl would have given much to have known erenow. That there was a difference in the power source became instantly obvious.

"Dat Voga!" he screamed with sudden realization. "Stop this instant! You don't know what you're doing!"

The padwar slipped one arm about the waist of Thuria. "On the contrary, I know precisely what I'm doing. I'm stopping you!"

Chapter Twenty-Seven

The Rage of Daxxus Nahl

DAT VOGA, ALTHOUGH REALIZING the futility of the act, kept the girl behind him to protect her in the event the unhinged man retrieved his ray device or attacked with his sword. With Daxxus Nahl between them and their planned exit, he was now forced to attempt a wild gambit. Pulling the frightened girl close against his back, he instructed her to clutch him about his shoulders and neck.

"Hang on for life, Thuria," he commanded.

He then pressed the equilibrimotor belt's power button, hoping the combined weight of them both would not adversely affect it; it did not. They shot into the air to the prescribed seventy-five sofads. With the insulators thrumming with energy, Dat Voga hit the control on the gauntlet—a miniature replica of the controls at his station with which he had become well acquainted.

In that instant he knew without a doubt that the power glitch had been solved; the nexus appeared instantly. Bright, powerful, and steady, it surrounded them in its lambent glow. The sphere hummed with such a resonance that the very molecules of air seemed to dance to the tune of it. Bits of dust and grit, disturbed from the ceiling of the enormous grotto, drifted through the safety netting, creating a dusty halo around the glowing sphere.

Supporting Thuria as best he might, they hung suspended

in the center of the nexus of energy. The power of the field was obvious, its presence discernible in the intense vibration of every atom in the vault. The color of the sphere deepened to a blue and then swiftly faded to transparency, while the background appeared in a distorted manner around its curving edges.

As the color of the nexus faded, the figures of Dat Voga and Thuria became ghostly shadows to the onlookers. Surrounding them was a spherical image of darkened sky filled with storm clouds tossed tumultuously. What looked like moonlight filtered through the clouds, but it was difficult to say with certainty because of an indistinctness in the sphere's center due to distortions curving along its surface.

Daxxus Nahl, caught in the grip of fury, howled. The Heliumite had thwarted him in his debased desire for Thuria, and now he had usurped the scientist's invention with the intention to derail his plans. His voice, when he spoke, assumed strange, tonal harmonics due to the disturbed atmospheric ambiance.

"Calculating calot," he screamed over the thrum of vibratory power.

He rushed to Dat Voga's station and began twisting dials and hitting switches to no avail, for he had been rendered powerless to stop the young padwar from Helium by his own design, which dictated that only the wearer of the gauntlets could control the machine. Daxxus Nahl must have foreseen a possibility that he would be within the nexus while another tried to stop him and had, therefore, installed the very safeguards that now thwarted him.

As the wearer of the gauntlets, he would have had complete control. And with the gauntlets, even were his laboratory destroyed, he could have returned to any portion of the globe at any time frame he wished simply by adjusting the time and spatial values via the gauntlet interface and triggering the return nexus. But destiny had it that another wore them, and so his fury knew no bounds.

"If you power down the nexus and descend this instant," Daxxus Nahl proclaimed, "I'll show mercy to you and your companions. But should you persist in this folly then know this: their torture and deaths commence this instant and there is nothing I do not know on the subject. I can wring pain from the human body in ways of which the scientists of today are incapable of knowing."

"You're a liar, Daxxus Nahl," said the shadowy form of Dat Voga. "I have no doubt you know how to torture defenseless captives, but how could a calculating beast like you know aught of mercy?"

"Power down the apparatus!" Daxxus Nahl screeched.

The padwar looked first at Carthoris, then turned and glowered at the scientist. His prince had given him his orders. Without uttering another word, he crossed his arms and locked the lug of the right gauntlet into the corresponding indentation on the left, then rotated his forearms horizontally until they aligned at which point the protective plate slid back into its recess with a soft *snick*.

A deepening hum resounded in the chamber for a moment, during which Dat Voga felt the gauntlets tremble as they took on a stored charge from the field.

Although Daxxus Nahl had yet to witness this aspect of the experiment, he recognized the effect, but he could only look on helplessly as indicators in the gauntlets glowed briefly with the emanations of their stored energy, indicating a full charge.

"Curse you, Dat Voga!" his distorted voice screamed over and over.

With no further hesitation, the padwar pressed the exposed button on the left gauntlet. On cue, the scenery visible inside the sphere became dark, while at the same time, from Daxxus Nahl's perspective, the forms of Dat Voga and Thuria faded and were gone as if they had never been.

A noticeable change occurred to the pitch of the humming equipment, and then it powered down as it was designed to do. It had successfully completed the cycle. Dat Voga was not there to see it, but the others saw.

Carthoris felt relieved because he knew his friend had saved Thuria from what to a woman of noble descent such as she would have considered a fate worse than death. That he might now die for it would not cost Carthoris any sleep as he had become accustomed, from the time he broke his shell, to a life of danger. And did his father's blood not run in his veins?

He always knew he would someday die a violent death because he lived violently. His only hope had been that, when his time came, it might be at the hand of a master swordsman rather than like a calot, trussed up where he could not even defend himself, and at the mercy of a lunatic.

Daxxus Nahl turned on Carthoris' bound form immediately and kicked him viciously with all his might. Zat Simpus, a look of ignorant glee on his demented and gloating countenance, pressed his face against the glass to better see the end of this despised enemy, not realizing that he, too, would be tortured and destroyed shortly.

Carthoris, his feet bound but having risen to his knees just before Dat Voga and Thuria disappeared, fell roughly upon his back with his legs bent painfully beneath him. His head rebounded from the floor of the laboratory, causing him to see starbursts. He hoped he would not lose consciousness.

He saw that a terrible change had been wrought in Daxxus Nahl. Whereas in the past weeks the man had acted with the objectivity of a scientist coolly studying a subject, now an unfettered mania possessed him. Unfortunately for Carthoris, he was now the sole object of the maniac's focus.

"The son of the Warlord of Barsoom—pah! And how easily snared!" Daxxus Nahl spat.

He punctuated his remarks with another kick at the prostrate man. This time, however, Carthoris rolled with the kick, so it did not land as powerfully as the last cowardly blow. He would have liked to have grabbed Daxxus Nahl by his foot and tripped him, but his hands were still bound behind his back.

Quick as a banth he continued his roll, coming back to his knees. He then rolled backward, sticking his legs in the air and, drawing his arms up over them, retracted his legs through the loop of his arms. Now his arms were in front of him.

Having recovered from his ill-landed kick, and having observed the maneuver of the bound man, Daxxus Nahl threw back his head and laughed, hard and maniacally. Tears of warped amusement filled his eyes; saliva, unnoticed, flecked his lips and chin as he stalked toward his helpless prisoner. He seemed to have become totally unhinged.

"I cannot wait, Prince of Helium, son of John Carter, supposed Warlord of Barsoom," he mocked, "to get certain devices I have in mind in your flesh. I designed them a thousand years ago and perfected them on natives I snatched from Ptarsas. Although I'm sure they haven't forgotten how to inflict pain on their victim, tonight we refresh their memory!"

And Daxxus Nahl lunged at Carthoris.

Chapter Twenty-Eight

Remodulated

Aside from the form of Thuria clinging about his neck, Dat Voga felt the sensation of moist, cool air. The laboratory had faded from sight and the blue nexus no longer surrounded them. A constant, sullen roar filled his ears as of a mighty, rushing wind, while above they beheld a sight few Barsoomians of his day have ever witnessed—a sky filled with dark, churning storm clouds.

The vapory forms were low and dark and were only visible because the nearer moon broke through the occasional rift in the cumulonimbus, bringing to view thousands of sofads of clouds stacked in thick layers rising into a nighttime sky. It was a terrifying and awe-inspiring sight.

Looking over a shoulder at Thuria, he called out and asked her how she fared. She had made neither movement nor sound since the remodulation but responded immediately. "I'm fine, Dat Voga, but I fear for Carthoris!"

That preyed on his mind as well. As he considered what might be done about the predicament in which he had been forced to leave his friend, a feeling of giddiness assailed him. "Thuria, do you notice anything strange?"

"Yes, I feel dizzy!" she answered. "How high are we? Do you think we're so high that the air is too thin to support life? I hope I don't faint, or I'll let loose of my hold and fall!"

The preset adjustment made to the spheron field had

functioned perfectly, and they were now over five thousand sofads above the surface of the planet. Were it daytime, they would see the Ptarsan Gorge below them, with the desert barrens stretching away to the horizon. But the scientist suspected the giddy sensation had nothing to do with altitude.

"No, Thuria, this air isn't rarified; quite the opposite. I think it's much more oxygenated than what we're accustomed to. As fantastic as this may sound, I believe we're becoming intoxicated from the air we're breathing!"

As if on cue, a great rent in the envelope appeared above them, the clouds parting to show a starry sky with both dim Cluros and his bright mate, Thuria, visible. The Heliumite and the girl from Zoquan gazed down to where the bright light of the nearer moon must be flooding the ochre sea bottom. Many haads away, a burst of lightning sizzled intensely, further illuminating the scene.

Expecting to see the great rift in the sea floor, they were shocked to instead see only water. The canyon was submerged, the immense body of water that covered it extending for as far as they could see, with nary a sign of land breaking the surface.

Dat Voga felt then probably the only quick stab of fear he had ever encountered in his life. But judge not too harshly one who has fought bravely and fearlessly beneath the banner of the Warlord of Barsoom—one whom John Carter himself was proud to call friend.

Although fully understanding what Daxxus Nahl hoped to accomplish, he was unprepared for the reality of its success. Thuria gasped as her eyes took in the scene below, and she came near to screaming out loud at sight of this vast body of water crashing in wave after wave of rolling swells.

It overwhelmed them. Many were there on Barsoom who had never encountered more water than that which could fill a wash basin. Of course, they knew of the Lost Sea of Korus near the Valley Dor; Dat Voga had even visited it once as a young padwar. But this! Titanic waves undulated thousands of sofads beneath their feet. The might of this body of water, its enormity and volume—why, the Sea of Korus paled in comparison with this colossus.

"He actually did it," he mused aloud.

"What did you say?" gasped Thuria. But Dat Voga remained silent, taking in the amazing scene beneath his sandaled feet.

The presence of the sea made it obvious that the time modulation Daxxus Nahl had preset was to a very distant point in Barsoom's past. The events in the laboratory had advanced so rapidly after the scientist caught them in their escape attempt that Dat Voga had not had time to evaluate the time settings.

The equilibrimotor belt Daxxus Nahl had modified to provide a safe means of arriving in a new time was still equipped with its small radium motor on the back. But the wings, which were typically strapped to the upper body to guide and stabilize the flier, were not present.

He had not guessed, when he had grabbed the gauntlets and the equilibrimotor, that he would be putting them to use. He had only wished to prevent Daxxus Nahl from using them. He did not recall seeing the wings but realized that he would not have taken them if he had, as he assumed that taking the gauntlets and the belt would be sufficient to stymie the scientist.

Currently, the two were hovering in a sky filled with billowing storm clouds and bolts of lightning unlike anything they had ever seen. Storms of this nature were impossible in their time. Below was a prehistoric sea, its glossy black waves hiding Issus alone knew what beasts. He and Thuria had to find a place to land. Having to shout to make himself heard, he explained their situation to her.

"Thuria, we need to get down . . . these electrical bursts! The belt is equipped with a motor, but we don't have wings.

We won't be able to direct our course against the wind! You need to get around front so we can use the motor."

Thuria, clutching Dat Voga's harness while he supported her, clambered around until she clutched him in front, grasping him about his neck, with his arms about her waist. With difficulty, he disengaged a piece of his harness and attached it to her and then back to himself to aid in supporting her weight, which would eventually tire them both until she fell into the sea.

"I need to let go of you with one arm briefly to start the motor," he shouted over the wind. "Don't be alarmed." Thuria flashed a brave smile at the padwar.

The man shifted her to one side, while he sought the controls with his other hand. His efforts were successful, and they felt a sudden thrust as the motor came to life. However, it tended to cause them to roll. He now realized how important the wing structure was in the use of an equilibrimotor, for both guidance and stabilization. They finally hit on a method that would allow them to be propelled without spilling them end-over-end, but they still had little control over their direction.

Wishing to drop lower and hopefully avoid the electrical activity, he incrementally adjusted the eighth ray control, dropping them in elevation until they were five hundred sofads above the waves. He did not wish to get too close to the surging surface for fear that a sudden downdraft might propel them into it; naturally, neither he nor Thuria were swimmers.

Although the motor propelled them, they attributed most of their lateral movement to the wind, which had become quite forceful. The wind's force increased, and then the skies broke loose and unleashed their full fury upon them.

For the first time in their lives, they felt rain—and lots of it. It came at them in sheets. They did not know it, but they were on the edge of a tropical hurricane that swirled them in a giant circle while the entire mass itself sped along chaotically over the surface of the churning sea. They were now at the mercy of gusts of wind reaching upward of one hundred and fifty haads per zode.

Much of the time they could scarcely breathe for the force of the wind. Interestingly, they noticed a strange anomaly relating to their inability to draw a breath, although at the time they could not discuss it due to the wrack of the storm. Dat Voga had discovered that he could draw a deep breath, and then not have to take another for several xats, and with no apparent discomfort. After mastering the trick of it, he quickly taught Thuria through pantomime. Breathing in this manner, they soon recovered their composure.

The canny scientist surmised that the lungs of the future populace of Barsoom must have evolved to take in greater quantities of the rarified air so they could capture the necessary amount of oxygen from the depleted atmosphere. Now in the past, their lungs were obviously soaking up the element on a scale of magnitude of perhaps four to six times that to which they were accustomed.

They had become intoxicated inhaling this prehistoric air! After realizing the atmospheric disparities, he became fearful the girl might succumb, and so quickly warned her to slow her breathing to avoid running a risk of oxygen toxicity until their bodies adjusted to this startling change.

The two were buffeted by the storm for zodes, though not long enough for Thuria to become an impossible strain on Dat Voga's harness. Directionally, they had become utterly befuddled. Riding the edge of the maelstrom, they were simultaneously spinning along the outer edge of the vortex, while the storm, whimsical and fickle, drove them in one direction after another.

Thuria tapped the padwar on the shoulder to get his attention, and when he looked at her, she indicated a direction by pointing. Looking, he saw stone cliffs illuminated by flashes of lightning.

Chapter Twenty-Nine

An Alarming Discovery

Crashing waves relentlessly assaulted the crag ahead of them, sending spray high into the air. From their position, the padwar saw that the bluff rose sheer from the sea for two hundred sofads. At their current altitude they would easily clear this.

Shouting to make his voice audible over the thunderous roar of the storm, he said, "We'll land and find shelter!"

Thuria vigorously nodded her head, blinking cascades of rain from her eyes. She did not bother to shout a reply. Both were soaked, cold, and miserable. While he had long since built up a tolerance to the cold night air of Barsoom, this drenching cold of the past was vastly different.

In his day, the air was dry and therefore the temperatures much more bearable than the wet chill that was currently freezing the two to their marrow. They were a bedraggled pair when they finally lowered themselves to the ground a couple hundred paces inland.

This was a very dark and violent Barsoom, and they were weary, but they could not yet pause to rest. Buffeted by gale-force winds and driving rain, he took the girl's hand and, with heads bowed against the elements, they stomped miserably through wet, waist-high vegetation toward a forest not far distant. Beyond the trees a series of cliffs reared that were visible when the lightning flashes illuminated the darkness. He had it in mind to seek shelter near the foot of them, hoping the intervening trees would blunt the force of the storm. Possibly they would find a cave.

The only storm of this magnitude he had experienced was the epic tempest that had carried away John Carter's daughter, Tara of Helium, and her flier. That event was marked in history, for on modern-day Barsoom, a slight wind or a puff of cloud is a rarity. Now, the trees here were bent over from the gale, giving them the appearance of dumb animals hunkering against the tempest.

The two discovered the darkness beneath this primordial forest to be so complete they would have been unable to see a hand in front of their faces but for the occasional flash of lightning, and Dat Voga's pocket torch. He always kept a torch in his pouch, together with other various small items that were useful when one was far from home. He thanked his first ancestor that he had found it in Daxxus Nahl's quarters.

They made their way to the foot of the cliff. As they had hoped, there was an appreciable decrease in the velocity of the storm. Although still violent, the intensity was greatly lessened by the intervening forest. This made conversation easier, although the noise of the wind ripping through the giant ferns was still significant.

The man made it known to Thuria that he wished to walk along the foot of the cliff seeking a hole or overhang—anything that might offer shelter from the wind and rain. Their first ancestor was with them. They had proceeded only a hundred sofads before stumbling upon an overhang reaching far back under the cliff. Inside was a dry floor, out of reach of the torrent of rain.

Uncomfortable from the wet and cold, he held the shivering girl to impart his body heat to her to make her more comfortable. For the first time in weeks, she felt a sense of security. The future was uncertain, but having escaped the clutches of Daxxus Nahl and the violence of this primitive storm, nature would no longer be denied. Laying her head back against the doughty warrior, she fell asleep, despite her discomfort.

The padwar wished to remain awake to maintain watch while the girl slept. Although so weary he could barely keep his eyes open, he did not know but that this might not be the den of some wild animal and did not wish to be asleep should anything return to this cave or seek shelter here as had they. Weaponless, he found himself armed only with his wits and ingenuity, having given his sword to Carthoris during the attack of Daxxus Nahl.

Daxxus Nahl! Issus, but he could strangle the man who had caused them to come to this sorry pass. Had that maniac only delayed his return by even a xat they would have been well on their way toward the ventilation shaft, and escape.

Thinking of the scientist made him recall the gauntlets and that he had no idea what duration had been used to set the time-frame modulation. Per Daxxus Nahl's formula, the modulation setting was derived based upon a given time variance, which was entered as a positive to modulate to the future, or a negative to modulate pastward. Although confident they were somewhere in Barsoom's dim past, it would be necessary to know exactly how far back in time they had traveled.

It had not been his intention to use the device, but the enraged scientist had forced his hand, making it imperative that he remove the gauntlets from the man's possession. When he pressed the button, his thought was that he and Thuria might find themselves outside the grotto in the sky above the gorge. For all he knew, nothing would have happened. It had been a chance he was forced to take based on the situation, his knowledge of the scientist's intellect, and the confidence the man displayed that, once the power problem was solved, the equipment was ready for use.

Careful to not awaken Thuria, he took out his pocket torch and began his first minute examination of the device.

In Daxxus Nahl's rooms, he had only had time to note and verify the working of the lug and the activation button. Now, he wished to decipher how one went about setting the modulation.

He discovered a plate upon the left gauntlet that slid to one side. Triggering the release mechanism, he opened the panel, exposing an array of tiny screens and a small fingerboard inscribed with Ptarsan hieroglyphics.

He thanked his first ancestor for his innate curiosity about the written languages of his world. While the spoken tongue of Barsoom is always identical, the written languages are unique from city to city. His interest had prompted him to get a basic understanding from his new friends in Ptarsas of their local written language during his brief stay there. Being widely traveled had also helped him to develop an affinity for learning new ones.

He recognized the markings after a careful study and deduced that he was looking at a screen to enter the modulation frequency. Since the frequency must be calculated out to a million decimals for accuracy—quite a considerable figure—the scientist had invented an ingenious method for entering the desired modulation in formula form, using standard symbols.

Dat Voga sighed with relief when he saw this. While he could calculate the modulation to the required degree of accuracy, entering that many characters on such a tiny input device would have taken quite a while.

He touched a button and noticed a small screen that began to glow with a faint blue tint; it displayed the current modulation value. He had memorized the cipher Daxxus Nahl had given him when his assignment was to engineer a means of blending the planet's spheron field into a seamless power source in combination with the gravitational and electromagnetic fields.

He now took out an article he was grateful to have placed there—his tiny computator. He had snatched the device from his bench as he made the adjustment to the power equipment during the altercation with Daxxus Nahl. He ran the displayed value in reverse, per the scientist's formula.

For accuracy, the duration value of the formulae is entered in tals, the smallest unit of Barsoomian time. He converted the returned value, his expression displaying his astonishment when he saw the result of the calculated duration. It displayed a result of negative one million and one years as the duration used to calculate the modulation value.

It seemed incredible to think that they were a million years in the past, but his eyes bore witness to the overwhelming evidence of the fact. Unbelievable though it might be, only at this point in time could one reasonably expect Barsoom to be covered in this much water and lush vegetation.

So, this was the time frame Daxxus Nahl was to visit to begin his goal of preventing the seas from evaporating, thereby wiping out untold masses who would never be hatched and forever changing familial and racial branching. The time frame made sense, as this was the approximate period generally accepted by the scientists of future Barsoom that the seas had begun their recession.

He could not have selected a riper time to study the seas, Dat Voga had to admit. Obviously, the people in this era were still in their prime. Had they begun to seriously abate, there would have been many more islands visible as the underwater mountain ranges began poking through the surface, creating new islands and archipelagos.

Dat Voga and Thuria had been blown by the hurricane over possibly hundreds, if not thousands, of haads before encountering this first sighting of land, although admittedly much of that had been in total darkness, with only flashes of lightning serving to illuminate the surface of the sea. For a while, he had begun to doubt the existence of any land whatsoever. If the seas had begun to recede, it was not yet obvious.

The padwar then noticed a chronometer advancing on one of the readouts. It currently displayed a value of seven zodes, forty-four xats, twenty-five tals. As he watched, it continued to advance. In a moment of clarity, he understood the intended use of this feature.

This chronograph automatically tracked the elapsed duration since arriving in this era. Dat Voga recognized once again the terrific depth and profundity of the arcane cleverness of Daxxus Nahl. The man undoubtedly was the most brilliant man he had ever met, perhaps who had ever lived. The importance of this chronographic reading would be of inestimable import when figuring the return settings *if one wished to return to a specific time.*

If he and Thuria returned using the same differential that brought them here but moving forward instead of backward by entering the million-and-one-year differential as a positive value, it would not take into account the time they had spent here. That meant if they were to spend two weeks here before remodulating, then they would arrive two-weeks after they had left—having left Carthoris at Daxxus Nahl's mercy for that amount of time! The man felt a chill run down his spine, and his face flushed with shame.

He should have thought of this fact himself and consulted his own chronometer the instant he had arrived. That interval would be paramount when he calculated the arrival point of their return to the future, which must be done to the nearest tal! He must subtract the time they had been gone from the time differential so that he could pinpoint their return to within moments after they had left so the madman would be given no opportunity to make good on his threats against the Prince of Helium.

Thinking of the modulation value caused him to glance at the input screen. After they rested, he would set the device and return to rescue Carthoris. He touched the small input device to enter a value, but the buttons made no indication when pressed. Puzzled, he tapped them again with the same result. Had it been damaged? Fearful, he then noticed a blinking input on the device and understood. Were there no bounds to Daxxus Nahl's conniving cunning?

He had set a safeguard in place, preventing any altering of his values. The man had the most paranoid nature of anyone Dat Voga had ever met. The padwar racked his brain for various patterns or symbols that would make sense for Daxxus Nahl to have used for a cipher, beginning with his age and any other information the man had mentioned, using it to derive dates, numbers, and combinations. After that he began entering various latitude and longitude coordinates. Nothing worked.

He began to grow frantic. If he could not solve this riddle, they would be stranded here forever, a million years in Barsoom's remote past. And no one would bring help to Carthoris and the Ambassador of Ptarsas.

The gauntlets were unusable with the currently stored value, as that would simply result in them returning to the exact point in time and space at which they had arrived, using up their store of power and effectively stranding them here forever. The modulations currently set were attuned to this time frame specifically; he must be able to enter new and precise values if they were to return to their own time.

Assuring himself he had gleaned all of import that he could for now and dejected after spending a full zode in failed attempts to unlock the device, he tried to stay awake until Thuria was rested enough to maintain watch. But he underestimated his weariness. Before he realized it, he had fallen asleep, both body and mind exhausted from the exploits of the last day.

Chapter Thirty

Beasts of the Wood

When Dat Voga awoke, a new day had dawned and the opening of their retreat was glowing with morning sunlight. The storm had moved on and Thuria sat watching him. As soon as she saw his eyes open, she flashed a smile and greeted him with the typical Barsoomian greeting.

"Kaor, Dat Voga. You're awake!"

"Kaor, Thuria!" He smiled in return.

She was a phenomenal young woman, he had come to realize. It was amazing for her to have endured what she had these past weeks and then to show such resiliency. He thought of the daughters of many of Helium's nobles who would be mental wrecks after being forced to endure the horror and privation she had suffered. Next, he recalled his discovery of the previous night and his heart plummeted. She was so happy that he hated to break the dismal news to her.

They were soon reminded by their bellies that they had not eaten for many zodes, and so, with tangible appetites, they sallied forth to see what nature would provide. The scientist determined that he would tell her the truth about their situation after they located food to assuage their hunger, not wishing to disappoint her any sooner than necessary.

Since his youth, Dat Voga had been familiar with the

mantalia bush that provided a nourishing milk-like fluid. He knew also of various fruits and nuts that were cultivated near the canals. He was unfamiliar, however, with what they might find in this time frame. He found himself pleasantly surprised when, upon entering this strange forest of cyclopean ferns and herbaceous trees, they encountered several nearby bushes full of ripened berries and fruits of diverse varieties hanging from limbs heavy with their burden.

Nor were they left long wondering which of these were safe to eat. With surprise and delight they observed numerous creatures dining upon the delightful-looking viands. Never could they have dreamed of so many examples of flora and fauna. Dat Voga, enchanted from the scientist's perspective, and Thuria, girlish in her simple appreciation of the beauty surrounding them, laughed as they strolled through a wonderful forest of a much younger Barsoom.

He told her of an old scientist in Helium; a man equally as unhurried in his stride as he was in his speech. He could speak tirelessly of the few surviving specimens of foliage of the modern day, to the utter tedium of those who listened. Dat Voga averred the man would doubtless be quickened with the vigor of youth were he to witness this veritable cornucopia of bush and tree and flower and grass.

Eating berries in the trees were tiny, many-legged, furry creatures who were so diminutive that Dat Voga could have fit two to three in one hand; with large, languid eyes, they watched the two foraging on the forest floor, resuming their meals after they passed. These seemed more curious than afraid, causing the padwar to guess they were unfamiliar with man.

They became fascinated with a two-armed, bipedal species that leaped from tree to tree as easily as a man might thread his way along a city street. Inquisitive, many of the creatures followed them until they ultimately became distracted, at which point they would scamper away, sometimes chasing and pulling one another's prehensile tails. These were considered odd by the two, who were accustomed to most beasts having six or more legs or arms.

There were several specimens that appeared to belong to the same genus but were different in size or markings. Some of these seemed at home on the ground, while others in the trees. And they saw herds of six-legged grass-eaters that Dat Voga eyed with the consideration of an epicure. His youthful body craved meat and here it was in aplenty.

It was the avians, however, that they found the most remarkable. In the forest were birds of every size, shape, and color. These were the first either had ever seen. Although the renowned Barsoomian scientist Ras Thavas had succeeded in manufacturing malagors, neither Dat Voga nor Thuria had ever seen one. These creatures were much smaller than the malagor, with some being about the length of a finger and others only half that size.

Delighted, they watched avians speed through the trees: the raptors in search of their aeries, and the nonpredatory birds hunting for the various fruits and berries that provided them sustenance. As he watched them darting this way and that between the giants of the forest, Dat Voga was reminded of walking the streets of Helium as a lad, enjoying the spectacle of fliers speeding overhead as they wended their way between the towers of the city.

The birds alone would have offered a scientist of his day a lifetime of study. Little evidence of them existed in the future. All traces of these delightful, colorful, and fragile creatures were lost during the ensuing millennia of drought, strife, and war after the seas receded. Those were dark times, when all but a small percentage of the flora and fauna of Barsoom became extinct. Seeing their delicacy firsthand, he no longer wondered that the disintegrating hands of time had effectively effaced nearly all evidence of their existence.

The thought caused him to pause in reflection as he and Thuria walked along a game trail. He looked wistfully about them. The girl stopped beside her friend and looked up at him with a questioning smile.

"I've never given much thought, Thuria, to what we of latter-day Barsoom have lost. The world of our time is normal to us since it's all we've ever known. I see now that, no matter what my wildest dreams might have conjured, had I attempted to visualize a primordial forest, it would be foredoomed to pale in comparison to its reality. What we've lost is more significant than I imagined. We traipse through a paradise whose visions will haunt me forever."

Thuria did not reply, but her eyes filled with tears as she looked from her friend to the beauty of their surroundings—a beauty unaware of a looming disaster.

A magnificent insect of many colors and multiple wings approached them, interrupting their somber observations. It paused briefly as if studying them and then sped on. Of such life forms were the two barely acquainted, for the Barsoom of the future is free from insects, with a few exceptions.

Here the air hummed with the sounds of their buzzing. Thuria's declared favorite was one of which Dat Voga knew the name, having once seen its rare fossil. "Look, Thuria, a fofal!" he exclaimed. "I have encountered its likeness in stone in a museum in Gathol." He recalled at the time being fascinated by its apparent fragility and beauty. He saw now that the fossil could never do the insect justice, for the impression frozen in stone could never reflect the animation of life nor the colors of this beautiful and delicate creature.

"In stone? Oh, but this is alive and amazing!" she exclaimed as she examined the colorful insect.

Its wingspread would have covered her small hand had it alighted, but for now it seemed content to lazily flit from flower to flower from which it drew its nourishment. It flew by flapping its four wings, rapidly and silently. After choosing a flower from which to feed, the wings ceased flapping and then the true marvel of its multiarticulation became apparent.

For then the wings would oscillate rapidly like a pro peller as it hovered, the only thing touching the flower being the long proboscis with which the insect drank deeply of whatever fluid it found therein. This fluid seemed to be its primary source of nourishment, for only upon flowering shrubs and trees did they find these silent and colorful creatures.

Thuria crept up on one. The creature began flapping about erratically at her approach, but eventually landed on her extended hand. Dat Voga tensed and was on the cusp of warning the girl against allowing the strange thing to touch her—but too late!

The insect landed on her extended finger and sat there, clutching her digit as its wings worked lazily up and down and its small, fuzzy legs brushed its face. Its multi-faceted eyes ignored the two as it attended to its task and then, jerkily, and erratically, it flapped away upon its mysterious journey.

Enthralled, they watched it climb into the upper terraces of a giant fern. Thuria laughed wholeheartedly with the sincerity of a child at the look of stunned concern on the padwar's handsome face. His frown swiftly faded to be replaced by a wide grin of relief.

"Its feet tickled," she said as she continued to giggle, carefree and joyously.

The lighthearted moment was shattered the next instant as a raucous din broke upon their ears a few paces from them within a thick patch of deep underbrush. To their ears came the sounds of heavy crashing, comingled with the snapping of tree limbs. A ferocious growl blended with frightened bleats.

A brief silence descended, where one could envision powerful jaws closing upon a soft throat, throttling the life from some hapless creature as it struggled to rise and escape the inexorable grip of its slayer.

Dat Voga motioned for the girl to follow and sought a

place of sanctuary. With no way to defend themselves, flight was their only option. He had been lulled into a false sense of security by the peaceful atmosphere surrounding them up to this point.

He cursed and silently scolded himself for not keeping a wary eye out. Why had he left the gauntlets and equilibrimotor belt in the cave? If they had the belt, they could have used it to rise into the air to safety instead of being trapped on the ground, surrounded by dense vegetation that made it impossible to see to any distance.

He soon located a tree with branches depending nearly to the ground. Into this they hastily clambered, with Dat Voga half expecting to feel savage jaws clamp onto their calves before he could reach safety. He encouraged the girl in low whispers, and Thuria proceeded to lead the way upward and then out onto a great branch drooping near the limbs of a gargantuan fern.

This fern was smooth for a length of fifty sofads above the ground and then sprouted several large and leafy fronds. Unless the predator could scale its smooth sides or follow the same path as they, the two should be safe from it. Here they crouched on the limb and waited. A creature emerged from the parting grasses, the sight of it ensuring the man they had made no mistake in their hurried flight.

The beast stood higher at the shoulder than a man's waist. But if he and Thuria stood side by side, they would not have been its equal in breadth. The creature's broad torso tapered downward to a narrow waistline, causing it to be slightly shorter in the rear and lending it the appearance of a battering ram. The two could not identify its species; it was truly a beast who had no modern descendant in their time.

The creature's body exuded an aura of immense strength, it being very muscular and covered with thick fur. The color of this coat seemed to have been derived primarily from dusky earth tones, being lighter along its midriff and darkening in outward gyrations until it became almost black at the head and feet. This shading would doubtless cause this thing to blend in almost invisibly in this forest world.

The head was short and wide, like its torso, its powerful jaws having dual rows of very white, angled teeth ending in exaggerated canines depending from the upper jaw and extending just below the lower, lending the beast what would have been an almost comical overbite had its overall mien not been so savage. The ears were short but had the misleading appearance of greater length due to short tufts of dark hair extending upward from the tips. These were constantly flicking this way and that as they searched for the sounds of prey or enemies. The eye was perhaps the strangest feature, being centrally located high on its forehead. It was large, perhaps half a sofad in diameter, and totally black in color so that the iris and the pupil blended into one large, ebon orb.

The creature was dragging one of the smaller varieties of grass eaters from the brush by its obviously broken neck. The poor animal's head dangled loosely, its delicate fur smeared in its own gore. The creature snarled when it spotted them, which it did instantly, dropping its prey to voice a bloodcurdling scream. Growling, it charged to the foot of their fern, which it viciously attacked as if it would uproot it.

Unsuccessful in tearing the tree down, it sniffed about, finally arriving at the foot of the tree they had initially ascended. Dat Voga cursed its perseverance and obvious intelligence. At the foot of the tree, it reared up on its short, muscular rear legs, grabbed a low hanging limb with its massive jaws, and attempted to hoist and claw itself into the tree. In this it failed, falling into the now trampled grasses. It had not been equipped by nature to climb trees.

The man thought they were in for a long wait, as the beast looked as though it intended to stand vigil until they came down to be devoured. But after a series of growls and snarls it sauntered back to its kill, which it grabbed and flung over one shoulder until it dangled down its back, obviously arriving at the conclusion that an additional meal that cost this much effort just was not worth it, no matter how good they smelled. Appearing exceptionally light of foot, it trotted off through the high grasses with the slain animal bouncing on its back, the predator's head turned slightly to one side where it gripped the carcass about its mauled neck.

"Never again," Dat Voga said, "will I be able to walk through those grasses as lighthearted as we did a few xats ago. I can't believe I allowed myself to become so complacent! It was foolish, Thuria, and I apologize. It won't happen again."

"Don't blame yourself. We were both mesmerized by the spectacle of this place! But it's too bad we didn't bring the belt and gauntlets. We could leave now before one of us is killed. If we make it safely to the cave, I'm for leaving at once. This opportunity is without equal, and as much as I would love to tarry, I feel we should be better provisioned to protect ourselves."

Dat Voga knew then he must tell her of the calamity that had overtaken them. Leaving out nothing, he explained the discoveries he made the previous evening.

"Unless we can decode the gauntlets' cipher, we're stuck here. If I had the right tools I could bypass it, but I don't. I'm not privy to its internal workings and we can't risk damaging it. I only hope this cipher isn't so obscure we can never guess it."

At first Thuria looked crestfallen. But as Dat Voga was discovering, she was the real deal. She sat pondering for a moment and then simply shrugged her shapely shoulders. "It'll come to you, Dat Voga, I know it will. In the meantime, we'll learn to live in this new world. I for one don't intend to become the next meal for that thing we just saw."

He looked at her in surprise. "It amazes me how you can be so optimistic. To me, our situation seems very bleak and hopeless."

She smiled at the distraught padwar, hoping to cheer him. "To be honest, I wasn't always so. When I was very young, I begged my father, who was then a dwar, to let me go with him on a field inspection. He tried to dissuade me, but my father was never good at telling me no!

"At the time there was some dispute with Ptarsas over irrigation in a section of outlying farmlands that both nations claimed; he was to inspect a detachment there. I thought it would be a fun day spent with my father—until a force of Ptarsans arrived and immediately attacked us. We were taken by surprise."

"Is your father all right?"

Thuria smiled. "I've never seen him so happy."

"What happened after the attack?" While she spoke, he watched the brush for signs of any other examples of their monocular friend.

"During the ruckus, my father tried to hide me. As it ended up, we were both captured along with a few of his warriors. Many of his men were slain. They loaded us on ships, and we were taken in shackles to Ptarsas.

"That must have been awful, Thuria," the padwar said softly. Theirs was often a barbaric world.

"Yes, it was terrifying. Later, arrangements were made for the release of my father and his men, but I, for some reason, Ptar Ras kept. He said it would teach Tul Torso, Jeddak of Zoquan, a lesson. It also taught me one as well."

"I'm sorry you've had to endure so much of captivity in your life. So that's how you came to live in Ptarsas, then?"

She nodded. "Yes. It was a frightening and hopeless situation at the time, Dat Voga—much as this."

Dat Voga looked thoughtful. "Obviously, everything turned out, because you seemed happy when Carthoris and I first arrived in Ptarsas."

"Yes, but it was not always so. Ptar Ras gave me to his youngest daughter for her slave. For a while, I was very unhappy. In Zoquan, my father became a thorn in the side of Ptar Ras to achieve my return. That is how he eventually became ambassador—Tul Torso could think of no one better suited, nor one with more reason to salve the tensions between the two nations.

"He so pestered Ptar Ras for my return that eventually the jeddak determined to release me. I think he did so as much to cause Darfa Quan, my father, to cease his importunities as he did as an overture of peace, since a continual state of warfare is taxing on any nation, great or small.

"But over those intervening years, a strange thing had happened. I'd become attached to the princess and vice versa; we'd become inseparable, and I no longer wished to return to Zoquan. I begged father to allow me to remain in her service."

Thuria went on to tell how her father could refuse her nothing, with the same being said of Ptar Ras insofar as his own daughter was concerned. Thuria remained in the retinue of the royal family of Ptarsas where her father, as ambassador to Ptarsas, became a frequent visitor. With this arrangement they saw vast inroads in the dealings between their two nations where diplomatic relations were often strained.

Dat Voga thought about her story. "Thank you, Thuria. You've reminded me that this is not the first seemingly hopeless situation I've been in, either. And, just as with yours, everything turned out all right in the end."

"Of course, I'm accustomed of old at being held captive by maniacs and facing dangerous carnivores in Barsoom's past!" she jested, smiling. They both laughed.

Having given the predator time to become occupied with its prey, they descended the fern. Dat Voga immediately picked up a large stick. "Come," he whispered softly to Thuria. The two retraced their path to the cave that gave them refuge the night before. The man knew now that they must have weapons, and toward this end he would bend his immediate efforts.

Chapter Thirty-One

Explorations

During the ensuing weeks, the padwar would have given much for a rifle. John Carter had shown him one that Tars Tarkas gave him as a token of friendship and mutual respect after the Warlord had visited the green man at his home. While typically a gift from one head of state to another would be unique, costly, and ornate, this was notable for its simple utility, being no more finely wrought than a rifle any green warrior might carry. How he wished he had it!

As had John Carter, Dat Voga appreciated it, despite its plainness, for he knew its accuracy to be such that he could have easily picked off one of the primitive herbivores that abounded here from five haads away. Eventually, though, he did fashion an effective, multitipped spear that, after much practice, he learned to use to bring down small game. He constructed it in the form of a trident, with the points in a triangular pattern so he would have more luck downing the nimble-footed creatures of the woods.

For defense he manufactured shorter, heavier spears for use against the savage beast with which they had the close encounter. He also made a wooden, swordlike weapon with a fire-hardened edge that he crafted over a period of several days, alternately heating and cooling the wood, then finally grinding it to a decent edge using a fragment of gergite found at the base of the cliffs.

In the manufacture of his armament, he found Thuria to be of inestimable value. Thanks to her people's familiarity with woodworking and expertise in all matters arboreal, she could aid in the selection of species of sufficient hardness for his purposes. It was also she who introduced the modern scientist to the lost art of fire hardening.

He found himself constantly thankful for his common utility pouch, which contained many useful items, including his never-failing pocket light and the simple tool modern Barsoomians utilize to produce fire. It was this last item he found the most valuable here. With it, they cooked their food and fashioned their primitive weaponry.

The padwar also fabricated daggers, of a sort, from stiff, hollow reeds. He ground one end upon stone until they attained an angled, sharpened point, while the other he wrapped with grasses to create a grip. Finally, the points of these were hardened.

After outfitting themselves with defensive weapons, which also ensured a means of obtaining game, Dat Voga climbed the cliffs, at the foot of which was their campsite, to take stock of the lay of the land. Locating an area that afforded plenty of foot and handholds, he began climbing, finding it easy going for one in fit condition. Thuria accompanied him, the girl also finding the climb none too difficult.

At the top of the cliff, they walked to a high peak from which they could survey their surroundings. It was during this survey that they began to suspect they were on an island, being able to see much coastline to the east, west, and south of them. At some distance from their location was a mountainous volcano, a common feature of tropical islands as Dat Voga recalled. It looked lifeless, to their relief.

They learned they had been blown here from the west, the direction of the craggy cliffs that plunged into the pounding surf they had seen on their approach. Their highland extended the full width of this end of the land-mass. The cliffs in which they had taken refuge scarred roughly half of this plateau and alternated in height from twenty to one hundred-fifty sofads, while the other half was covered in jungle verdure, falling gently to the sea on the southeastern side.

The land to the north beyond these cliffs was a mixture of rolling, grassy hills together with dense tracks of forest, and with a constant declination in elevation toward a wide valley. From this region of forest and grassland rose the volcano, with the trees and vegetation advancing only partially up its rocky slopes.

Occupying the foothills were large tracts of forest alternating with swathes of grassland. The latter were dotted with various species of grazing animals ranging from tiny four- and six-legged, timid little creatures of about knee height to giants that dwarfed anything with which they were familiar.

One beast of note had so many legs it reminded them of an enormous version of the many-legged insects they found in the forest beneath rotting timber. Covered in shaggy fur, the mountain of flesh trod ponderously over pastures covered in flowering plants, lowing and bellowing, and leaving a meandering path denuded of foliage. On its back, birds perched, piping and picking parasites from the hide of their enormous conveyance. Their nests were interwoven in the brute's fur, indicating they lived on it permanently.

With time, he and Thuria became proficient at retrieving fruits and nuts, and even discovered an edible tuber while observing a long-snouted creature digging them from the ground using its curled claws. Out of necessity, they learned to do more than subsist in this strange land.

After arming themselves, they hiked the distance to the volcano, scaling its sides with little difficulty. Near the top they found a natural ledge running about to the opposite side. Following this path, they arrived at its highest point.

Here they could see to a greater distance than previously. Between these observations, and later walking the perimeter, Dat Voga surmised they were on an island of approximately five haads in width and fifteen in length. It narrowed at the end upon which their cave resided, where there was a natural harbor with sandy beaches on the southeastern side. The whole presented a striking vision of beauty such as they had never before seen.

They continued their climb to the crater's rim where they were delighted to find a lake residing in the core of the dead mountain. The interior slopes above the mirror-like surface were covered in lush vegetation. As they watched, a prehistoric malagor rose and flapped lazily toward the rim carrying a large fish in its beak. Cresting the summit, it flew away toward the north. Birds of various species dove into the lake to retrieve prey while others waded near the shallows.

They observed a bird disappear in an explosion of water, and guessed the beautiful lake housed predators as well as prey. They stood for a long time, drinking in the beauty of the unfamiliar scene. The hum of the insects, the variety of wildlife, and the shining lake in the heart of the dead volcano combined to form an extraordinary image.

Never once, however, did they see any signs of human presence during their wanderings. They concluded the island was uninhabited by man, being peopled only by the sundry wildlife, and scarcely a day passed when they did not see something new. Being used to a world populated only by a handful of examples of the animal kingdom, they found the myriad flora and fauna breathtaking.

They descended the volcano, wishing to make it back to their cave before sunset, having begun their trek at daybreak to avoid spending a night exposed in the forest. Judging by the sounds they heard after dark, many of the carnivora were nocturnal hunters. A primordial forest can be extremely dangerous to those yet ignorant of its many perils.

After the encounter with the calban, the name they coined for the one-eyed predator, Dat Voga fashioned a rough boma he could use to barricade the low entrance to their hollow in the cliff side. The suddenness with which the creature appeared, and the ensuing savagery it displayed, awakened them to the grim reality that all was not idyllic here as they thought when they first laid eyes on the wonders of this prehistoric world.

Fearful a hunting calban might attack them in their sleep, Dat Voga narrowed the entrance to their cave by leveraging large pieces of fallen stone from the cliffs into position. Using tough, fibrous grasses he fashioned a gate from saplings laboriously felled with a primitive axe. The gate was crude, and he eyed it skeptically before calling Thuria to inspect his craftsmanship.

She smiled supportively and said it was the sturdiest door she had ever seen. Modest as it was, though, it did give them a sense of security, offering as it did a certain measure of protection. They were still getting acquainted with their new home, and so deemed any security better than nothing.

Months passed on the island, and during that time they found the calban to be the greatest predator with which they were forced to contend, although it was not the only hunter of the forests. Luckily, the creature's numbers were not great, with their quantity being just enough to offset the birthrate of the quick-breeding herbivores.

Although extremely fierce, the calbans were easily frightened away when confronted by the spears of the humans. It seemed the beasts were not accustomed to hunting anything that fought back, their natural prey being the peaceful grass eaters that existed in plenty. Stunned by the sharpened points wielded by these strange, two-legged beings, they were invariably spooked to run howling through the forest, issuing their strange cries of warning to their fellows.

One day, while making their way through a natural clearing, they were surprised by a low growl from a clump of brush; this was followed straightaway by the charge of a calban. It came at them with the awkward, sideways shuffling gait the creature used to intimidate its prey, growling ferociously. They were both armed with their primitive spears. In the past, shouting and thrusting their weapons toward an aggressive calban always resulted in the barrel-chested beast leaving; but for some reason, this one acted differently.

Dat Voga cast his heavy spear when it appeared intent on attacking. With practice he had become very proficient; the spear drove deeply into the beast's side, eliciting a roar of pain and wrath. The shaft of the spear, dragging along the ground, disrupted the calban's attack, giving the man time to draw the sharpened stick he called his sword.

Thuria ran in, stabbing the injured beast with her own spear while her companion assaulted it with his wooden sword. The edge they had long since discovered to be completely ineffectual against the thick hide of the beast, but the tip, with Dat Voga's expert thrust, found the creature's vitals.

Even with this last wound, the calban yet strained to get at and maul the two. Thuria, having toughened up much during the months spent in these wilds, clung with determination to the haft of her spear. Dat Voga leaped to her side and grabbed it as well, trying to prevent the beast from clawing either of them, which it made great attempts to do. They were jerked from side to side in the calban's efforts to come at them as it dragged itself across the torn-up turf by its front feet alone.

Together, they held on as the tough beast at last convulsed and died. It was their first victory against their primary enemy on the island. The man commented on the hardiness of the beast, and the tenaciousness with which it had clung to life. They wondered what caused this one to attack, when in the past its kind always fled when confronted by their spears.

They had finished crossing the clearing and entered the forest when Thuria stopped, holding up a hand for silence. "Shhh! Dat Voga, I hear something."

He paused, concentrating. And then he heard it—a soft mewing coming from the nearby brush. Tentatively, they moved forward, ready to spear anything that threatened them. It was Thuria who discovered the source of the sound—a calban cub, obviously only a few days old, hidden in the thick grasses near the brush from which the calban had charged.

They guessed its mother had been moving it when they happened across the two humans and, not realizing they would not have interfered with the new mother and her cub, maternal instinct had prompted her to attack to preserve her offspring. The cub hissed and spat at them, causing them to smile. It was tragic, but there was no way they could have known the reason behind the charge, nor could they have responded any differently.

Dat Voga commented, "It's too bad, but the tiny waif will never survive without its mother. I suppose we should dispatch it." He prepared to thrust the same spear through the wee bundle of fur that only moments before he had withdrawn from the body of its mother.

Thuria stopped him. "Hold, Dat Voga! I want to try to save it."

The man was skeptical. "You're only going to raise a killer that'll slay us in our sleep, Thuria."

He might as well have argued with a stone, for the girl remained resolute. She caught up the cub by its scruff, the cycloptic creature twisting and striking in vain attempts to bite and scratch her. She smiled at its efforts for its bite lacked the force to hurt and its claws were tiny and ineffectual.

She spoke soothingly to it; soon she could stroke it, petting its downy fur and allowing it to sniff her.

Eventually it settled down, but it never ceased its plaintive wails for its mother. The girl from Zoquan cradled the wee cub to her breast and spoke in low tones to it as she and the man from Helium walked the trail back to their cliff-side home.

Just before dusk, as they approached the edge of the cliff above their cave, Dat Voga made a lucky kill, bringing down a nice-sized mammal. Below them, where the forest had already turned black with shadows, tiny flashes of luminous colors flashed sporadically, specks of light that, from their vantage point, looked like twinkling stars. They eventually learned the lights were emitted from a nocturnal insect that appeared in the evenings.

Using his rough implements, the man cleaned the carcass and cut away what they wished, and approached the cliff down which they must descend. Pausing, they watched the sun dip into the watery horizon. They continued to gaze upon the wondrous sight, enthralled by its supernal beauty. And then, not wishing to risk the climb in pitch blackness, they descended to their cave.

That night they celebrated their victory over the calban by roasting fresh-cut steaks from the flanks of the herbivore. These fur-covered creatures were odd at first, but later they found them to be immensely palatable when grilled over an open fire, the meat periodically drizzled with the juices of a tart fruit of which they had become particularly fond.

Thuria captured the juices and melting fat dripping from the steaks into a bowl-like leaf that she offered to the calban cub. That first night, however, it disdained everything she offered it, preferring instead to remain curled in a sad, pitiful, furry little ball. Its single, ebon orb reflected the firelight as it watched them nervously, occasionally offering up a mournful wail for a mother that would never again heed its cries.

Chapter Thirty-Two

Life by the Sea

The man and the girl loved the roar of the nearby coast. The sea! They took to life beside it as though they had lived their entire lives there, never dreaming they would so enjoy being near it. Many afternoons were whiled away playing upon the strand and wading in the warm surf. Dat Voga swore that were he to return to his own time he would never again sleep as soundly as he did here, within hearing of that sullen roar.

Aside from the ocean, the additions of dawn and twilight were also unique to them. In their own time the transition was near instant, the sky going from starry darkness to light of day and vice versa in only moments due to the tenuous atmosphere of the future.

But in this time—Issus! Neither could find words to describe these skies and do them justice in the telling. The sun looked double its size in this thicker atmosphere, turning into a swollen, red disk at dusk with a horizon erupting with flaming hues of yellows, oranges, reds, and heliotrope; they found the spectacle to be without comparison. They often rose early to witness the dawn and would occasionally walk to the cliffs to see the westering sun sink into the sea.

The beauty of Thuria's celestial namesake was mesmerizing when the nearer moon sparkled over the water at night. She fairly flew across this prehistoric sky, casting her reflection and dancing light on the satiny surface of the sea, making something magical of her nightly journey.

Sometimes when he thought of the future, he found himself wondering what this person or that was doing. Then he would catch himself, realizing they were yet unhatched. Both found this aspect of their situation the most confusing. The simple act of thinking of friends, and then realizing they did not yet exist, was so disconcerting they felt they could never grow accustomed to it.

Nor were these aspects of this older Barsoom the only phenomena they had noticed. Since their advent here, their skins had assumed a deeper shade of red. At first Dat Voga attributed this to a trick of the prehistoric sunlight which, as viewed through the haze of the lusher atmosphere, seemed more reddish than the sun of the future. But at night, when they were illuminated by firelight, he saw their skin looked much more vivid than it had by the same source of light in the future.

Eventually he attributed this to having nothing whatsoever to do with the light, but rather the higher oxygen content somehow affecting their epidermis. He noted that the affect seemed especially pronounced the more active they were, such as when they hiked to the volcano or the beach, when their breathing became accelerated.

Not long after their adoption of the calban cub, the padwar decided to try his hand at fishing to vary their diet, having heard of the palatability of the rare aquatic creatures of their own time from one Tan Hadron. He had heard the warrior's account firsthand of the difficulties encountered trying to capture them, so decided he would utilize his multi-tipped spear for the purpose.

Armed with his trident and sharpened fronds, and with Thuria carrying her calban cub, which she had named Aava, the two hiked to the sea one morning with the goal of spearfishing in mind. They visited this stretch of beach nearly every day. Never tiring of it, it was not uncommon for them to spend the day in the surf, watching odd creatures scuttling about the sand.

This day they came as primitive anglers, the man earnestly imploring Thuria to quiet her calban, who of late had become voracious in her appetite for things to chew on, an occupation she engaged in with lustful growls. The girl laughed gaily—he took himself so seriously while she, a carefree spirit, simply enjoyed being alive and playing with her cub.

They had previously discovered an area north of the natural harbor where a great headland of rock extended far out to sea. Resembling a pier for straightness, this narrow, rocky ledge formed the northern boundary of the natural harbor while a curving extension of the island formed the southern. From there he decided he would bring home his catch.

Having Thuria remain a short distance away with Aava (who he feared might frighten away his prey), he hiked to the end of the promontory. Although they were unable to carry on a conversation due to the roar of the surf and wind, he would be careful, he said, not to go so far that he would fail to hear her if she called. Ever solicitous of the girl's safety, he did not wish to become so preoccupied as to not note if something was amiss.

He found a location that allowed him to look over the edge into the relatively calm harbor and watch for movement. He had taken the precaution of attaching a length of braided grasses to the end of his spear to prevent his losing it; this also ensured him a means of retrieving his catch.

Dat Voga was not a swimmer, so he had no aspirations of diving after his spear. He never ventured into water any deeper than that in which he might stand upright with his nose in the air. It might have chilled him to know that near its terminus, the headland dropped perpendicularly on its north face for a thousand sofads, a grim reminder of the staggering forces that had formed the isle.

Squatting on his haunches, he watched intently for movement in the freakishly blue water. With his mind intent on his task, it took a few moments to register that Thuria was yelling excitedly. He could not make out her words, but she was waving her arms wildly to get his attention. He realized then that she was indicating something beyond him. Turning, he at last saw the cause of her excitement.

Unbeknownst to him, a large creature had crept from the sea onto the promontory and now sunbathed on the same rock from which he fished; it watched him lazily. He had no idea if it would prove dangerous or not, but at first glance it did not appear menacing.

The creature was a behemoth, approximately the size of the modern-day thoat. Its colors ranged across the entire spectrum of drab grays and browns; it regarded him quizzically with four black eyes. Its multiple rows of flippers along each side suggested it possessed tremendous speed in the water, while its face possessed a sad, comedic expression that made him smile.

He was considering speaking to it to note its reaction when, without warning, from the deep, northern side of the headland the ocean heaved upward. Breaching the surface was a creature whose immensity staggered the mind, and only a portion of it rose from the water. It twisted its body sideways, its cavernous maw opening to reveal multiple rows of ebon teeth the length of a man's forearm.

With a sickening crunch the massive mouth slammed shut upon the poor, flippered beast. On one side of its maw, a portion of its prey was visible where the hapless creature squirmed in its death throes. As the monster crashed back into the sea, its enormous mass caused a swell to cascade over the headland, swamping the man.

Questing for a hold, his hands grasped a piece of protruding rock, which he clutched to avoid being sucked into the sea as the wave receded. Soaking wet, he stood and turned to wave reassuringly to Thuria when, as capricious fate would have it, he stepped upon one of his own round daggers that had apparently dropped from his belt.

His foot flew out from under him as the sharpened reed rolled beneath his foot, catapulting him head foremost into the harbor. Realizing the calamity that had overtaken him, he succeeded in drawing a single, deep breath just before he knifed into the sea. The man descended rapidly for several sofads before, kicking and flailing in panic, he stalled his descent. He had no idea how to swim back to the surface and any effort on his part only caused him to move further from shore and to sink ever deeper.

Fortunately for Dat Voga, the southern side of the promontory was shallower. The water here was only a couple hundred sofads deep—a depth he eventually plumbed to the full, coming to rest on the sandy bottom. Had he fallen off the side from which the leviathan emerged, he would have plunged a thousand sofads before being crushed into a jelly.

He knew he had only moments before his oxygen-starved lungs would force him to inhale seawater and drown. He wondered why they were not already burning for air. He glanced upward to get his bearings, hoping he would not spot the leviathan nearby. The water was unusually clear, and he could discern the slope of the bottom, which he followed toward shore, still unable to swim.

In this manner he continued, seeing many strange creatures. He yet gripped his trident, which had been tethered to his arm; with this he speared a large fish that had ignored him to its own detriment. Carrying his wriggling catch with him, he struggled up the incline of the firm, sandy bottom, marveling that he yet lived and determined to continue walking until such was no longer the case.

Above, Thuria looked frantically for Dat Voga. She ran to the spot where she watched him fall into the sea and found his dagger lying where he had dropped it. She retrieved it and, in tears, called his name as she stared

Breaching the surface was a creature whose immensity staggered the mind.

frantically into the depths, searching for any sign of her lost friend.

The calban cub whimpered, being unfamiliar with the strange behavior of her mistress. The red girl petted Aava and stroked her fur, more to soothe herself than the cub. Thuria had started making her way slowly back to land when she saw something a hundred sofads to her south. Soon she identified it, crying aloud when she recognized the lost padwar.

With great difficulty, the padwar had continued to walk along the sandy bottom, climbing the incline. He was not sure how long he had been underwater but guessed several xats had passed. He had paused to look behind him, peering down the grade into the inky depths in case the leviathan should slip upon him unawares. His ancestors alone knew what else dwelled in that deep pit of water.

Finally, his head broke through the surface. He took a deep, grateful breath, but realized he could have continued holding it for much longer as he had not yet begun to suffer for lack of oxygen. He was ecstatic. Prior to arriving in this wild, primitive world, Dat Voga had never feared man or beast. Then, when he saw the mightiness of the great ocean, he had known an instant of fear. Now, he feared it no more.

He knew primitive man had swum in the deeps, for he had seen the paintings depicting such scenes in million-year-old murals in ruined cities across the surface of his dying world. He now decided that he, too, would learn this lost art. Now that he had survived his first dunking, he was filled with self-confidence. He could not wait to tell Thuria!

Thuria ran to the beach and across the sand to meet him as he waded ashore. He had a large fish on his spear and a wide grin split his handsome face. Dat Voga noticed that his skin had taken on a lesser degree of its customary vibrancy by the time he emerged from the sea, but that now that he was breathing normally it was resuming the shade it had taken since arriving on the island.

And then Thuria was asking him questions faster than he could answer them. Finally, he was able to assure her that he had never felt better. If he had been her brother, she could not have been more solicitous for his well-being. That evening, for the first time in their lives, they tasted fresh roasted fish.

The next morning, after reaching their cliff top to observe the sunrise as customary, they noticed a commotion at the volcanic mountain. Swarms of birds were flying about the rim in hectic chaos. Dat Voga had a dreadful premonition at the sight and decided they should examine this more closely. The volcano looked extinct, but one could never be sure what occurred within the bowels of a planet. It might be nothing; maybe a calban had slipped over the rim and wrought havoc?

After preparing strips of smoked meat to take with them, they left. If they needed anything else, it would be found as they traveled, there being plenty to forage in the forests. Moreover, natural springs abounded, and from the crater lake a beautiful stream poured from the side of the mountain to cascade in a rough falls. Even had that not been the case, the modern Barsoomian can go a long time without water, for their bodies have become accustomed to the lack of it.

They had little by way of adventure on this latest trek to the volcano. They were jumped by one calban; but as they were each armed and alert, they were prepared for him. The calbans of late seemed to be confused because of a tiny, young female cub who bounced along beside them, Aava always growling at those who presumed to accost her mistress. In this case, she snarled at the bull, causing him to pause with a quizzical look on his face. Then he bound into the foliage where he could be heard crashing through the underbrush as he raced away.

With no further misadventures, they arrived at the rim of the volcano after scaling its craggy sides, during which time Thuria had carried Aava in an improvised sling for fear the little one might slip on the smooth rock and injure herself. Upon reaching the top they looked down in shock. Where the last time they visited they had found a pristine, blue lake inside the interior of the volcano, they now saw nothing but a vast field of mud that bubbled and plopped. Tendrils of smoke, or steam, trickled from the surface.

Alarmed, they turned to retrace their path down the side of the cliff to the now well-worn trail that led to the cliff they called home. The squawks and calls of birds, confused at what was happening to their home, filled the air around them.

Dat Voga was troubled, but just how much so he hid from the girl. If this volcano became active it could destroy the island, rendering it into an unlivable wasteland depending on the violence of the eruption. He glanced over the verdure of the forests to where the sea lay shimmering in the midday sun. He remained entranced by its beauty, but he saw that now it had become a prison. They had lived on the island for half a year.

Chapter Thirty-Three

A Storm

THE ARRIVAL OF THE TWO HUMANS in this primitive world had been at the onset of a violent tropical storm. And while that storm was fierce, carrying them away while caught in its merciless grip, it was typical of such, with similar instances occurring throughout the year. In fact, they were on the island only weeks before they saw a repeat of the monsoon that kept them inside for days.

At this latitude, one day was very much like any other, for they were in the tropics. The temperature remained constant, with two distinct times of the year when rainy, tropical storms reigned supreme. The island had advanced into its second wet season, and while they were accustomed to light showers almost daily, the frequency and ferocity had begun to appreciably escalate.

To two who had never known such, they found the increase in powerful weather exciting. They could scarcely believe the high-running seas and the height and force of the ocean during these vicious hurricanes.

While hiking across the tableland upon which they dwelled it happened that a storm of extreme magnitude formed rapidly. On a whim, they visited the cliffs above the sea. Standing on the edge of the western rim, with the storm on the cusp of bursting loose, they watched the waves crashing into the cliff, some surging nearly to the top, the vibrations palpable in the ground.

Out to sea, the skies darkened while ominous flashes of lightning crackled in the distance. The sky filled with dark gray clouds. Amazed at the storm's turmoil, they watched for a while and then beat a hasty retreat, wishing to return to their shelter before they were caught in a downpour. Once there, they started a fire and were content to remain inside for the remainder of the evening.

The daylight was cut short by sinister clouds, the rapid movement of the shifting grays menacing in the darkening sky. This would be no typical storm. The sun deepened to a purplish-red, then hid its face behind the thunderheads as the wind gained force. Of a sudden, and without further preamble, the deluge broke. Fortunately, their cave entrance sloped upward, as the light from their campfire reflected on a deepening pool at its foot.

They could not see from their refuge inside, but the typhoon sounded horrific. Land slips occurred, and from the nearby growths of giant fern came the sound of falling trees and splintering wood. Over all rose the cacophony of rushing wind and pounding rain that fell in torrents.

A massive cliff south of them collapsed from the volume of water rushing into it from above. Untold tons of gergite crashed into the tropic forest, wreaking death and destruction upon the unfortunates hunkered down in the foliage where they had sought refuge at the foot of the cliff. The sound of the avalanche was audible above the din of the storm, and the concussion shook the ground violently.

The volcanic lake, lately a murky mire from subterranean activity that had only worsened of late, now filled with fresh rainfall, causing landslides on the interior rim that mixed with the mud-filled lake. Steam gushed forth across its turbulent surface, jetted from fumaroles below.

On the volcano's steep outer flanks, the runoff rushed in floods, creating rivers in the forest and valleys, and carrying mud, trees, and rock out to the sea. Had they made their way to where they could see the landlocked harbor, they would have seen surges a hundred sofads high crashing ashore and forcing their way deep into the forests.

If they had chosen to move their camp closer to the shore, they would have been slain outright, never standing a chance against the surging, tidal onslaught. The strip of rock from which Dat Voga had fished now lay completely submerged beneath high, running seas.

The explosive detonations and lightning strikes made them wonder if they were the direct targets of an enraged deity. It seemed to the two humans as though the storm paused over their shelter and cried, "Now, witness to the full my power!"

At times, the thunder boomed so concussively it caused tremors in the ground that dislodged small rocks and debris from the walls of their cave. Dat Voga feared the floodwater might rise into their cozy redoubt and trap them, or the powerful concatenations might collapse the roof. The air became pressurized from these enormous discharges of energy. When he could make himself heard, he advised Thuria to keep her lips parted to equalize the pressure.

The lightning strikes were so frequent now that the smell of burnt ozone singed their nostrils, and a metallic tang could be tasted in the air. It proved to be a sleepless night as the very real threat of the storm raged outside.

The man refused to try to sleep, in any case, preferring to keep watch so they would be aware of the first sign of danger. He urged Thuria to rest, but she could not sleep. Nor could Aava. The poor beast remained ensconced in the lap of her mistress, who stroked her fur as the cub remained stock still with the exception of her single eye, which roamed about in fright.

The storm raged all night and into the next morning and for two more successive days without sign of abating. On the evening of the third day, it seemed as if the hurricane became aware that it could not defeat the humans in their lair, so at last it lifted its siege and began to subside.

Within the next couple zodes, the winds over the island finally died and the rain ceased completely. On the morning of the fourth day, they saw blue skies again. They crept from their cave to survey the damage. Trees had been downed everywhere, and the forest was submerged in standing, knee-deep water. Crisscrossing the terrain were newly formed runnels while the familiar ones were bursting their banks or had changed their courses.

Climbing the cliff where they could survey a great portion of their end of the island, they saw the extent of the damage the storm had accomplished. Rivers of mud made their oozy way to the sea, which no longer looked blue, but instead had become a sullen brownish gray, a mixture of topsoil and silt thrown up from the bottom. Gazing at the devastation, the two marveled that they had managed to survive the horrendous storm.

The day after the hurricane had deposited them on these shores, there had been no aftermath such as this. Dat Voga recalled the recoiling of the trees as they hunkered against the onslaught. As soon as the wind and rain had abated, the trees had stood back up. Now, many were down, having been wholly uprooted by the ferocity of the tempest. Others had been snapped off, their jagged remains stabbing upward into the rain-washed sky. He saw it would take the island years to recover.

Dreading what he might find, he turned toward the volcano. Steam issued from the crater, above which he discerned no bird activity. The wildlife that once made their homes there had long since relocated to the north end of the island.

Later that afternoon, the padwar heard a muffled report reminiscent of radium explosives discharged at a distance. It had been difficult to distinguish exactly from where the sound originated, but he instinctively climbed the cliff and gazed toward the not-so-distant prominence near the middle of the island.

The report had obviously come from this region. The mountain was now issuing much more smoke and steam than before. He stared for several xats and then turned and faced the natural harbor, wondering if they should just take to the sea, but knowing it would be only to perish beneath the waves or by some great leviathan.

To remain here and be blown to bits he found unthinkable. He envisioned Thuria incinerated in a fiery blast, or crushed by falling stone, or cooked alive by vents of steam and super-heated gas. The unbidden visions caused him to wince. The girl was like family now. He could not allow harm to come to her

For a time, he felt he was falling in love with her. But before he could be so inconsiderate as to broach his feelings for her, she had smilingly compared him to her brother, Quan Cluros. Her words caused him to bite his tongue and seriously consider his feelings. Later, he was happy and relieved to realize he felt similarly.

He was happy because he felt such a kinship toward her and he took great comfort knowing she did for him as well, while the relief came from the fact that he had remained silent when he had been mistaken about his feelings. If he were to have revealed what had been in his mind, it may have caused considerable awkwardness, perhaps driving an unbridgeable wedge between them.

He had a young sister the same age, and so he would think of Thuria as he did Vala, whom he loved to imagine safe at home. It was with the consideration of an older sibling now that he endeavored to make Thuria's life safe and comfortable while they were stranded here due to his actions. Admittedly, it had not turned out as he had hoped. He spent every evening with the gauntlets, but thus far to no avail.

His survey of the volcano complete and dejected at his

inability to come up with a plan of escape, he returned to the cave. The evening was soddened as only ones who have endured the travails of a hurricane in the tropics can understand, making him grateful for storing up firewood. Other than the fire, the young scientist saw only one bright spot—the personality of the girl, Thuria.

She always had an optimistic outlook which served to bring the brooding padwar a smile. He could not stay morose for long in her company. She scolded him for feeling responsible for their dilemma, reminding him that he took this course of action as a spontaneous reaction to the danger they had been in, and at the command of Carthoris.

The next day the sun and sky appeared as if there had never been a storm. The color of the sky was a beautiful blue, with one of the most stunning sunrises they had seen to date. The sun looked enormous, the air already feeling bright and warm. They decided to walk to the cliffs to survey the changes in their harbor.

As they topped a rocky outcropping allowing them to view the scene below, Dat Voga pulled Thuria suddenly behind the rocks. Below them, anchored in their harbor, sat a sailing ship.

Chapter Thirty-Four

Aboard the *Tycheus*

From an altitude of five thousand sofads, the armada from Helium sailed beyond the continental shelf and out over the moss-covered dead sea bottom of the former Throxeus Ocean. Several haads to the southeast, beyond sight over the curvature of the horizon, were the ancient ruins of dead Xanator. Carter intended to approach Ptarsas from a direction different from the flight plans of Carthoris had called for.

Earlier, they set down briefly to debark a special force with orders to thoroughly search the path of the ambassadors from Helium. Carter's idea was that this small, ground-based group would have the ability to peer into areas invisible from the air, and could then approach Ptarsas unobserved under cover of night.

This force consisted of a small number of handpicked green men who Carter placed under the expert command of his great friend and ally, Tars Tarkas. They were the obvious choice, since no one could cover ground as fleetly as a green man on the back of a thoat.

Carter did not doubt that, barring a flier mishap, the two missing men had arrived safely at their destination. Of all the navy men with whom he was personally acquainted, these two he would pit against any odds and expect nothing short of success, he was so sure of their abilities.

The *Tycheus* headed southwest until they flew out over a great depression in the sea floor, at which point Carter commanded the dwar to make their course south. Now that these two waypoints in their journey had been reached, he sought out Dejah Thoris.

He found her at an observation post at the bow of the vessel. This was a gunnery position, the warrior having been ousted by the princess who now occupied his station. She wished to be of whatever aid she might be in the efforts to find her son and Dat Voga. She stood there, the gun ignored, her eyes straining forward over the mossy plains and formations of the desert, although she knew her son and his companion had not flown in this direction.

Carter paused and smiled with understanding at that perfect, straight, poised form before he opened the hatch leading from the bridge. Stepping onto the forward deck he joined her, the wind fresh and cool in their faces.

"I'd heard we had a new deck gunner of passing fairness! You look as though you might single-handedly win a war with the Ptarsans, my princess."

She knew he but teased her and beamed into his smiling eyes. "If that is what it takes, my chieftain." From long practice, she nestled into the powerful arms of her mate.

Knowing her deep concern for their son, he said more seriously, "We're on the lookout for this so-called Ptarsan range. On our current approach we should converge on it as it bears west. At that point, it's our intention to await darkness before proceeding on a course parallel to the range, watching for signs of civilization."

Dejah Thoris did not reply. She knew these details already and knew as well that John Carter but repeated them to reassure her. She inhaled deeply and let her breath out slowly, feeling its warmth immediately stolen away by the cold, night air as the ship knifed forward at tremendous speed. Somehow, her mighty mate always knew exactly what to do and precisely what to say.

She said aloud, "I think I am ready to go back in." Taking one of his hands in hers they left the forward watch station and headed for their quarters.

From his position inside the control cabin, Dwar Brik Lakko nodded to a warrior standing by. "You may resume your post."

"Yes, sir!" The young man slipped through the door.

Seeing the forward gun position once again manned, Brik Lakko resumed his concentration upon his gauges. Night was upon them now, so on his wireless, he announced, "This is *Tycheus*. Running lights only."

Chapter Thirty-Five

Departure

THE SAILS OF THE VESSEL sitting in the natural harbor hung in tatters, drooping forlornly from her yardarms except for a small number of lesser sails that had been rigged to propel the vessel beyond the promontories into safe anchorage.

A small craft, used to sound the harbor on their approach, had been drawn up on shore. From it, men had issued who were still visible as they walked toward the forest. It was apparent to Dat Voga that they had come upon the scene shortly after this craft struck shore because a couple of the sailors had yet to debark. Those who had approached the edge of the forest had paused to await the stragglers.

The deck on the main vessel bustled with activity. Men yelled instructions and answered calls, each of them busily engaged in clearing debris from the decks. Sails, apparently torn in the storm, were removed and spares brought up from below. New rigging was pulled through tackle and fresh sail hauled upward.

This was all very mysterious work to Dat Voga and Thuria, neither having seen a sailing vessel before. During his tenure in the Heliumetic Navy, the padwar had visited the Sea of Omean, where he had ridden in the converted fliers used as ships by the Black Pirates. But there could be no comparing those to the vessel below. To see this ship with one's own eyes evoked admiration and astonishment—sitting there as though drawn from Barsoom's remote past. The handsome young padwar smiled at that thought and reminded himself that this *was* Barsoom's remote past.

He knew historians who would give their first hatched to see this. Not for the first time he wished for his instrument used for capturing images. But it had been left aboard Carthoris' flier. The sights he had seen these past months often caused him to wish he could capture images that instead he must be content to keep within his mind's eye.

Having watched the crew debouch from the beached vessel and scatter into the forest, the man and the girl retraced their steps to their hideout to discuss these things. The location of their cave would not be obvious after the damage suffered by the surrounding forest. While just prior to the storm there had been a well-worn path leading to their cave, the trail now lay submerged beneath standing water and debris consisting of broken branches and fallen fern.

Scanning the ground for anything that might betray their presence, the two entered their domicile, pulling their protective boma closed behind them. Once they settled in their customary seats, Thuria opened, "We can't remain hidden from these men, Dat Voga. We must avail ourselves of this opportunity to escape. With the volcano showing signs of imminent eruption, to remain here is to court destruction."

She had summarized their predicament succinctly and perfectly. He had to agree. There seemed nothing else to consider in the matter but for one thing: how to determine if these were the type of men into whose tender mercies he was willing to entrust Thuria? If they were the type that would kill him and misuse the girl, then they were better off to stay where they were and take their chances with the volcano.

He was also unsure whether they would be able to

communicate with them. To think that they spoke the common language of modern Barsoom was simply beyond the pale of belief, so they could only assume they would have a language barrier to cross.

If it were only his own hide to consider, the decision would be easy—he would go to these men and trust to his fighting skills to carry him to safety if they proved dishonorable. Since embarking on this mission to rescue Thuria, however, he had found it increasingly difficult to make decisions regarding the safest alternative to dangerous situations with his usual alacrity.

Thuria sensed his confliction and laid a hand on his arm. "Dat Voga, you mustn't try to protect me from everything. I'm very resilient. Although I appreciate the nobleness of your gesture, and the reasoning behind it, this decision must be made for the good of us both. We must see if these men will take us off this island and trust that we can deal with whatever situation arises."

He had to smile at her straightforward, and sensible, speech. "You're brave and wise beyond your years, Thuria. Come on, then. We'll go see what manner of men these are. But we go armed." The two girt themselves with their primitive weapons, Thuria with Aava cradled in her arms.

One thing uppermost in the mind of Dat Voga was the equilibrimotor belt and the gauntlets, neither of which could be easily hidden. Their only option was to take them and hope for the best. Placing the belt upon Thuria he donned the gauntlets, having instructed her in the use of both and explaining the science of the latter inasmuch as she could grasp it.

Zoquan and Ptarsas were not as advanced as other cities of the modern day so she was unfamiliar with many of the terms, nor was she a scientist or mathematician, but she understood enough to use the gauntlets could they but solve the riddle of the cipher. The equilibrimotor belt she could use as a means of escape should it prove necessary.

It would not take her away very quickly without the wing, but at least it would carry her out of reach.

She had retained the filmy garment she wore the day they departed from Ptarsas, having kept it safe in the cave as it would not have lasted navigating the forests. She did her best to arrange the belt to be hidden beneath it and her leathers, a token attempt since her raiment was scant at best.

Dat Voga mounted the gauntlets to his forearms, hoping he could pass them off as ornamental and not be quizzed about them too closely. Taking one last glance about the cave that had sheltered them for months, they headed for the beach.

It was with difficulty that they followed the trail they were accustomed to taking to the harbor which had suffered much from the storm. About halfway down they heard savage growls and the shouts of men coming from just around a bend. Running forward, they came upon a scene that in another instant appeared destined to end in tragedy—a great, bull calban stood over the still body of one of the sailors, the beast's slavering jaws spread wide above the face of the man as it glowered down the trail at his fellows.

The friends of the stricken man shouted and thrust at it with their spears in an effort to frighten or distract it. This without doubt caused the creature to hesitate, as typically its kind strikes and immediately goes for the kill.

It surprised Dat Voga that the calban had attacked such a large body of armed men, leading him to guess the victim to have been somewhat ahead of the others, or that the recent storm and volcanic activity had unnerved the creature. The sailors were hesitant to cast their spears, he could only assume for fear of harming their comrade if he yet lived.

From Dat Voga's vantage point uphill, the broad back of the calban presented a splendid target, with only the legs of the fallen man being visible. Reacting instantly, the red man charged the calban.

In less time than it takes to tell, Dat Voga's arm flew back and then sped forward, his missile launching from his outstretched arm smoothly and powerfully. The trident flashed through the air and buried itself to the haft in the spine of the beast, in the center of its broad shoulders. He did not stop there.

Allowing his momentum to carry him forward, he slammed his second spear into the side of the animal, which had fallen to its belly after his trident struck it. The tip of his heavy spear plunged behind its right shoulder and passed diagonally through its body to protrude out its broad chest. The beast shuddered as it struggled to rise, only to collapse once more upon the fallen man, stone dead.

Dat Voga and Thuria had expected to meet these people, and so were unsurprised by their presence. However, the sailors nearly came out of their leathers at sight of these two, who, with their rough-hewn implements and unusual pigmentation, looked savage indeed. They recovered from their shock and ran forward to help the padwar, who was attempting, alone, to shove the calban's heavy body from their comrade.

Together they rolled the beast off the sailor, half fearing they would find a dead body. Instead, to everyone's surprise, the man sat up dazedly as if awakening from a nap, rubbing an angry welt upon the back of his head where he had struck a stone when the calban pounced upon him.

This fellow's popularity became immediately apparent to the two from the future. The sailor's comrades laughed in relief and felt him over for wounds. They all spoke at once, asking him questions: Was he injured, did he hurt? It was to Dat Voga's utmost surprise and relief that he realized he could understand these men!

Apparently none the worse for his experience, the sailor's comrades explained to him what had occurred while he had been unconscious beneath the savage beast. The object of the calban's attack now turned to face his savior.

"Who are you? Do you live on this island? Why did you save me from the calban? And your skins! What manner of people are you? I've never seen such as you before!"

The pronunciation of some of the words sounded different to the modern ears of the time travelers, but not so much that they were unable to understand him. They continued to size up the first prehistoric folk they had ever seen while answering the man's questions. "My name is Dat Voga, and this is Thuria. We were blown here in a storm and have been stranded here for months. As to why I saved you from the calban, you may attribute it to the nature of my people. We help those in need as we're able."

Indicating the dead carcass with a foot, the padwar continued. "The storm must have maddened it, or perhaps it was in *must*. Thuria and I have faced these creatures many times, alone and with only these rough, wooden weapons. We were coming to meet you because we hoped to seek permission to depart with you when you leave."

"You're not native to this island, then?"

"No, we aren't." Dat Voga indicated a peak visible through the trees and ferns. "For weeks, the volcano has shown signs of awakening. I think it will erupt soon and when it does it will destroy all life on this island. When you were beneath the calban, I saw that I might rescue you. It is now my hope that in coming to your aid you might in turn help us."

He saw looks of confusion appear on the faces of the sailors as he spoke and realized his speech sounded decidedly different from theirs, both in accent and enunciation. But he was not left long to wonder, for the man he rescued replied immediately.

"It is a strange thing you did, risking your life for a stranger. However, I am indebted to you for saving my life and I'm sure it will go a long way toward winning your rescue from this island. I do have to ask, what is this word 'volcano' you used, and why is it your manner of speech is so different from ours?"

Dat Voga was relieved that his introduction to men of this age was going well. Pointing once more to where the mountain disgorged an immense volume of smoke and fumes, he said, "A volcano is the fire-mountain, over there. As to our manner of speech, we come from a faraway land, and it's evident that both our appearance and dialect differ from yours. At least *most* of the words are the same, for which I thank the ancestors!"

Glancing at the smoking mountain, the men nodded their heads collectively as if the word now made perfect sense. Dat Voga had been surprised at the fellow's mention of the word "calban," as this word he and Thuria had coined, or so he thought. They had given the creature an appellation that made the most sense, a word by which they could refer to it in conversation.

"How did you know that we had named that creature a calban?" he asked curiously.

The man looked quizzically at him. "Because it *is* a calban. What else would I call it?"

Dat Voga was stunned. He could only attribute this anomaly to the inexplicable laws of parlance that held sway in his own time that caused all nations to speak an identical language. Apparently, a word for anything new encountered by any Barsoomian would be the same word everyone else would invent, no matter what person invented it first, or in what time frame the word was contrived. This was the first time in his life he had experienced this law of nature firsthand, although he was at a loss to explain it.

It seemed then, that at this point in time, these people were satisfied to continue using a descriptive phrase for the volcano, with 'fire-mountain' seeming to work just fine for them. He suspected that when they did invent a word for this phrase, that it would be the same word he had used.

While they conversed, the padwar observed these men of a bygone age. The color of their skin he found surprising, it being as white as a thern's, albeit tanned from exposure. Their hair was different, for they wore no wigs as did the therns, instead sporting thick locks ranging from blond to auburn to brunette that hung to their shoulders. Their bangs they confined with a band of leather, or the cured skin of an aquatic animal, this same material being used for their harness, which they decorated with feathers or the teeth of carnivores.

The sailors wore similar dress, consisting of a leather harness with protective strips of leather that swung from the wide belts about their waists. These had O-rings at the bottom and metal clips on the opposite end that attached to metal bars riveted to their belts. These strips hung to about mid-thigh. Dat Voga later learned that these were easily removed and attached to one another to form long utility straps they used frequently.

Many of the sailors sported facial art, or paints daubed upon other parts of their bodies, with no two designs being alike, the entire effort appearing to be one of individual taste rather than any sense of national or familial unity. They wore upon their feet a simple sandal, the top being supported by the simple expedient of crisscrossing straps that wound up and about the lower calf to just below the knee.

Each carried a short, heavy spear with a gaff hook upon one end and a sharpened point upon the opposite end sheeted in a white metal, so that the entire affair would be dangerous no matter which end they chose to use. The haft of the weapon was interlaced with thin strips of leather to afford a sure grip when the weapon became wet from the spray encountered at sea.

Their features were regular and their teeth white and healthy. Being a military man, Dat Voga noticed short bows among their number, carried upon their backs, while quivers full of short, staunch quarrels hung from their belts. Others had short swords slung over their backs, leaving the grip protruding above one shoulder and within easy reach. The padwar had never familiarized himself with the bow, the weapon having become obsolete before his time and long since replaced by firearms.

Each of the men looked to be an attractive example of the

physical perfection a body might attain when cared for as it had been designed to be—active, clean, and living close to nature. The entire ensemble he thought to be one of primitive beauty and health, and he found himself greatly admiring these ancient ancestors of modern-day Barsoomians.

As they studied the sailors, they, in turn, were similarly sizing up Dat Voga and Thuria. While noticing Thuria's great beauty, they did not overtly stare which reassured the young scientist. He saw them eyeing each article of clothing and weaponry. He guessed they might be wondering why these were so incongruous. Their harnesses and his pouch were well tooled, but their weapons were unskillfully made. These two were certainly a mystery.

After only a brief pause during which each party took in the strangeness of the other, the man whom Dat Voga rescued spoke again.

"I am Gar-Noh-Dar, Second Osar of the *Prachus*. Come, we shall take you to Gan-Toh-Gan, who is odar. It is he who will decide if you are to accompany us, or if you will remain here. I'm uncertain, however, in what manner he might respond to your woman's pet."

As though sensing she was the topic of conversation, Aava, the calban cub, nestled deeper in the arms of her mistress and whined, her large, black eye darting nervously from face-to-face. Dat Voga, his gaze level and unblinking, ignored the sailor's comment about the cub, returning instead to another statement the man had made.

"Thuria is not my mate, Gar-Noh-Dar. She is, however, under my protection." He wished these men to know from the onset that he would fight for Thuria as if she *were* his mate. "And we shall abide by whatever your odar decides regarding the cub."

The man glanced curiously at the two but refrained from asking any questions. "We shall proceed," he said.

Chapter Thirty-Six

Orovars

They were making their way back to the harbor and their beached boat when Dat Voga recalled an unfamiliar term the sailor had mentioned. "Gar-Noh-Dar, what exactly is a 'prachus'?" Although unfamiliar with the word, for some reason it connoted feelings of savagery and watery depths.

Gar-Noh-Dar laughed. "Not *a* prachus, *the Prachus*," he corrected. "It's the name of our vessel. You are right, though—prachus is more than just a name. Our vessel is so-called after a voracious fish that, thank the shades, exists only in small numbers, being exceeding rare. They attack and eat their victim while it yet lives. They're highly prized, for their skins are incredibly beautiful when cured."

Dat Voga observed a shudder pass briefly through Gar-Noh-Dar's frame. "You've encountered them before?"

The sailor nodded. "I watched them devour a comrade who leaped overboard to retrieve a fishing spear dangling in the water underneath its safety float, the hollowed husk of a barra nut. As his fingers closed on the nut, they attacked, his body stiffened, and he began to scream. It seemed to go on forever—listening to him scream in agony as the prachus devoured him. When they had finished, only the barra, floating in his blood, remained."

The padwar listened to the grim tale in silence, hoping

he never found himself floating among these man-eaters from which there could be no escape.

They soon arrived at the beach where Gar-Noh-Dar detailed four men to retrieve water from a nearby source of which Dat Voga had apprised them, saving them time they said they would have otherwise spent scouting. He garnered from this statement that it must have been their first time on this island.

The red man helped the sailors propel their beached craft into the surf after seeing Thuria safely aboard with her calban cub. As they pushed off from the shore the cub surprised them by flying into a panic, finding itself upon the surface of the sea in a bobbing contraption that was simply too much for her fragile nerves. With a yip and a bound she jumped free of Thuria's grasp, leaping overboard and swimming right past Dat Voga, whose focus was diverted with launching the craft.

Thuria cried out in dismay. Dat Voga looked up from his labors to see the poor cub, soaking wet and with her sodden fur flattened against her tiny body, galloping up the strand as if the devil were on her heels. Straight into the jungle she ran at high speed, the foliage swallowing her in an instant. By this time they were committed to the launch, so he told the girl he would come back at a later time and find the poor thing. For Thuria's sake he lamented the loss as she had become attached to the orphaned waif.

As they rowed toward the larger vessel, the Heliumite found it difficult to stifle an exclamation of appreciation. He did not wish to broadcast to these primitive progenitors that he had never seen a ship of this type. As they drew nearer, it became obvious the vessel had been crafted with an acute eye toward quality.

Nothing of this nature had survived to his day. They knew from faded murals and ancient writings that their ancestors had sailed the seas, but as to the details of the appearance and construction of their vessels they only had the vaguest idea and no hint of their true beauty. The padwar glanced at Thuria to see her reaction. She was obviously impressed, her eyes also drinking in the lines of this man-made wonder.

As they drew closer, Dat Voga could not fail to notice the beautiful carved figurehead of a nude woman upon the prow. The fact that she had been carved in the nude caused him no wonder, as his people went about daily in scant attire. Rather, it was the attitude of the carving, her expression, that he found so arresting.

Carved by a master sculptor, the maiden's exquisite face bore an adventurous mien of eager curiosity, one that gave the impression she could not wait to see what lay beyond the watery horizon. Her level gaze stared resolutely forward, her mane of flowing hair almost lifelike, as though captured in the act of blowing in the winds of the high seas. Her left arm stretched forth as though reaching toward distant shores and strange ports of call, while her right arm strained toward the aft, beckoning her crew onward. The lively maiden-of-the-prow had then been artfully encased in hammered bronze to help her weather the salt spray.

When they came alongside, a sailor fore and aft grabbed hoops along the waterline with their gaff hooks to pull their boat against the larger vessel, where they secured it by tackle. Having tied off, they clambered aboard the *Prachus* using a woven rope ladder hanging over the side to the waterline. On the main deck they found their eyes drawn involuntarily upward into a veritable maze of rigging. The ship was immense, being multidecked, and having three main masts.

From the main deck two flights of stairs, one on either side, climbed to a secondary deck from which a clearer view ahead might be had. On the railings, Dat Voga noticed a metal he did not recognize left in its native silvery-white color. He knew it could not be forandus or aluminum steel, as it would be hundreds of thousands of years of until they were invented.

Bronze was also utilized extensively, easily identified by its golden hue. Being untarnishable, he knew it would be an excellent choice for marine vessels. What the other metal might be he could not guess, but its dull appearance contrasted agreeably with the polished bronze fittings.

The sails that he initially thought to be of cloth he now saw were manufactured from the skins of an immense animal. The great masts were the strong yet flexible boles of finished and polished tree trunks. These were fabricated from a tight-grained species of tree and were light in color with attractive contrasting streaks of darker grains; the railings were of a similar material.

The decking, stairs, and cabins were of a different species, with a dark, purplish-red cast that the man of the desert found stunning. The planks that formed the hull were possibly of the same material as the decking but had an application of a coating he later learned resisted the wear of the tide, the coating giving the hull a glossy sheen in contrast to the plainer oil finish of the decking.

Gar-Noh-Dar, watching the changing expressions on their faces, smiled. "I see you're impressed with the ship. You should be! She's the finest of her class. This is the latest of Hal-Roh-Kim's designs to sail from Horz. He's doubtless given us up for lost by now. That storm nearly sent us to the bottom. But she stayed afloat, the *Prachus* did, although it tore away almost every bit of her sails before we could furl them."

Gar-Noh-Dar allowed his own eyes to roam along the familiar lines of his vessel. When he spoke next it was with obvious pride. "She's a fine ship."

Dat Voga admitted, "Gar-Noh-Dar, I can honestly say I've never had the pleasure of boarding a more beautiful ship in my life. Perhaps you can show us the vessel in more detail after we speak with Gan-Toh-Gan?"

Gar-Noh-Dar agreed, directing them to follow him to the afterdeck, where he expected to find the odar in his quarters. Each sailor they passed paused in curiosity to observe the Heliumite and his lovely companion. Their vibrant red skins and black hair were striking in contrast to the sailors, although the beauty of the handsome pair would have drawn attention anywhere, no matter the epoch. Upon knocking on the door of the odar's planning room, a deep, robust voice bid them enter.

The odar sat at a table with his First Osar, one Bim-Gon-Dar. Gan-Toh-Gan was without doubt a man of measured self-control, as he never batted an eye at the strange and barbaric sight of the two who presented quite the spectacle with their strange garb, and the foreign appearance their skin-color lent them among this fair-skinned folk.

The man exhibited the signs of advanced maturity, having a thick beard, a rarity on Barsoom—in Dat Voga's day, anyway—with a good bit of iron showing in his otherwise thick, dark hair. He had an expansive chest, and his body was well-muscled. His features would be considered handsome in any time frame, with eyes as blue as the harbor. The man possessed a wholesome, honest appearance the Heliumite found reassuring.

However, Dat Voga remained on guard, for he was ever apprehensive when he felt Thuria to be at risk. He noticed that his breathing had quickened. Glancing downward, he saw the crimson tint of his breast deepening and slowed his breathing, causing the coloration to lessen.

He saw that Thuria displayed no sign of nervousness at all, but then she was not one to fret about her own safety. This man held their lives in his hands; and even though Dat Voga had saved the life of one of his sailors, they must wait and see what he would do, as the padwar thought it unwise to ever assume anything in any situation.

Ignoring the two strangers for the time being, the odar turned to Second Osar Gar-Noh-Dar. "Report, osar, on your findings."

All eyes turned to Gar-Noh-Dar as he relayed, with

complete veracity, what had transpired on the island—the calban attack, the advent of the two strangers, the saving of his life by Dat Voga, and a summary of their conversation. He finished by informing the odar of the man's aid in locating water and that he had detailed four men to fill water casks while he brought these two before the odar.

Odar Gan-Toh-Gan turned to Dat Voga. "You have my thanks for saving the life of my officer—it is a life, I should mention, that I value highly, being that he's my only son. You have permission to take up quarters aboard our craft and will return with us to Horz, the shades of our ancestors permitting. Now, Thuria—be you the mate of this man?"

The direct question came suddenly, but Dat Voga knew if they were to be assigned quarters aboard the odar's vessel, the question of their association would have to be settled. Before he could speak, Thuria answered.

"No, Odar Gan-Toh-Gan; we are but fellow travelers. But, more than that, I owe him my life. But for him, I would have been the slave of an evil man and certainly have taken my own life erenow. And while marooned for these six months on yonder isle, he has tirelessly made every effort to secure first my comfort and safety before thinking of himself."

It was a simple speech yet it declared clearly their relationship to be pure. Also, it indicated that Dat Voga would risk his life to protect her. This seemed to be well received by the odar, who smiled approvingly. "It seems you have comported yourself with bravery and integrity, Dat Voga, during what anyone would consider singular circumstances. Well done."

"Now," he continued, "osar, you will return to your unfinished business ashore. We have no idea what else may happen there since no man ever saw this place before today; fetch our men back aboard as quickly as you can. Osar Bim-Gon-Dar, if you would show our guests to their quarters. You may quarter Dat Voga with Osar Gar-Noh-Dar.

"As for the girl Thuria . . ." He paused and smiled at her

before continuing, "Give her the empty quarters of Hal-Roh-Kim and his mate; I am quite sure they will not mind."

As they left, Thuria threw her arms about the old sea odar and hugged him. "Thank you so much for helping us," she cried.

The odar seemed affected by her obvious sincerity and clearly spontaneous gesture. He smiled down at her and replied, "You're welcome, daughter."

Dat Voga took this to mean the girl would be under his protection as if she were his own kin. Fortune had indeed smiled upon them to have thrown them into the company of such as the odar and the crew of the *Prachus*, a ship whose name belied the beneficence of those who served aboard her.

Having been shown to his quarters and not having anything to deposit or keep him there, Dat Voga asked permission to return abovedecks to see if he could lend a hand. His spears he had left imbedded in the corpse of the calban, while his sword he had discarded after joining Gar-Noh-Dar's band. They had served their purpose and would have been useless had the sailors proved to be aggressive, armed as they were with quality weapons.

He knew nothing of sailing but determined to perform whatever manual labor he might to earn his and Thuria's keep. Thuria had remained in her cabin, saying she wished to freshen up and rest. Coming back on deck, the padwar of time-distant Helium was once again impressed with the vessel.

It really was a fine ship in every sense. The crew seemed good-natured and must have been well-bred indeed, as no colorful remarks were made about of his appearance, which differed so markedly from theirs. He watched a group of sailors rigging new sail and approached them, asking if they needed assistance. They saw that the stranger wished to help, and so, smiling, they waved him over and showed him how to perform their work.

He said honestly, “Where I come from, I labored as a scientist. I’ve never worked on a ship before.”

“Don’t let that worry you,” laughed one, jabbing an elbow into a companion’s arm jestingly, “neither has Rok-Tu here!” The sailors all joined in a hearty laugh at their companion’s expense. “By the time we reach Horz, you’ll be rigging as if you broke your shell on this very deck,” another reassured him.

Dat Voga smiled and bent to his ropes, learning how to tie knots and rig sails on a vessel that sailed a million years before his time. They sat in the harbor for a week replenishing stores, some of which had been ruined in the storm, and completing needed repairs. The padwar became of immense value. He helped spear fish and kill and cure grass eaters, and showed them various water sources and fishing spots, for by this time he knew the island as if he had been hatched there.

With the volcano imminently closer to eruption, the sailors were understandably anxious to put some nautical haads between their vessel and the island. A constant billow of smoke and fumes now poured continuously from the fire-mountain, and at night they could discern a glow in the sky over its summit. They could hear rumblings from within the mountain, and men returning from outings on the island reported feeling the ground shake from tremors.

Try as he might, Dat Voga never came across the wee calban cub of Thuria’s. The girl was distraught at the loss of the beloved bundle of fur and mourned her terribly. He hated to see Thuria suffer so but was helpless to do anything about it. The cub was, after all, but a tiny speck on a large island.

As did her friend from Helium, Thuria, too, soon adjusted to life aboard the ship, lending a hand with the daily work where she was able in the performance of many useful chores. Both were thankful to be treated in a friendly fashion by these total strangers, the timing of whose arrival had been impeccable. While for the most part they had enjoyed their time on the island, with the impending eruption looming they were glad to have the ship's deck beneath their feet.

At last the day arrived when Odar Gan-Toh-Gan announced that they would leave with the next tide. Those last remaining xats that the ship sat in harbor the two from the future spent on deck, looking at the island that had given them a home for six long months.

Leaning on the balustrade at the stern of the ship, both presented a different sight from the day they had come aboard the *Prachus*. Their apparel had been worn to tatters, so Odar Gan-Toh-Gan saw to it that they were outfitted with new garb. The quarters of Hal-Roh-Kim's mate had already been outfitted for her, so there were plenty of articles from which Thuria might choose. In addition to a new harness, the odar added a slender dagger that would prove useful in her daily duties. This she fastened to her leather belt and girt upon one thigh.

Dat Voga's old harness and pouch had suffered from the humid atmosphere of the tropics and was in sore need of replacement. The new harness given him was of a different design from that of the modern day, consisting as it did of the waist belt and utility straps favored by the sailors. It contained a built-in pouch running lengthwise across the front and kept out of sight beneath the utility straps, a design feature he appreciated since it prevented it from swinging in pendulum fashion upon his hip in the manner of his pouch from the future.

His wooden sword and sharpened fronds were replaced with a dagger and a short sword for which he was grateful. He had been given a longer sword as well, the blade heavy, but razor sharp. This he stowed in his cabin, it proving far too long and ponderous to carry while performing his duties, while the short sword was adequate for most needs.

He kept the latter lashed to his outer thigh so it would not swing about and get in his way after he began training to work in the rigging.

Encircling Thuria's waist was the equilibrimotor belt, and upon Dat Voga's forearms were the bronze gauntlets. Naturally, they were quizzed about these strange articles. While finding it distasteful to prevaricate, they could not readily admit what these items in actuality were. So, they were forced to claim these were articles of their station in their country and leave it at that. Being that their appearance and accents were so foreign, their explanation seemed natural and was not questioned.

Although unique, neither of the items were decorative, being utilitarian in appearance; Daxxus Nahl was not one to waste time on artistry. Dat Voga asked Thuria to disguise the equilibrimotor belt as much as possible, as with its radium motor it drew the most attention. He felt that the less it was noticed, the less they would have to field questions about it.

She disguised it by way of a lavender cape she found in the Lady Hal-Roh-Kim's articles that she tied about her slender waist. The odar had given her permission to wear what she wished, insisting the lady would not begrudge a damsel such as Thuria anything she needed.

In short order, the time came to put to sea. A call to up-anchor was heard, and then taken up and repeated. Two sailors began turning a large capstan to haul in the anchor. Several small sails were added to catch an offshore breeze. The sails took the air as a man starving for a breath as they swelled with the wind. The red man glanced upward into the rigging and swollen sails, silently taking in the wonder of the sight.

From the stern, the sight of the island was ominous. The peak of the volcano was no longer visible, a pall of doom seeming to hang over the entire island. The cliffs where they had made their home were obscured by dense smoke, which saddened him as he would have liked to have seen them once more. In less time than he could have imagined, they struck the open sea.

Gantahns, the first he had seen up close, swam carefree alongside the ship, their sleek skins glistening in the sunlight, all uncaring of the doom looming not far distant. He had watched these graceful creatures at play in the harbor, but they never came close to land, preferring to keep just offshore.

Those aboard the ship began to hear claps far louder than thunder, and rumbles originating from the bowels of the landmass. Dat Voga and Thuria remained at the stern, watching as their temporary home slowly began to disappear in smoke and the haze of distance.

They were eight or ten haads away when it exploded. From their position it appeared that half the side of the volcano blew out to sea. Red streaks of burning rock flew thousands of sofads into the air, a plume of smoke and rock dust billowing outward, growing more and more voluminous with each passing moment. Giant fragments of rock rained down, plumes of water geysering into the air with their impact in the sea.

"Oh, Aava," Thuria murmured, her eyes brimming with tears.

Shortly afterward they felt the first waves caused by the upheaval and disturbance of the seabed pass beneath the ship, possibly to cause tidal effects on distant shores. The padwar turned to look at Thuria to note her reaction and saw tears streaming down her cheeks. She wiped them away and smiled up at him bravely. He placed an arm about her shoulders to offer what comfort he may.

He noticed movement and turned to see Gan-Toh-Gan. The odar nodded and then turned and climbed the stair to the odar's deck where he entered his planning room. He did not understand their seeming attachment for this island, which to him would have been nothing more than a prison.

How could he know that, to the two castaways, the

island—for all its inescapability—in their minds and hearts had assumed the status of wonder? To them it was a magical place where they had been given the unimaginable gift to see, appreciate, and immerse themselves in beauties lost to such as them, the inheritors of a dead and dying world.

There, they had walked among giant ferns and forests teeming with a myriad of life forms. There, they had seen for the first time the beauty of the sunrise and the sunset. There, too, they had witnessed rain—a phenomenon unknown to their people in the far-flung future. They had splashed in the ocean, listened to bird calls and the musical trills of insects, as had their ancient ancestors.

And now they witnessed the island's destruction—an omen, perhaps, of what would eventually come to pass for their beloved Barsoom. No, Gan-Toh-Gan could not have understood, and they could not have explained it. But if he could have seen into their hearts, he would have no longer wondered that their eyes were not dry.

Chapter Thirty-Seven

Azaria

IT IS A BOON OF HUMANKIND, and one for which its members should thank their creator, that not for long may the vicissitudes of life prey upon their spirits. The sorrows of today evaporate and are soon forgotten, with the joy of living, the thrill of surviving, and the miracle of discovery ultimately triumphing.

So it was that the castaways did not for long lament the loss of their paradise. Odar Gan-Toh-Gan saw to it they were both kept too busy to dwell on it. And anyway, these two from the future were not the types to sit idle and mope.

For two days, however, Thuria suffered the tortures of sea sickness in her cabin. When she got her "sea legs," as the sailors called it, she sought out the odar for duties to keep her busy. He was impressed with her pluck, as many women would have been content to sit in their cabin, given the option.

It appeared to the sailors as if the red man had broken his shell on a pitching deck at sea. Coming as he did from a desert world, he had never heard of sea sickness, and but for poor Thuria's sufferings, he would have never been introduced to it, since he never suffered it.

The padwar spent his days aloft, learning the art of sailing on the high seas. Naturally, he spent much of his time doing the menial tasks sailors are happy to get out of. Yet even these were new to a man who came from a world without seas and sailing vessels. He recognized in these chores the fundamental value of the craft these men of a bygone era sought to teach him.

This ship had been to sea only a few short weeks for her sea trials when she was blown off course by the storm. A new enterprise, she had been conceived by Hal-Roh-Kim, a wealthy merchant and member of the nobility of Horz who owned a fleet of trade vessels. Of all his ships, this one he deemed his greatest design, being three hundred sofads in length, and fifty across her beam.

It was nothing for Dat Voga to stay aloft all day, swinging from one point to another. Soon, he could trim and furl with the best. On one such day, having spent most of the day aloft, he discovered a piece of damaged rope, a section they had missed replacing when the ship was being refitted after the storm. He reported it to an osar and was rewarded by being detailed to fetch a spare.

The rigging was stowed in the forward keel, deep below the waterline. Three decks were below water, with one above, this being the main deck with a command cabin located aft. This command cabin was surrounded by transparent glazes with an internal walkway in the form of a promenade, giving crew members access to topside cabins without having to go outside, an advantageous feature during a storm.

The ship's steerage lay in the command deck, with the odar's quarters and planning room located toward the stern. An observation deck sat atop this command deck, from the heights of which most of the ship's fore and aft could be surveyed. There were two sets of stairs for accessing this command area, one located fore and one aft, while the observation deck could be accessed only through steerage.

This last feature had been incorporated by the designer, Hal-Roh-Kim, in the event of mutiny or attack, with the idea that the officers might barricade steerage, preventing any access to the observation deck, from which vantage point they might direct defensive efforts.

Access to the storage holds were located fore and aft, with stairs leading belowdecks to the crew quarters, which had a capacity for one hundred and fifty men. The officers' quarters were located below the command cabin with berths for twenty officers, and spacious accommodations for the ship's owner. The latter were the rooms assigned to Thuria, with Dat Voga occupying a less pretentious room with Gar-Noh-Dar.

Belowdecks, one could navigate from hold to hold via companionways. At intervals a bulkhead, or a primitive attempt at one, would intercept a companionway. At that point, one navigating these dark passages would be forced to ascend to a top deck hatch, these being kept open during fair weather with men assigned to ensure they were closed at the onset of a storm.

In the event the ship's signal bell summoned all hands to quarters, or a call to arms, the officers were to ensure these were closed. Hal-Roh-Kim believed it paramount to seal the ship into its various compartments, his thought being that if one or more compartments were flooded, then perhaps the sealed remainder would keep the ship afloat, or delay sinking until the crew could abandon ship.

Still unfamiliar with the dark holds of the vessel, Dat Voga went below, trying to recall the maze of directions the officer had given him to the rope storage. He descended to the lowest deck where he could discern the sound of the sea rushing beneath the keel.

When he was alone in the holds, he would retrieve his pocket torch to navigate the dark recesses. But he did not wish to be seen by these primitive people using either it or his modern gadget for starting fire. In his other hand he carried a primitive torch used by the men of this time, an economic alternative to the more expensive radium torches, both of which were far less effective than his futuristic light.

While looking for a storage marking cited by the officer, he heard a sound ahead of him. The sound called to mind an ulsio, these dark passages reminding him of the pits beneath ancient cities. He told himself the ulsio had probably not yet evolved into the hideous creature it would become in his day. Then it occurred to him that its ancient progenitor might be more terrible than its modern-day descendant.

Pausing at the thought, he steeled himself and continued. He was determined to learn what made the rasping sound originating from behind several storage containers. Moving forward cautiously, he took mental note of the layout of the stacks of boxes securely lashed to the subdeck, the boxes forming narrow passages shrouded in the shadows cast from his light.

He estimated the number of steps that would take him beyond a row of boxes opposite the area where the sound originated, and then, dousing his light, he quietly stepped forward. Reaching what he estimated to be a point opposite the sound, he touched the switch on his pocket torch. In the light was a tall, dark figure that gasped in surprise and retreated.

A dagger was clutched in one hand of the figure, one he was relieved to note looked human although he could not make out its features due to the heavy folds of an overhanging hood draped over its head. He suspected he had just discovered an enemy of his newfound friends, lurking in the dark, waiting to unfold Issus knew what diabolical plot.

Dat Voga reached behind his shoulder and withdrew his sword, the steel singing as it left the leather scabbard. He heard a muffled gasp as he drew the weapon, prompting him to speak. "I don't wish to harm you, but neither will I allow you to harm my friends. Come now, lay down your weapon and come with me."

With an exasperated sigh, the figure flicked its dagger.

Dat Voga saw that the dagger's trajectory would be short, and so, supposing the figure meant only to startle him, he did not flinch as it thudded into the boards at his feet. He picked up the dagger and slid it into his belt, then motioned the figure toward him.

As the cloaked figure brushed past him, it flung its hood back to reveal a mass of hair surrounding the whitest, fairest face he ever saw. Stark beauty stared up at him with flashing eyes filled with wrath and fire. He now saw the mysterious figure was that of a woman, one with an obvious and distinctly disdainful opinion of Dat Voga.

"Oh, why did you have to come down here just now?" she cried, angrily. "Now they'll return me to my father, who'll force me to mate with that horrid calban of a Zit-Tar-Phak!"

The comments, flung in rapid succession, left him astonished. He started to reply but found his mouth had gone as dry as an ochre sea bottom while his tongue clung to its place, refusing to allow him to speak coherently. He had never been one to be shy around women, so he was at a loss to explain his speechless condition.

After the woman passed him and started down the companionway, he realized with chagrin that he still held his modern torch. Hoping she would fail to notice, he turned on the archaic lamp hanging by its hook on his belt, and quickly switched off the other, returning it to his pouch.

Wincing at the greatly reduced radiance, he was not left long in doubt to the fact that the woman noticed it, too. She immediately looked over her shoulder at him.

"I'm not a silly girl—I noticed you swapped out the lights. Why did you do so?" she demanded.

He did not know how to answer her. He hated to dissemble but, momentarily stumped, said, "You must be mistaken, my lady."

She replied with an agitated, "Humph!" Then she asked suspiciously, "Why did you call me lady just now? I have never seen you before. Do you know who I am, perchance?"

The red man replied honestly, "No, I only called you thus because I didn't know your name, while your station speaks for itself."

The woman did not reply. Coming to a bulkhead, she began to climb. Dat Voga followed close behind her so she could not give him the slip or slam a hatch on his head. But when she came to her feet on the next level, she extended her hand to take the lantern to free his hand, as he was holding it in one hand while climbing with the other. He was surprised at the offer of help but accepted the aid.

He smiled at her as he came to his feet. Her own face was emotionless as she handed him the torch. Then her eyes flashed up and down his muscular form, her brows knitting in perplexity.

Guessing the cause, he volunteered, "You've noticed the coloration of my skin. I come from a distant land—my companion and I. Although we look different, I can assure you, you'll come to no harm from either of us."

One perfectly chiseled eyebrow raised archly. "Do I seem fearful to you? And anyway, I noticed something different in the way you speak already, so I knew you were not of Horz—or anywhere with which I'm familiar."

She continued the rest of the climb to the main deck in silence, continuing to offer to hold the lantern for Dat Voga at the exit to the hatchways. For a prisoner, she was certainly considerate, he thought.

Eventually, the woman's curiosity got the best of her. "Well, where do you come from, or must I pry it from you with a gaff hook?"

He smiled. "A little island in the middle of nowhere. You've probably never heard of it."

At last, they came to the second deck from which a stair climbed to the main deck rather than the ladders they had used to exit the depths of the holds. Here they climbed side by side, Dat Voga returning the torch to the hook on his belt. As they stepped into the light of day, he noticed sideways glances from the woman as she took in his alien appearance.

He found her captivating, and easily the most beautiful woman he had ever seen. He recalled the great beauty of the many women he had courted in Helium, but they all paled in comparison with his primitive princess. He caught himself with a start, realizing he had called her "his princess" in his mind.

He smiled as one of his erudite peers in Helium came to mind—one who delved into the devilish maze of the Barsoomian psyche, who would enjoy exploring his thought and its deeper connotation. He believed he had just had what John Carter called a "Freudian slip," although he did not know who Freudian was, nor what it was he had slipped upon to become so famous because of it.

"Why are you smiling?"

The woman was staring at him. Her question wiped the amused look off his face, which he replaced with one of a more serious nature, one more befitting the circumstances of escorting a prisoner before the odar, where the malefactor might face stiff penalties for her presence aboard this ship. He thought it best that he remained quiet.

The thought of his pocket torch came to mind. He hoped she would have the discretion not to disclose what she had seen. As they came through the opening onto the main deck, all eyes turned their way. There were broad smiles, and he heard many murmurings. He thought he heard a few sailors utter a name, but he did not catch it. He saw that they recognized the woman.

As he escorted her toward the command deck, he whispered, "You seem to be known among these men. Who are you?" Now it was the woman's turn to smile and not answer. And then a great booming voice interrupted them. "Azaria! By the shades, girl, what are you doing aboard the *Prachus*? Old Hal-Roh-Kim will have my hide!"

The girl smiled genuinely into the face of the stunned odar. "Kaor to you, too, dear Gan-Toh-Gan!"

Dat Voga, seeing that Gan-Toh-Gan knew the girl, started to withdraw, intending to retrace his steps to finish what he originally started out to do—fetch a piece of rope.

His tone serious, Gan-Toh-Gan barked, "Come with me, Azaria!" He turned and stormed toward the stair that mounted to the command cabin but glanced at the red man who hastened to make his exit. "Dat Voga, you come, too. I want to hear your side of this as well." Then, casting a stern glance at the woman beside him and shaking his head in disbelief, he strode toward the stair.

Dat Voga indicated the stairs, which he still found difficulty in navigating, being accustomed to the ramps of the modern day. "After you, my—that is, Azaria, was it?"

The woman smiled a confident smile as he stumbled over her name. "Of course, my—*Dat Voga*, was it?" she whispered, emphasizing his name in playful mockery.

Chapter Thirty-Eight

Smitten

For the first time in his life hearing his name fall from the lips of a woman caused a thrill to run up Dat Voga's spine. His eyes feasted on the vision of that perfect figure as she went up the stair before him. She was stunning! Her toned limbs were as the purest, whitest marble, with a form and tone that might be considered an example of flawless perfection.

Now that they were in the light of day, he saw that her hair shined a deep auburn, a color he had been unable to ascertain in the deep recesses of the hold; he had never dreamed of its like. Thick and luxurious, it was piled into a simple bun at the back, but with a single thick, coiling lock dropping to a shapely waist. Two ornate gold pins protruded from her coif.

Her hood had been a disguise she had adopted to aid in blending in the darkness of the storage holds. This she had doffed, showing her trappings underneath to be simple and scanty. Her poise indicated nobility and wealth, for no one walked and carried herself as she did without years of training and tutoring.

As they carried out the exchange with the odar, Dat Voga had noticed how delicate were the features of her face. Her eyes were of the deepest azure; he never would have guessed eyes could be so blue. He found it almost unbearable to wait until they reached the odar's cabin to study her fascinating features more closely.

Passing through the command cabin door behind her, he found himself alone with the woman and the odar. With a silent gesture, Gan-Toh-Gan bid them sit, while he selected a carafe and poured himself a glass of water.

"Now," he barked suddenly. "I want to know all!" The man's tone did not brook any nonsense.

Dat Voga began, "I'd been sent to fetch—"

Gan-Toh-Gan interrupted him with a staying hand. "My apologies, Dat Voga. First, I wish to know why Azaria is on my ship and why I'm only now learning of her presence. Azaria, I've known you since you broke your shell, and you know I feel toward you as if you were my own daughter. I can only guess how Hal-Roh-Kim must feel right now, not knowing the whereabouts of his only child!"

Hal-Roh-Kim was the man who owned the *Prachus*! Dat Voga studied her while her eyes were on Gan-Toh-Gan. The man commanded respect. All the former playfulness and banter Azaria had exhibited earlier vanished beneath the odar's gaze. This did not surprise him. In his mind, he had already compared the man to the greatest odwars of Helium, nor did Gan-Toh-Gan fall short in the comparison.

He detected no hint of rebellion when she answered. Reflected in her eyes were only the respect and adoration with which she obviously held this old sailor, and repentance when he likened her to his own daughter. But her expression changed to one of firm resolve at mention of her father.

"I never intended for you to know I'd stolen away on your ship. You were to go to Xanator where I intended to disembark, never to return to Horz. My father has of late urged me to choose a mate. He has become obsessed with it, while my only desire is to aid him in his efforts to govern his interests.

"I know he loves me, but I feel he wishes he had a son

to entrust his business to instead of a daughter. Apparently, he's mentioned this to his many associates, for recently I've been plagued for my hand from all sides, the most insistent being Zit-Tar-Phak, son of Tal-Phak-Tal. He's a rival merchant in Horz whose name I happen to know you're familiar with."

At mention of Tal-Phak-Tal, the odar's head jerked as if he had caught scent of something objectionable. "Oh yes, I'm familiar with him." His tone was one of disgust. "He is the oiliest daksor I've ever had the displeasure of doing business with!"

Dat Voga interjected, "What exactly is a daksor?"

Both Horzians looked at him and shook their heads. While he was looking at Dat Voga, Gan-Toh-Gan recalled he had another to interrogate. "How did it transpire that you discovered Azaria?"

The padwar related his story to the odar and finished by saying he should go check on Thuria and get back to work.

Azaria arched one eyebrow. "Ah, you mentioned you had a companion." She ran her eyes up and down him playfully. "Is he as rubicund as you?"

The padwar smiled at the directness of the question. "Nearly so, yes, she *is*."

Gan-Toh-Gan said, "You should see him when he exerts himself; he fairly glows! You'll love these two, Azaria! They've never been at sea before but have taken to it like a couple of gantahns. The crew loves them. We found them stranded on an island in the middle of nowhere. A beautiful place—or rather, it was. But I'll leave it to Dat Voga to tell his story."

Throughout the oration, Dat Voga's eyes never left the beautiful eyes of Azaria.

And she, her gaze locked impishly on his, said, "Yes, Dat Voga; you'll have to tell me your story sometime."

As one hypnotized, he finally tore himself from the cabin

and went forward. His heart pounded forcefully inside his chest, and he felt that if night had fallen, one might have found his path by the glow emanating from his own skin.

By then, word of Dat Voga's discovery had reached the ears of the officer-on-deck, who sent another to fetch the needed rope; he told Dat Voga to take the rest of the evening off since his shift was nearly up. Restless, the red man sought Thuria, wishing to tell her of his experience.

He found her near the bow mending a harness. Opposite her on the deck sat a box of odds and ends; upon this he sat. Thuria beamed when she saw her friend. She looked happy, and fairly glowed at her work, causing him to feel sea life must truly be agreeing with her.

"I heard they caught you belowdecks with a strange girl," she said, smiling mischievously.

Dat Voga looked stunned. "Is that what they're saying? It was nothing like that!" And then he saw she was laughing, and he smiled.

He recounted Azaria's story of being the daughter of the owner of the ship and how she had fled Horz to escape mating with someone she did not love. He also detailed his discovery of her in the holds and admitted the effect she had on him.

These two had by now triumphed through so many trials together that he found it easy to confide in her. He had strong, familial feelings of kinship for Thuria, and would have laid down his life in defense of hers.

Although at one time he thought he had deeper feelings for her, he now realized that rather than losing a potential mate, he had gained a cherished friend. He could recall no closer bond in his life than the camaraderie he felt for this little slave girl. Recalling her introduction by Ptar Ras, he now understood why the jeddak so loved this pure and beautiful maiden from Zoquan.

By the time he finished, Thuria had a broad smile on her face. "Why, Dat Voga," she exclaimed in surprise, "I believe you have feelings for this girl! How is that even possible? You only just met her!"

The man leaned on the railing and stared sightlessly out over the sea. "I know, Thuria, it makes no sense. My mind tells me I'm confused about my feelings, but my heart tells me I'll never be happy if I don't spend the rest of my life with Azaria."

Chapter Thirty-Nine

Lost

DAT VOGA CONTINUED TO GAZE across the sea where a glorious sunset unfolded. The girl, watching the patrician profile of her friend, finally joined him and turned her gaze toward the stunning sea.

She thought about his sudden and possibly futile love for the daughter of Hal-Roh-Kim, who had fled her home and condemned herself to exile to escape a loveless union. It called to mind Thuria's dear friend, Tahn Dih, who had faced a similar situation with Zat Simpus.

The sun, dipping into the ocean, caused the sea to look as red as blood. She glanced at one of the gauntlets where Dat Voga's arms rested on the railing and hoped they could solve Daxxus Nahl's cipher. Her friend had explained the ramifications of their spending the remainder of their lives in this bygone era. The potential for damage was incalculable.

The least modification of someone's path might cause millions of people to cease to exist. Even the brief time they had been here already might have compromised the future. It was imperative they return, as soon as possible, to their own time.

While they were alone on the island, it had not mattered so much. Even so, they had worked every day to solve the cipher. Now that they were in separate quarters, they had been prevented from working on it together, although he assured her he did so on his own when Gar-Noh-Dar was absent.

They had been quizzed on more than one occasion about the gauntlets and the equilibrimotor, and always had they told the same story—that they were articles common among their people. But it would not coincide with their story if they were seen poring over the secret panel on the left gauntlet each night.

The days sped by. They visited frequently at the spot near the bow where they would discuss the goings-on of the day: Rok-Tu pinched his finger in a capstan, or Kal-Vis-Tok speared a magnificent gantahn, or Kun-Bor misplaced a chart. When alone, they would discuss their desire to return to their own time frame so they could come to the aid of their friends who remained in the clutches of Daxxus Nahl.

Of late, however, Thuria began to notice long silences where she guessed her friend daydreamed about the girl, Azaria. This worried her, for Dat Voga and the young woman were separated by an unbridgeable gap—he from the far future, and she from the dim past. Either of them would be out of time in the other's world.

Weeks had sped by since they had put to sea, during which time the refugees learned much of the fickleness of life aboard a sailing ship. Blown off course during the tempest, they now floated upon an immense, watery plain with no idea in which direction lay land. Gan-Toh-Gan's idea to find their way home called for backtracking in the general direction from which they had been blown.

The path of the *Prachus* had been as erratic as theirs when they were at the mercy of a hurricane months earlier. The wind and currents had forced the vessel out to sea further than it typically ventured, the Horzian sailors preferring to keep within sight of land when possible and navigate by familiar landmarks.

Gan-Toh-Gan was confident they had been blown in a

great circle that started out westerly, but gradually turned and brought them around in an easterly fashion, thousands of haads to the south. Thus, as near as they could reckon by the position of the sun and the stars, they held their course northeast, hoping to strike land, at which point they would follow it until they recognized a shoreline, or met someone to advise them.

At the end of his day, Dat Voga sat at the spot where he and Thuria were wont to meet in the afternoons, mending pieces of worn rope as he had been taught by one of the many sailors he had befriended. His likable personality and uniqueness made him popular with the other men, and he had had no problems making friends among these early progenitors of his race.

He was engrossed in his work when someone surprised him with a friendly, "Kaor!" Caught unawares, he looked up to see Azaria, and felt his heartbeat quicken. Her musical laughter, sounding low and untamed, floated out over the water. Beaming, she sat beside him.

"Why, Dat Voga, you're fairly glowing at sight of me! Is it a problem for you, knowing me to be of noble descent rather than the homeless stowaway you first thought me? Or could it be that . . . ?" Her eyes squinted with her teasing smile.

The red man was embarrassed because his heart did indeed race when he found himself in her company, and he guessed the girl to be fully aware of the fact that she flustered him. He could not help but smile in return, appreciating the dimples in her cheeks and the flash of ivory in her beautiful smile.

"It would be dishonest for me not to admit that my eyes have never gauged your equal in loveliness," he avowed honestly.

"So, you *are* enamored with me. I knew it! Well, you're a strange suitor to be sure. I've never seen a man with such red skin. I must admit, you have a certain charm, especially when you glow so," she teased.

"If my glowing pleases you, then I am happy for my radiance," he said, playfully.

"From the short time I've known you, you seem an honorable man," she continued, ignoring his implication that he pleased her. "To be sure, your intelligence seems little short of uncanny. I've heard tales of your helping the men in their work with ideas of a fantastical nature. It seems you're endowed with quite a bit of analytical fortitude. Tell me, are all from this unknown island so gifted?"

"Well," conceded Dat Voga, "mayhap not all."

Azaria smiled—a genuine smile this time. "Somehow, I thought not."

Chapter Forty

ABOARD THE *PRACHUS*

WHEN HE PONDERED HIS TIME spent aboard the *Prachus*, Dat Voga compared it to recalling happy memories from childhood, except that these, being fresh and new, were clearer. Often it seemed to him he lived vicariously through a primitive man who spent his life on the sea; one to whom the things of the future—flight, time travel, radium rifles, and towers rearing into the sky—were things he did not consider because he was not even aware of their existence.

His days were filled with learning the parts of a vessel and how to chart a path by the constellations. He trimmed sail during nighttime squalls with the deck of a rolling, pitching ship a hundred sofads beneath him, while stormy gusts and wind-driven rain tried to rip him from his precarious perch. He speared fish and swapped stories beneath the majestic moons and calm skies at twilight.

The thought came to him as he went about his work that he could not recall the last time he had dwelled on his former life—and he marveled. Even when he and Thuria sat together to chat, it seemed they most often discussed what they had seen or heard or done aboard ship that day.

Of late, Azaria had begun joining them, so naturally they could not always speak of their peculiar dilemma. He had become entranced with life at sea. With his growing love for the daughter of Hal-Roh-Kim, it came to him that while he was with her, he was happier than he had ever been in his life.

Azaria stood at the helm with Thuria when he approached this afternoon. The two girls had become fast friends and they now shared the quarters of Hal-Roh-Kim, Azaria's father. After meeting the girl from Zoquan, Azaria confided to the red man that she thought her quite the most exquisite woman she had ever met—a compliment Thuria repaid in kind.

More than that, Thuria came to adore the fair-skinned Orovar. She assured her friend that she approved of his choice, although in her mind she still did not understand how the relationship could end happily for these two who could not be together without revising the future in unpredictable ways, as he had explained it to her.

He was thrilled, however, with Thuria's approval. Since their advent here, she had become the closest thing to family he had, so her endorsement carried for him the same weight as would his sister's.

Approaching the chatting girls at the bow, he caught the trail of their conversation and realized they were watching colorful water birds at play. These swooped and dived into the ocean only to emerge with a spray of water an instant later, chirping and whistling while keeping pace with the *Prachus*. Since being thrust into the remote past, Thuria had become captivated with the wildlife, which was still strange and new to her, and was always curious about it.

He heard her say, "Oh, Azaria, how beautiful they are!"

Azaria laughed. "Why Thuria, one would think you'd never seen phlegas at play!"

Aware that too many instances such as this might draw suspicion to their ignorance of the commonplace, he interrupted with, "Kaor, princesses! I've just heard from Gar-Noh-Dar that they deem this a perfect spot to do some fishing and swimming to give the men a few zodes of leisure. I've decided to learn to swim, so I'll be joining them overboard."

Now Azaria looked at him in surprise and asked inquisitively, "You come from an island and yet you can't swim? How can that be, Dat Voga?"

Thuria arched her eyebrows at a reddening Dat Voga. He had mentioned to her before about not giving the others reason for too much curiosity about them. "Yes, how can that be, Dat Voga?"

He realized instantly that he had just made a similar mistake, that of admitting ignorance of something from this time with which he should be familiar. "Suffice it to say, I just never learned—but today I'm going to rectify that. Gar-Noh-Dar said he swims better than a gantahn and has volunteered to teach me."

"Pah!" Azaria scoffed, immediately. "I can outswim Gar-Noh-Dar; gantahn indeed! I'll instruct you myself. Come, Thuria! We must select fitting leathers for swimming. I'm sure my mother will have examples constructed from wassaen hide. Oh, they make elegant leathers! They're so tight fitting you can slice through the water like a fish. And we'll need diving knives. You can never guess what you might come upon."

The two sauntered off, chattering as gaily as phlegas, leaving the man standing where they had left him. Just before they disappeared into the hatchway to their quarters, Azaria turned her head in time to catch Dat Voga still watching them—or rather, watching her. She flashed him a knowing smile.

"We'll see you shortly—islander!" she teased.

Still smiling, she spun and disappeared through the hatchway, her bubbling laughter drifting back to Dat Voga. Sighing, he smiled and shook his head in wonder.

After sailing nonstop for days, the ship gradually slowed as men aloft furled the sails. Shortly, a great anchor, cast solid from the unknown white metal the padwar had noticed the first day he came aboard, splashed into the sea.

When he inquired about the unknown metal, the odar told him he believed it to be of a bronze base, alloyed with a liquid metal found in the tropics near fire-mountains. These were smelted in certain ratios along with what the padwar took to be radium ore, from the odar's description.

The man went on to say that early experiments to combine these metals failed until they thought to add the white, rocky ore. This resulted in horrid, noxious fumes, causing terrific illnesses until they learned to mix it properly without exposing the metallurgists. The liquid bonded with the bronze ore, the radium being the catalyst, resulting in the former liquid forming a new solid.

The whole formed an extremely dense, strong, tarnish-resistant alloy that proved useful where excessive wear might occur, or where one wished an object to be very dense and heavy—such as the anchor of the *Prachus*. Dat Voga aided the crew in some of the final details, tying off sail and taking in loose rope. While they always seemed cheerful to him, the sailors now appeared joyous, singing lustily as they worked.

When Dat Voga commented on this observation to Gan-Toh-Gan, the burly odar grinned. "If you think them happy now, you should see them when we raise the sight of land after weeks at sea! They'll sing and carry on like children. They're fearless, and any one of them would leap overboard to poke a brobdoganth if it was nipping at you. And they love simple things; but don't let that fool you into thinking them simpletons. Many of these are the offspring of affluent families or the sons of nobility. A sailor's is a wonderful life, and they love it."

The small boats used for shuttling men and supplies from shore were being prepared for launch, the men breaking into various parties in readiness for fishing and sport. Many had appareled themselves in aquatic leathers, these being especially able to resist the effects of salt water. Each had a serrated knife lashed firmly to an outer thigh. Having donned these leathers himself, Dat Voga joined the two young women at the stern.

"Now, observe closely, Dat Voga." Approaching the rail, Azaria climbed onto it, the sunlight glinting from her radiant, white skin.

"I shall be," he replied honestly. His level gaze never left the curvaceous form of the daughter of Hal-Roh-Kim. Placing both feet together, the girl executed a perfect dive, entering the water with scarce more than a ripple.

Gan-Toh-Gan nodded his approval. In his best needling tone, the odar said, "Now, see here, young Dat Voga! There's no shame in conceding to Azaria's superior skill, as the girl practically broke her shell in the sea! Attempting to duplicate that dive, in the wake of such obvious perfection, could cause a man all manner of perturbation. But if you're up to it, let's see what you can do!"

Grinning at the challenge, Dat Voga stepped up on the stern rail, a wide, solid structure. Having performed a graceful sweep underwater, Azaria resurfaced a short distance away and smiled teasingly up at Dat Voga.

"Jump—islander!" she called, never missing an opportunity to bait him.

Recalling Azaria's posture, he adjusted his feet as he had observed his prehistoric princess position hers. He took several deep breaths, his skin fairly glowing from his deep and rapid breathing. Azaria, watching from below, observed the palpable glow of the man, her gaze intent on his handsome face.

With all eyes upon him, the young Heliumite leaped into the air, his back performing an arch in close approximation of Azaria's. At the last instant he knifed his hands, tucked his head, and entered the water.

The coolness of the sea closed over his head—considering it was his first dive, his entry had been well executed.

Aboard the ship, Thuria clapped her hands and laughed happily, along with Gan-Toh-Gan, who was both surprised and impressed.

"I thought you said he couldn't swim!" he exclaimed.

The girl grinned. "He can't—but obviously, he can dive."

An equally impressed Azaria smiled up at the two standing at the gunwale. Shaking her head in disbelief, she took a breath and dove to see how he fared. While having entered the water almost flawlessly, Dat Voga found he still had the same tendency to sink, just as he had the time he fell from the headland. He attempted various movements to prevent his sinking further, resulting in a reaction exactly opposite of what he desired.

Seeing that the Heliumite had sunk to a depth of several sofads, Azaria swam down to him, fearful of finding him gasping in seawater. Watching her approach, and noting the worried expression on her face, he ceased struggling and awaited her. He felt calm and experienced no discomfort at all in holding his breath, just as when he fell into the harbor.

The thought came to him that she might believe him to be in trouble because he had not told her of his unusual ability to hold his breath. He had seen no way he might broach the topic without having a lot of explaining to do.

As she swam close to him, her hands instinctively reached for him. He let her take him by the hand, not because he feared drowning, but because he could not resist the desire to take her hand in his. He then indicated that he wished her to demonstrate how to go up.

Azaria realized he was in no danger and that he wished the swimming lesson to begin in earnest. She saw then how brave he had been, leaping into the sea with no knowledge of how to swim to the surface. She showed him how to hold his hands and move his arms, indicating how he should move his lower limbs, as well. Together they slowly rose toward the surface.

When he broke through the waves, he wore a wide grin on his handsome face. Azaria, her lungs starving for air since they had been underwater for a long time, caught her breath and watched the smiling and unperturbed Dat Voga as he told Thuria of his experience. He seemed to be breathing as easily as if he were standing on the fantail with Gan-Toh-Gan.

After catching her breath, she exclaimed, "Dat Voga! Your dive was superb, but we need to work on your recovery! But, how is it you're not gasping for air? You were underwater longer than I was, and my lungs were burning!"

Not wishing to lie to one he cared for, he said truthfully, "It's my belief that where Thuria and I come from, our lung capacity has become greater than yours here. We're both able to hold our breath for a long time." He did not bother to explain that by "here" he meant her time, not her geographical region.

"Well, it's marvelous and I wish I could do that! You'll have to show me just how long you remarkable islanders can hold your breath."

He already knew her to be a creature of intelligence for she possessed an inquisitive nature, a necessary trait if one is to learn. But he now become doubly impressed that, when faced with an aberration such as his astonishing ability, she did not shrink from it, but instead displayed an innate curiosity.

"Certainly. We can experiment. Truthfully, I don't know myself how long I can hold it. I've also noticed that during prolonged physical labor that would cause most men to pause and rest many times, I can continue without stopping."

The padwar looked at Thuria. "Jump, Thuria! I can now show you how to easily return to the surface!" He was obviously proud of his new skill.

Grinning, Thuria called to the two below, "I will! Look out!" She took a quick step to the top of the baluster, barely pausing while she poised her slim form in the same position Azaria had taken. She then made a fine, graceful dive, entering the water with barely a splash.

Unlike her friend though, Thuria seemed to take to the task of navigating underwater more naturally. Although he and Azaria reflexively dove under to aid her, she had already begun to move steadily toward the surface.

Thuria had waded in the surf while on their island but never essayed to go beneath the water, as Dat Voga had accidentally, it seeming too foreign to her to do so. Dat Voga was impressed at her display of courage; for where he had first plumbed the depths unwillingly, she did so now bravely and of her own volition.

As the three surfaced together, laughing and talking, they heard a loud shout from above them. "Beware below!"

They barely had time to note a blurry body coming at them with the velocity and unexpectedness of a meteor out of a clear sky when Gar-Noh-Dar, legs crossed, trunk upright, and a big grin splitting his face, hit the surface with a clap like a peal of thunder. His entry caused a cascade, splashing the three in their faces. Surfacing, he chortled at his joke.

Azaria yelled, "Gar-Noh-Dar!" Then she began splashing the man with her hands. They all started laughing and splashing. Gan-Toh-Gan, still at the rail, laughed uproariously at his son's antics.

"My children," he boomed, "I return to my duties; keep a wary eye out." With that the odar strode toward the steps leading up to the command deck.

Taking instruction from both Azaria and Gar-Noh-Dar (for although Azaria had undermined his vaunted skill, he was an excellent swimmer), the two neophytes began to learn an art that went largely unpracticed in their own world of the future.

At its present position, the *Prachus* lay at anchor in a shallow area of the Throxeus where the depth was at most a couple hundred sofads—shallow as compared to other areas of the sea where several haads might cover the depths.

The red man found the bottom intriguing. He discovered that he could dive down a hundred sofads and, in the amazingly clear water, see the bottom where strange rock formations jutted from the seabed. Lying upon its side on the sandy bottom were the remains of a wreck, the lines of its hull unmistakable.

He had no idea where their position might be relative to modern-day Barsoom but, in gazing upon that sandy sea bottom, he had to wonder if he had ever torn across this stretch upon the back of a thoat or flown overhead in a one-man scout flier. It might be that upon some occasion he had sailed over these very plains upon the gunnery deck of one of Helium's gargantuan battleships of the skies.

It did not take much imagination to envision the scene below as it would appear from this elevation in a flier with naught but the thin air of the future between himself and the seabed. The ochre bottom would be brightly lit by the same sun visible above if he looked upward, the swollen orb just passing midday in its course. He found the daydream so intriguing that he had no idea how long he floated there, a hundred sofads below the ocean floor, lost in his imaginings.

Overhead he could see the swimming figures of his friends. Azaria and Gar-Noh-Dar, both near Thuria, had surfaced. Scattered at varying distances from the ship were sailors, swimming, or fishing from the boats. Flitting here and there were fishes of amazing variety while entire schools of them reminded him of the flocks of birds he had observed on the island.

He had been underwater, he guessed, approximately twenty xats without surfacing. Not knowing what strange side effects remaining below for so long might cause, he decided to surface and get a breath to be on the safe side. For all he knew, he might black out without warning and drown.

Thuria, he discovered, had the same ability to hold her

breath for an enormous amount of time. Swimming slowly back toward the surface, he determined to ask her to accompany him, feeling that she, too, would be interested in the sight of the sunken vessel. He had no idea how long the view would remain, since the angle of the sunlight surely had something to do with the quality of visibility at that depth.

After hearing of his discovery, the red girl's curiosity was piqued. The others were fascinated by his description, but neither could hold their breath long enough to venture that far down. They would dive a short distance and watch their strange, new friends and then resurface while Thuria and the red man continued their long dive into the depths.

At last, they reached the position he desired to show the girl. Pointing, he watched as Thuria's face took on a look of intense interest, a grin spreading across her beautiful face. While he was looking at her, the look on her face changed from one of excitement to one of concern. Her eyes widening, she stabbed a finger downward. He snapped his face away to see what she had discovered.

His smile faded; it was a brobdoganth.

Chapter Forty-One

Fish-men of the Deep

THE LEVIATHAN, the same as that with which he had had the near scrape on the island, had just heaved into view. It was swimming unconcernedly just above the sandy bottom. The rows of tusks and horns, which swept upward in every direction from its snout and down the great length of its enormous body, were plainly visible.

While these timid creatures tended to stay away from the surface unless the hunt for a meal brought them upward, they were dangerous if, in their curiosity, they approached too closely to a ship. They could render a vessel into flotsam with their enormous mass and their bony protuberances, which could break a keel with little effort.

Dat Voga touched Thuria on her arm to get her attention and pointed upward. They needed to warn the odar and the others immediately; they began their ascent. As he glanced down periodically, it seemed the great beast would swim on, ignoring the surface dwellers.

Looking up at his friends, he saw Azaria waving at them frantically. She, too, had spotted the great fish and could not know if they were aware of it or not. He nodded to indicate they had seen it, but then, glancing down again, saw the real reason for her gestures. The brobdoganth was swimming at them in an almost vertical ascent. Having spotted their movements, it sought to investigate.

With the closing proximity Dat Voga noticed something odd about the creature that he had been previously unaware of, for he had never heard it mentioned when the sailors spoke of their experiences with these monsters. There were several strange shapes clinging down the length of the body to the horny protuberances, shapes oddly reminiscent of the human form.

He shot rapidly upward, urging Thuria on and feeling an impending doom as though they were to be devoured alive by this creature. Its maw was so massive it could have swallowed them whole. The idea of one of the girls being devoured by this giant of the deep was too horrid to contemplate—they must return to the *Prachus* without delay.

Looking down at the rising leviathan, he was wondering why the seemingly inevitable had not yet occurred when he saw the creature make a sudden stop just beneath them. From their perches down the length of the beast, manlike creatures, pasty white with dead-black eyes, shot upward with the speed of gantahns.

The red man could scarcely believe the velocity with which their pursuers closed the gap between them. He observed that, rather than feet, they were furnished instead with large, finned appendages, and subtle dorsal fins ran along their spines. They were webbed between their fingers and beneath their arms to midway down their sides. Along their long, sinewy necks, gills were visible, indicating that these creatures spent their lives underwater.

Their hands were extended for him as they sought to grab his feet. Seeing that they intended to drown him, he drew the serrated knife from the scabbard at his hip and faced them head-on. He hoped Thuria would know he did this to buy her and the others time, and that she would not seek to come back and aid him. Right now, he needed to focus on this enemy, not on her whereabouts.

He tensed as he prepared to come to grips with the strange creature cutting through the water toward him.

Its teeth were bared in a grimace as it came for him, the pasty skin of its fingers ending in dark, curved talons. Its mouth opened wide, causing its lips to peel back above its gum line, revealing black, angled teeth that looked like they could saw through a gantahn. The creature's rapidly receding forehead ended in a shock of thick, black anemone-like tufts that waved and writhed behind it.

As they grappled, he realized this thing had an immense advantage over him. In its native element, its skin was so slippery that the man, his fingers closing on what would be its wrist, discovered that only with the greatest difficulty could he retain his grasp. At last, he jerked his knife hand free from the creature that sought to keep the blade from its flesh.

Pulling his feet up, he kicked outward with great effort, contacting the thing in the pit of its belly. It instantly doubled up. Too late it realized its danger and found itself unable to avoid Dat Voga's blade as he slammed it home in its neck.

He heard a resonating gurgle, sounding oddly modulated underwater, as the thing cried out in its death throes. Glancing upward, he saw others of the creatures tugging at the lower limbs of Thuria and Azaria, who had made it to the surface. They were attempting to drag them under. Daggers in their hands, both girls sought to slice the creatures' grips from their ankles.

Thuria spent as much time underwater as she did above, taking the creatures on in their own element to prevent them from drowning her friends, not fearing the creatures herself. Seeing humans come at them underwater seemed to take them aback. Dat Voga watched a webbed-fingered hand float free, trailing black gore, after Thuria's knife severed it at the wrist. Again, he was impressed with the girl's backbone.

Across the surface, the sailors fought the creatures. The pasty beasts capsized boats and pulled men over the gunwales to get them into the sea where they would have the advantage.

But they found the men, when they had their gaffs in hand, to be no mean antagonists. Many hacked, pasty-white corpses bobbed lifelessly, oozing thick, dark blood.

Gar-Noh-Dar found himself engaged with two concurrently and having a tough time of it. When he gave his attention to one, the other would rush him from behind, its long claws curled to rend the man's flesh. All about the ship, similar battles were being carried out. The boats, their crews having heard the cries of battle, were returning, fairly flying across the surface from the sailors' efforts to succor their comrades. Several of the dead bodies floating on the surface, however, were human.

Ripping his blade from the body of his opponent, the red man swam briskly toward the girls to help them fend off the attacks. He hoped to get both back aboard the *Prachus* before either were harmed.

As he swam toward them, he recalled a yarn with which Gan-Toh-Gan regaled a rapt audience one night when several of them gathered on deck beneath the moons and stars, swapping stories. The memory instantly galvanized the red man.

The odar had told of coming upon bits of floating wreckage years before, indicative of the sinking of a ship. Among the wreckage floated a living man, the sole survivor. Wounded grievously but still alive they had pulled him aboard, giving the man small amounts of food and water to revive him. It was obvious to them, however, that he would probably not survive his ordeal.

He had been in the water for days, he told them, awaiting some savage, toothy fish of the deep to drag him down to a horrid death. He had prayed to the mighty shades of his great ancestors that a group of prachus would not sniff him out, and was grateful for the reassuring sensation of solid decking beneath him once more.

The dying sailor said that his ship had been attacked by

green men who had beset them using gantahns and brobdoganths, towing strange vessels of bizarre design resembling giant seashells. From these unconventional craft the green men issued in prodigious numbers. They swarmed the railings with swords, flails, and iron bars, not attempting to take prisoners, but seeming rather to joy in the slaughter of the humans.

They fought as best as they might to repulse the boarders; at some point during the fray, the wounded man was knocked overboard. Seeing the green men retreating from the ship, he thought they had been repulsed by his mates. Then he saw a green man, perched atop a brobdoganth, gripping the massive array of horn in his hands to steady his perch. The green man appeared to be concentrating intently, focusing his gaze on the great beast.

Slowly it moved forward. Then it appeared to catch the concept of what the green man wished and with a surge and almost a roar from its open maw, it rushed the ship. At the last it launched itself into the air and came crashing down, mouth first, onto the ship. It snapped its jaws shut with a deafening crunch, the timbers shattering as if made of confetti. Those in its path were destroyed in an instant.

The remainder, those that were not directly beneath the creature when it crashed onto the deck, were tossed into the air to fall amid the wreckage from which the monster thrashed in its attempts to extricate itself. This it did by the simple expedient of writhing its body from side to side, its massive horns alternately impaling and ripping men asunder as it dismembered the vessel.

Just prior to the impact, the green man who issued the telepathic commands had slipped into the sea and swum to one of the shell-shaped vessels bobbing nearby. The brobdoganth slid back into the sea, the ship all but broken in half and shoved beneath the surface from the creature's ponderous weight and its efforts to free itself from the shattered timbers of the decking and ribbing that had become wedged and jammed in its horned extensions. The creature continued its onslaught until nothing remained but fragments with no resemblance to the ship it had been.

Then the green men, astride the creatures that they had learned to control telepathically, heaved off and departed, leaving the lone human survivor floating in the blood of his fellows. He made no outcry for he did not wish to attract the attention of the green men for fear they would come and rend him. He spotted captives who were crying out at the destruction of their craft and the slaughter of their countrymen in acts of wanton cruelty; they were carried off for torture and death.

What had taken the odar many xats to tell came back instantly to the red man, giving him the germ of an idea. In his time, it was common, among both red men and green, to use telepathy to control their irascible mounts, the humble thoats. He stopped his ascent and attempted to sense whether any telepathic commands were being issued to the great beast hovering below. Shortly, he detected it, a slight mental susurration. One of the fish-men was urging the beast to snap the ship's keel and send it to the bottom.

Glancing about, he saw one in the direction from which the sensation originated. It was paramount he stopped the humanoid creature. Diving, he focused his own mind on the brobdoganth while swimming rapidly toward the fish-man. He strained his mind to the uttermost, unaware if he penetrated the thick haze of the fish's dull intellect or not, combating simultaneously the telepathic commands of the pasty fish-man he attempted to reach in time to slay before it could wreak its plan.

He was aware of the possibility that the creature, accustomed to the signal of these base humanoids, might ignore his commands, which would have the accent of a foreign mind. He could still detect the signals being sent to the brobdoganth, and the intent of the message, but they were becoming fainter. He just might be succeeding in subduing the enemy's telepathic control of the creature's brain.

He drew nearer the white aberration that slowly undulated its limbs as it floated and directed the actions of the leviathan, which had hesitated, confused by the conflicting thought patterns. The vile fish-man sensed its danger. Spinning suddenly to face him, it opened its mouth in a silent roar of rage. Dat Voga had broken its concentration. Sending one last telepathic command himself at the brobdoganth with all the intensity and focus he could muster, he closed with the hideous travesty of humanity.

He had slain several of these things, but still could not accustom himself to their appalling visage. This one was huge, larger than himself, well-muscled, sleek, and slippery as slime on a rock in the Great Toonolian Marshes. They fought silently, grimly. In his mind's eye, the man from the future could still see the bodies of his friends floating upon the waves above him, the clear water stained with their blood; the scientist's face reflected his rising anger and determination.

The battle would not be a protracted one, the Heliumite would see to that. He could not afford to waste time when his friends were dying. The thing made a sudden rush toward him. Timing it, and with both hands upon the hilt of his dagger, he slammed his arms powerfully upward, the knife catching the creature behind its teeth in its lower jaw, penetrating upward through its soft palate and slamming through its brain to finally pierce the top of its skull.

Giving the knife a vicious wrench, he felt rather than heard the bone crack in its skull. With a powerful tug, he jerked free the heavy, serrated blade, which came out with bits of flesh clinging to it while blood gushed from the gash in the creature's flesh. The grotesque white body, its limbs splayed wide in death, floated free, dark cruor continuing oozing from its inanimate form.

Only now could Dat Voga risk a look to see if the leviathan had obeyed his last desperate commands, or if the humanoid fish-man had succeeded in directing the behemoth's actions; he was grimly satisfied to see the brobdoganth gobbling up the white creatures in great mouthfuls. They were fleeing in stark terror at the creature's sudden change in allegiance, as it now proceeded to completely ignore the remaining humans.

Swimming back to Thuria he saw that she was holding Azaria's head above water while the fish-men were swimming away at unbelievable speed, easily outstripping the giant beast. The fish-men dove for the deeps, which had become impenetrable due to the blood and changing angle of the sun's rays; the sandy bottom could no longer be seen as distinctly as before. As he approached the girls, he directed the brobdoganth to hold and await his next command, unsure if it would obey or not.

He arrived at their side to discover Azaria unconscious and Thuria almost in a panic as she attempted to detect signs of life in the other girl, this being difficult to accomplish while floating amid all the carnage surrounding them.

As he came alongside, Thuria gasped, "She was dragged under by two of them. I fought them off and got her back to the surface. We need to get her out of the water!"

Together they managed to swim Azaria to the ship and hoist her aboard, where Gan-Toh-Gan was busy issuing orders. The odar stiffened when he saw the seemingly lifeless body of Azaria in the red man's arms. He rushed forward and aided in lowering her limp form to the decking.

The ship was a hive of activity as the bodies of slain sailors were retrieved; the corpses of the fish-men were simply ignored and relegated to the scavengers of the sea. Dat Voga, while not a medical doctor, nonetheless possessed some basic knowledge in the field. The girl had inhaled a quantity of seawater after being pulled under by the fish-men. To his immense relief he resuscitated her using revivification methods that are taught to every young recruit in the navy.

Untreated, she would have died then and there, possibly never regaining the deck of the ship alive. Medical knowledge of this type was yet unknown, so the padwar thanked his ancestors he had been here to save her. As she sat up, painfully coughing up the brackish sea water from her lungs, her arms went automatically about Dat Voga's neck. She could not see the tears of fear and anger in the red man's eyes, emotions wrenched from deep within after witnessing the girl's close brush with death.

He held her steady as she stood to her feet. To Thuria he said, "I have yet one more thing to do."

He stepped to the rail and did not pause for an instant, but rather leaped immediately into the sea, which he would never again fear. He swam out to the gigantic creature that reposed nearby, awaiting him, as he had ordered it. Taking a great horn in each hand, he gazed steadfastly into one enormous eye as, concentrating on its small brain, he issued his commandment—a decree that he put so much effort into he had no doubt but that the creature would continue for years to obey if that's what it took to accomplish its goal.

He instructed the beast to seek out those who had enslaved it and wreak a terrible vengeance on them. He ordered it to never cease in its efforts other than in finding sustenance for itself, until those who escaped had been destroyed. He imposed upon it that he wished it to remain free from their vile control. As to the fish-men, it would hunt them until they were extinct, or it expired.

His anger burned with intensity at the nearness to death the creatures had brought Azaria, and for the wanton attack that left so many of his friends lifeless. Only with great effort did he resist the urge to clamber aboard the giant and ride with it into battle.

He knew the great beast would find them eventually,

surprising its onetime masters when and where it discovered them, immediately devouring and destroying them without preamble. After his last command, the creature did not hesitate but, turning, dove from sight, heading immediately in the direction in which the red man last saw the humanoids fleeing.

Aboard the *Prachus*, all watched to see the outcome of his approach to this giant monster that they held in almost superstitious fear, that fear sailors hold for certain creatures of the deep, those who instill in them wonder and dread, fueling their stories that become myths. Azaria, fearful for him, clutched Thuria's hand convulsively, wishing to call out to him, but fearful of how the behemoth might react should she do so.

Seeing the actions of the great fish, however, and the red man now swimming easily as he returned to the vessel, Azaria involuntarily spoke.

"Has anyone ever seen such a man?" she said hoarsely.

Thuria shook her head in disbelief at her friend from Helium, and then she replied. "No, Azaria. I don't believe his equal has ever lived before."

Chapter Forty-Two

Burial at Sea

THE ATTACK LEFT THE CREW of the *Prachus* stunned, yet they knew they must ready the ship and leave that death-haunted place. Gone, however, was the singsong mood when they had made ready for a day of sport. For a time, they would wear sullen expressions of anger and grief at their losses.

Those the fish-men had slain were twenty in number, whose corpses now lay in orderly fashion upon the forward decking. The bodies of the fallen had been washed and garbed in new leathers, then festooned with bright blades at their hips, unused from the stores. Finally, they were sealed in fish-hide sail, to the outside of which was then attached a shiny, new gaff.

Dat Voga stood on the command deck alone, having assisted in these preparations, awaiting the established time for the burial of these friends and comrades. He leaned on a rail above the rows of the dead, gazing at where only that morning he and the girls had joked and laughed. His gaze climbed to where the sea met a horizon filled with stunning clouds.

The beauty he beheld was at odds with the grim mood on deck. A man of war, he knew how swiftly the tide of battle could overwhelm, and was not unfamiliar with the macabre hollowness immediately following a battle, when one felt the immense relief to have survived mingle with the unutterable loss of friends who had not.

He and Thuria had no idea what was to come, never having experienced a burial at sea. The crew began moving toward the bow. From below and exiting onto the deck came Azaria and Thuria. Their simple garb consisted of white leathers, with ceremonial capes falling from one shoulder. Their hair was arranged simply and unadorned, for they were here not to attract attention, but to honor the fallen. Bright blades swung on their hips.

Dat Voga descended the stair to join them. He himself wore only a simple harness with a cape made from some creature he never knew existed. He walked forward to stand beside Azaria, who smiled to acknowledge his presence. Her eyes were sad, but her chin was firm and level.

These were a proud and beautiful people whom he was grateful to have been afforded the opportunity to meet—they being legendary in his day. For these were the ancestors his people invoked daily in their oaths and prayers. At times when he was among them, talking and laughing, he felt as might a man in a fable who met and mingled with the gods of myth—only these were very human.

They loved and swore great oaths; they labored, risking life and limb in the performance of their duties aboard a ship on an unpredictable sea—a sea that would woo them one moment and try to drag them to their deaths the next. For this sea, quite different from what those of the future might imagine, held troubling secrets—arcane knowledge that could slay one unprepared to meet her wiles with an equal measure of his own cunning.

The odar exited his cabin and made his way to the stern past the waiting crew, and the patient dead. Pausing, he stood with his back to the sailors, his long hair blowing over his shoulders while he gazed at the very horizon upon which the padwar had just been gazing. As Dat Voga wondered what the odar was thinking, the man turned to address the assembled.

Dat Voga could tell by the psalm-like quality that the rite was ancient—a sacrament of which the men of the future knew naught, for it was not destined to survive the cataclysms to come. The odar's voice rose in the form of a singsong chant.

"I am odar. I am odar of this ship—I am Gan-Toh-Gan. I am Gan-Toh-Gan, and I knew these men. I knew these men that upon the decking lie, which the sea hath slain. Here before me is Bak-Noh-Dok. I knew him well. He loved the sea. He served with honor."

In unison—except for Dat Voga and Thuria who knew not the rite—the crew repeated: "Here before us is Bak-Noh-Dok. We knew him well. He loved the sea. He served with honor."

After this simple passage, two sailors approached. They carried a single, great link of dense anchor chain. This link they attached to Bak-Noh-Dok's feet where a loop had been sewn in the body's wrappings for the purpose. They lifted the body then, four additional crewmen stepping forward to assist so that all proceeded smoothly, and the body was accorded the utmost respect.

The odar removed a circular hatch that the red man had not noticed, revealing a chute. The six sailors approached the shaft with their grim burden. Inserting first the weighty segment of anchor chain, they gently let the body down into the chute, a pair of men stepping aside as they lowered their burden until only one pair of sailors held the body by loops at the shoulders.

These continued to lower the dead sailor into the chute until his head disappeared and, synchronized perfectly but with no visible or audible signal, released their hold upon Bak-Noh-Dok. A low *ploosh* was heard as the body entered the sea beneath the ship.

As this last pair of sailors returned to their positions, the odar continued. "Here before me is Kal-Vis-Tok. I knew him well. He loved the sea. He served with honor."

"Here before us is Kal-Vis-Tok. We knew him well. He loved the sea. He served with honor."

And so it went down the long line of the dead until the last. After hearing the initial eulogy, Dat Voga and Thuria joined their shipmates in the simple burial chant in paying homage to the fallen, by now considered friends after spending so much time at sea with them, and in delivering their comrades' bodies to the deep.

Once the burials were accomplished, the odar sealed the hatch. Ever afterward the young man from the future could never look at that hatch the same after witnessing the remains of so many friends disappear into its macabre opening. The dismal business completed, there was a flurry of activity to get underway.

Under command of the First Osar, the red man swarmed up a mast to his station. For a while the girls remained at the bow, watching as each sailor ran to his task. All were anxious to hear the hum of the rigging, to feel the rolling swells of the sea beneath their keel and smell the fresh sea wind in their face.

In short order, the sails billowed, and the ship surged forward, seeking a piece of land the men could recognize that they might get their bearings and sail for Horz.

Dat Voga was leaning on a rail in the bow, gazing thoughtfully out over the sea, when Odar Gan-Toh-Gan joined him. The latter eyed the red man thoughtfully for a moment. "That was an amazing feat, what you did, today," the odar said. "You have a similar ability as that possessed by the green men, who also can control the beasts of the sea with their minds."

"Odar—" Dat Voga began.

Gan-Toh-Gan held up his hand. "You do not have to

explain, Dat Voga. You and Thuria are different, obviously in more ways than one might see with his eyes. You saved the *Prachus* today, and the lives of many of my crew who would otherwise have perished. We learned today that the fish-men use mature brobdoganths in much the same fashion as the green men. For all I know, one of them stole the idea from the other. I would guess that the fish-men witnessed the actions of the green men and emulated them; a gantahn has more imagination than a fish-man, in my opinion."

"I feel I may have acted rashly," admitted Dat Voga. "I sent the brobdoganth after those who attacked us. I told it not to stop until it hunted them all down. I was so angry, Gan-Toh-Gan! Azaria . . ." He could not bring himself to finish the thought.

"Good!" Gan-Toh-Gan exclaimed. "They killed my men! And they nearly killed the girl! I'm just grateful not to have to bear word of her passing to her father. Old Hal-Roh-Kim would tie me to the prow and sail around the world, using me as an anchor in ports of call if anything happened to his daughter on my watch! Don't you worry about those fish-men, Dat Voga . . . brobdoganths must also eat!" With that the odar clapped his hand familiarly on Dat Voga's shoulder and left him to see to the mysteries to which an odar of the high seas must attend.

After waiting for Gan-Toh-Gan to ascend to the command deck, Thuria approached her friend. "Azaria is resting," she informed Dat Voga. Glancing behind her to be certain no one might overhear, she continued in a low voice, "Dat Voga? What are we to do? We can't continue to have such encounters; you have said so yourself."

Dat Voga nodded, and sighed. "I know, and you are right, Thuria. I may have gone too far, sending that great beast after the fish-men. I was out of my mind with fear for Azaria, and anger at those who had put her in peril." The man paused, his skin beginning to take on its characteristic glow, bespeaking the odd reaction his body had to the denser oxygen of the past and his rapidly increased breathing when he became excited. "Luckily, it was only fish-men. It would be far worse if it had been a group of Orovars we had to fight. Every interaction with a Barsoomian may potentially affect the future in unknown ways."

The two from the far future became thoughtful, staring out to sea. After a while Dat Voga broke the silence. "I will spend more time working on the gauntlets, Thuria, every free xat," he promised. "We must return to our own time while there is still one to return to. John Carter has undoubtedly sailed for Ptarsas to demand an accounting for our long absence, Daxxus Nahl has Carthoris and Voss Borgas at his mercy and knows not the meaning of the word, and there is the very real dilemma our world faces with the potential for disaster should our atmosphere plant suffer another catastrophic failure, as it has once before. We must mine that radium."

Dat Voga turned to face the Ptarsan girl and smiled reassuringly. "Do not fear, dear Thuria. I will somehow find a way to unlock Daxxus Nahl's gauntlets so we can return to our own time, because we must! Meanwhile, we will do all in our power to not influence the past. And just think," he added with a smile. "We are about to see one of the most famous of ancient cities as it existed in its glorious past. Is that not exciting?"

Thuria grinned at her friend. "Maybe a little," she admitted. And then she turned her face to watch a swollen sun fall toward a sparkling and mysterious sea.

The saga of Dat Voga will continue in

Gauntlets of Mars

About the Author

Chris L Adams spent years playing guitar in various bands and during that time was more of a voracious reader than a writer. After his last band collapsed, he turned from writing songs to writing stories, including *Dark Tides of Mars* and its forthcoming sequel. In addition to writing, Chris also dabbles in painting; the cover art for his previous novel, *A Savage from Atlantis*, was created from one of his paintings. Chris resides in Southern West Virginia with his wife and daughter.

About the Illustrator

An award-winning illustrator, Douglas Klauba was born and raised in Chicago, and is a graduate of the American Academy of Art. His paintings have been included in the art annuals of *Spectrum: The Best in Contemporary Fantastic Art*, the Society of Illustrators, and *Imagine FX* magazine. He was Artist Guest of Honor at the 2016 Burroughs Bibliophiles Dum-Dum convention, and he previously provided artwork for the books *Tarzan Trilogy*, *Untamed Pellucidar*, *Tarzan and the Valley of Gold*, *The Girl from Hollywood Centennial Edition*, and *Tarzan and the Forest of Stone* published by Edgar Rice Burroughs, Inc.

Edgar Rice Burroughs: Master of Adventure

The creator of the immortal characters Tarzan of the Apes and John Carter of Mars, Edgar Rice Burroughs is one of the world's most popular authors. Mr. Burroughs' timeless tales of heroes and heroines transport readers from the jungles of Africa and the dead sea bottoms of Barsoom to the miles-high forests of Amtor and the savage inner world of Pellucidar, and even to alien civilizations beyond the farthest star. Mr. Burroughs' books are estimated to have sold hundreds of millions of copies, and they have spawned 60 films and 250 television episodes.

About Edgar Rice Burroughs, Inc.

Founded in 1923 by Edgar Rice Burroughs, one of the first authors to incorporate himself, Edgar Rice Burroughs, Inc., holds numerous trademarks and the rights to all literary works of the author still protected by copyright, including stories of Tarzan of the Apes and John Carter of Mars. The company oversees authorized adaptations of his literary works in film, television, radio, publishing, theatrical stage productions, licensing, and merchandising. Edgar Rice Burroughs, Inc., continues to manage and license the vast archive of Mr. Burroughs' literary works, fictional characters, and corresponding artworks that has grown for over a century. The company is still owned by the Burroughs family and remains headquartered in Tarzana, California, the town named after the Tarzana Ranch Mr. Burroughs purchased there in 1919 that led to the town's future development.

In 2015, under the leadership of President James Sullos, the company relaunched its publishing division, which was founded by Mr. Burroughs in 1931. With the publication of new authorized editions of Mr. Burroughs' works and brand-new novels and stories by today's talented authors, the company continues its long tradition of bringing tales of wonder and imagination featuring the Master of Adventure's many iconic characters and exotic worlds to an eager reading public.

Visit **EdgarRiceBurroughs.com** for more information.

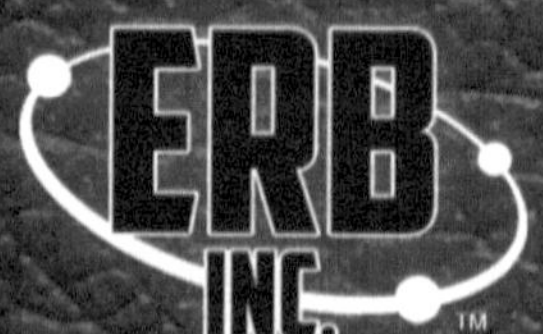
ERB
INC.
TM

THE FIRST COMIC BOOK ADVENTURES EVER PUBLISHED BY EDGAR RICE BURROUGHS, INC.!

JANE PORTER®: THE PRIMORDIAL PERIL

32-PAGE, FULL-COLOR COMIC BOOK

WRITTEN BY MIKE WOLFER

ART BY ROY ALLAN MARTINEZ

JANE PORTER® AND THE CITY OF FIRE

74-PAGE, FULL-COLOR GRAPHIC NOVEL

WRITTEN BY MIKE WOLFER

ART BY MIRIANA PUGLIA

EDGAR RICE BURROUGHS UNIVERSE™ ILLUSTRATED EPICS™

ERB INC.™

AVAILABLE EXCLUSIVELY FROM ERBURROUGHS.COM

www.ingramcontent.com/pod-product-compliance
Lightning Source LLC
Chambersburg PA
CBHW030423310726
48979CB00009B/1586/J

* 9 7 8 1 9 4 5 4 6 2 6 0 3 *